Jane Carter lives in Goulburn, NSW, with her husband, Richard. Raising five children, farming, and helping to run a livestock transport business kept her busy until a few years ago when the last of the children left home and she started writing. Her first book, *A Dream Of Something More,* was published in 2009. Although she worked in film and television before she was married, forty-four years in the country have made her passionate about rural Australia, the farmers and the townies she lives among. She loves their stud sheep, adores her grandchildren and anything at all to do with boats.

Jane loves hearing from her readers. To get in touch with her, please visit janecarterauthor.com.

I0610342

Also by Jane Carter

A Dream of Something More

High Country Secrets

Jane Carter

First published by Momentum in 2014
This edition published in 2014 by Momentum
Pan Macmillan Australia Pty Ltd
1 Market Street, Sydney 2000

Copyright © Jane Carter 2014
The moral right of the author has been asserted.

All rights reserved. This publication (or any part of it) may not be reproduced or
transmitted, copied, stored, distributed or otherwise made available by any person or
entity (including Google, Amazon or similar organisations), in any form (electronic,
digital, optical, mechanical) or by any means (photocopying, recording, scanning or
otherwise) without prior written permission from the publisher.

A CIP record for this book is available at the National Library of Australia

High Country Secrets

EPUB format: 9781760081157
Mobi format: 9781760081164
Print on Demand format: 9781760082543

Cover design by Danielle Maait
Edited by Kylie Mason
Proofread by Dianne Blacklock

Macmillan Digital Australia: www.macmillandigital.com.au

To report a typographical error, please visit momentumbooks.com.au/contact/

Visit www.momentumbooks.com.au to read more about all our books and to buy
books online. You will also find features, author interviews and news of any
author events.

For Skye

1983

Why was the music these days so awful? She turned the radio off. Fabulous sounds they'd had in the sixties—The Beatles. The wonderful Abba of the seventies and then, ten years on, it was all rubbish. Madonna even sounded dreadful.

Come on.

It was dark and she didn't have a lot of time left. She glanced at her watch. Hurry up. On cue, the battered and rusty ute paused briefly across the road before pulling out again. With a little laugh, she turned on her engine and followed it. Where to? Did it matter? She looked over her shoulder at her beautiful five-year-old son, sleeping soundly, as he always did. He'd be okay. An earthquake wouldn't wake him now. The car turned down a laneway and stopped. They were surrounded by the ghostly white snow gums that always gave her the shivers. Or was something else doing that to her? Anticipation? She pulled up behind his ute, wound down the window a little and then got out and went to the passenger side and opened the door.

"I thought you weren't coming," she said, sliding in.

"I come when I can. You know that. Come here."

Thank God for the bench seat and column shift. Thank God he was here, and her mind began a strange kind of crossing-off of things from a long list of thank-yous.

What was wrong with what she was doing? It was incredible. How could this be bad?

Yes, for pulling me on to you, thank you, for he was like a warm heavy mattress, but his arms were strong around her and he quickly pulled up her shirt and rubbed her nipples. Thank you, yes, she sighed into the softness of his throat and he smelled of animals and hay. Delicious.

Her pants were gone. When had that happened? Maybe she'd done it. Two warm, strong fingers rubbing her. It was driving her crazy. Her knee was pulled up and he was inside her and thinking was beyond her. Only thank you.

Afterward, he lit a cigarette and passed it to her. They lay snuggled up to each other, his arm draped over her shoulder. He lit another. In the sudden flare of the lighter she saw his mouth. He had the most beautiful mouth. Full, sculpted.

"Put the window down—I need to hear him if he wakes up." Now she could tell him what to do. "I'm not supposed to be smoking. I'll have to chew gum on the way home. Shower."

"No, you smell wonderful." He nuzzled her neck and she laughed. "He won't be home tonight. I'd like to think of you with my smell all over you."

"This is getting complicated. I saw your wife yesterday, at the school. Your son and my son are friends. I don't know what to do."

"Nothing. Nothing can come of this. I told you before. This is what we have. Sex. I told you this. I can't resist you. You can't say no to me. So for a little time we enjoy the moment. Okay."

She finished the cigarette and stubbed it out in the ashtray, almost overflowing with butts. "I know. I know." She sighed and snuggled back into his chest one more time. "We should stop." But she didn't have the slightest idea of how or when.

But she did know why.

This was very unlike her. Not true to form. When she tried to talk sense into herself, she would put it off and even argue back: Not now. I'll think about it next week, or tomorrow. It was as though she had a little piece of something that was still hers, something that didn't have to measure up or be pulled apart and criticized. She could be herself, just for a moment in time. Of course, it was like walking a knife edge and if anyone found out, she'd be dead. Yes, she was crazy.

He shrugged, said nothing.

"I want to be back in time to watch Dallas. *Poor Bobby, that wretched JR, I hope he get what's coming to him. But he's just too clever." And she was gathering clothes. Dragged her undies out from under him. Pulling down and pulling up. He watched her, then straightened reluctantly and she slowly did up the top two buttons on his shirt.*

"Goodnight." She kissed the tiny piece of chest she'd left exposed. Where the collar bones met.

Chapter 1

Jessie's nose itched. The dusty wooden floors, the faint moldy smell of the red-upholstered seats, the darkened, cavernous hall—just standing there brought the memories flooding back. How amazing that she'd finally got old enough to say, "I remember when". Wow.

People scurried past as she walked into the lobby of the familiar theater. Not one person she recognized. No, there was Sue Benson, who'd been in charge of the box office forever, buried in lists and seating plans over in the corner. She stopped at the wall of photographs. There she was, aged fifteen, in a witch's costume with wild, green hair and blackened teeth in a production of *Macbeth*. That had been one of the Christmas productions. She'd been able to get to enough rehearsals in the October holidays to be allowed to do it. Being away at school mostly prevented her from being in the plays the theater put on. But, boy, there had been some memorable occasions when she'd fought tooth and nail to be in them, not to mention some dastardly rivalry with

Belinda for the main parts. She grinned. There she was in *The Secret Garden*. And there was her mother, in *Summer of the Seventeenth Doll*. She *looked* about fifteen. That was a long time ago but then, the community theater had been around for fifty years, at least.

And wouldn't they all get a shock tonight? Her eyes were dancing and she couldn't contain another grin. Jessie Cranfield was back.

"Jessie!"

Hearing the familiar voice, she whipped around and opened her arms to hug the slight figure of her mother, in skinny jeans and a pair of long leather boots, bearing down on her.

"You're here in perfect time! It's lovely to see you. Let me look at you. I always love your hair like that. Have you brought a dress?" Her mother had taken her by the arm and was propelling her forward without drawing breath. "Come and I'll show you where to get dressed." She stopped abruptly. "Where's Alan?"

"I've left him to have a walk around the town." Funny, her corporate-savvy fiancé had appeared a little nervous about spending one-on-one time with her family and had been quite happy to disappear for half an hour. It had all slotted in so perfectly: Alan had to come down here for work and she got to show him off and spend some time at home. "I think I know where to go. This place hasn't changed that much."

"Heavens, don't say that too loud, we've just put twenty thousand into renovations."

Jessie hung up her dress bag and looked around the dressing room. Seeing the comfortable leather sofa and chairs, she laughed. "Okay, this is an improvement."

"Music? Have you got it on a CD? Here, give it to me and I'll go and give it to Phillip. This is such a good song, I love it."

Jessie handed a USB stick to her mother with a smile.

"Oh, these things always confuse me. Just when I think I'm catching up," she said and off she marched. Clare Cranfield, mother of two, loyal wife to Lex Cranfield, scion of one of the town's oldest grazing families. This theater had always been her mother's passion. She was quite a different person here from the woman she was on the farm.

The Irish blood of Clare's antecedents and the Scottish blood of Lex's had resulted in two children, one straight out of Scotland—Jessie's brother, Fred, and the other pure Irish—herself, which made for some interesting family arguments.

How she had ended up quite so Irish, Jessie didn't know, as the Cranfields had been in Australia now for six generations and in the Monaro for five of them.

It had been her irresistible mother who'd asked her to come and sing tonight. At least, Jessie couldn't resist her. "Please, Jessie, I need you to be there. There's no point you being back in the country if you can't come down and see us occasionally." So here she was at a benefit to raise money for a project for kids with disabilities that her friend Belinda had been putting together—or trying to—for the last couple of years. Belinda hadn't been quite so polite: "You get down here or else."

Not that she'd needed much persuading. Show her a stage or a microphone and you'd likely get knocked over in the rush. She'd been told they would try to pair her up with a singing partner, but she hadn't heard any more about that.

Jessie loved her dress. Black taffeta with a peplum, London to a T. She took her prized Stella McCartney pumps out of the most incredible shoe bag she'd ever seen and put them neatly together on the floor. She couldn't resist fabulous shoes—Alan didn't know the half of it—but for a confidence boost, they were perfect.

Wandering backstage, she pushed her way through the curtains to stand at front of stage, squinting into the lights. There was her mother, down below, talking to a man—it must be Phillip, the musical director. If that's what you called him; in these amateur shows, everyone did everything.

"Hell, if I didn't know before, I'd know who you were now—you are the spitting image of your mother. Hi, Jessie."

And hadn't she heard that before, although she could never see it. "Phillip, good to meet you." She supposed she did have the auburn hair but the similarity ended there—she towered over her mother.

"Michael's running late," Phillip called up to her. "Thank God you're here on time."

"Michael who?"

"Michael D'Larghi. He's been held up, but he said he should be here in time."

Her stomach dropped. They couldn't be serious. Her mother looked equally surprised. *Michael D'Larghi.* Suddenly this singing assignment took on a totally different aspect. Now she was nervous. Goosebumps spread up her arms. Ridiculous. She was a different person now. She'd show him singing.

Michael almost didn't make it. She was waiting in the wings, quite prepared to go on by herself. To be truthful, she'd have preferred it. They were being introduced by the compere when a tall figure came swiftly along the hall behind the stage. He was dressed in black and all she could see was the top of his shiny brown curls as he ran up the stairs toward her. He hadn't changed—he still looked like some god from ancient Roman times dropped to earth, as though he'd just leaped out of a chariot. He stopped short when he saw her and looked somewhat disconcerted, just for a second, before hitting her with that smile of his. She'd forgotten how tall he was. She hadn't forgotten the smile.

"Jessie?"

"Hi, you're cutting it fine." She handed him a microphone.

"Sorry. Good to see you. Ready to go and knock 'em for six?" He gave the mike a professional tap.

"Better get your breathing right first."

He just laughed, held out the other hand, winked at her and they walked out on the stage.

"Great choice," he whispered to her. He was looking at her, at her dress, but he must mean the song she'd chosen.

"Thank you." Her arm, the one he held, felt weird, as though it had sparks shooting up and down it. There were the opening bars and they started to sing.

His eyes held hers and she couldn't look away. Deep, warm, melting; was that the music or his voice? Hell, she'd never sung like this before. It was as though he was pulling her up with him. She was so strong and she was flying. And she could hear them, their voices blending together—it was a though the words of the song were being wrung out of her.

Then it finished. In the silence she could hear herself taking deep, rasping breaths, sensed Michael doing the same beside her. The crash as she returned to earth. The lights were blinding her. The audience started clapping. Then they were whistling and yelling. She could barely see into the audience. Her mom was standing and clapping, looking slightly shocked, before her face was transformed by a beaming smile, as though saying to everyone, "That's my Jessie." Then she saw Alan, her fiancé, he was up too, next to Fred. Remember to breathe. She didn't want to let go of Michael's hand. *Don't let go of my hand, Michael.*

*

Back at the Five Oaks homestead, Alan was still going on about Michael D'Larghi.

"Come on, Alan, knock it off. I haven't seen him for years. He was running late and I didn't even meet him until we walked on the stage together. The whole idea was to raise money for Belinda's project, Growcare, remember?" Jessie lay back on the sofa in her family's sunroom, swinging one leg slowly back and forth and watching him pace up and down. This was annoying—the only word for it. When in living memory had the men in her life—her dad, her brother and now Alan—ever given her any credit? They still treated her as if she were twelve.

"Mom, do you want some help?"

"No, I won't be a minute," her mother called from the kitchen.

"All I've heard from you for weeks now is how important this D'Larghi is, how I've got to make an appointment with him, and then you get up in front of the whole town and you can't take your eyes off each other. And since when did you become a singer?"

That was almost an accusation. Jessie shook her head and laughed. "I'm having trouble working out if I should take that as a compliment or an insult. I sing all the time. You knew I was having singing lessons in London with Malia. You know I love that song. I sing it a lot."

"Have you any idea how I felt, seeing you, being ... *intimate* with that idiot?"

"Michael D'Larghi might be described as a lot of things, but idiot isn't one of them." It was so still outside. Through the window behind Alan she could see the countryside brightly lit by moonlight. The stone outbuildings had defined shadows—as did the fenceposts on their march across the bald landscape. Her family rarely pulled the curtains at night, only if it was very cold. There certainly wasn't a problem with privacy out here, maybe the odd kangaroo stopping by to have a look in.

"He's a friend of Fred's. They were at school together until Fred went away, but I haven't seen him for," she added the years up, "thirteen years. Good Lord." A slight exaggeration; she might not have laid eyes on Michael for thirteen years but that didn't mean she hadn't heard about him or the D'Larghis. They were always in the news, going from strength to strength. Michael had been quite a hooligan in those early days. Her dad was always saying to Fred, "Whatever you do, just don't get involved with that crowd." She'd never understood it, he'd always appeared quite the dashing hero to her. But he was much too old, and he'd never even have known she was alive. Well, he did now. She wondered if he was getting the same dressing down from the girl with brown eyes who'd been eyeing her off so suspiciously.

When they'd told her she'd be singing with someone, she hadn't expected Michael D'Larghi. Seeing him again was such a shock—and that strange reaction, that whoosh, when he'd winked at her and her stomach plummeted and he'd taken her hand to lead her onto the stage.

Nuh, it was just nerves.

"Hey Jessie, that was some performance tonight." Fred walked into the room. He lived with his wife Sonya and their twin babies in the manager's cottage, and he ran Five Oaks with their father. Fred had the Cranfield's thick red hair and blue eyes. Jessie had the blue eyes but her hair was a darker red and she'd missed out on the freckles, mostly. She tried to make a face to warn him to play down his comments, unfortunately with no success.

"I didn't know you and D'Larghi had a thing going."

Jessie rolled her eyes. She had often considered killing her brother and thought now would be a good time. Fred had to be totally insensitive—how could he come in and say something like that, even as a joke? She glanced at Alan; he looked as if he might burst a blood vessel.

"It was a joke, Alan, honestly. Tell him, Fred." Fred just gave her an exaggerated wink. And she gave up. "It was a pity Dad couldn't make it. And Sonya."

Her father hadn't come to the fundraiser. That wasn't unusual. There was always something in the way. Tonight her mother said it was one of his prized stud heifers calving.

"You know Dad, he hates those nights Mom gets involved in. Can't hear properly, he says. And my beautiful wife is coughing and spluttering like a dog. I can assure you, you wouldn't have wanted her in the audience tonight. But she's spitting mad she wasn't there."

"Jessie." Her father came in from outside, stamping his feet and rubbing his hands together from the cold. He gave her one of his bear hugs, lifting her off her feet. His cheeks were icy. "It's been far too long, Jessie. How are you, girl?"

"Good, Dad. You okay?"

"Yeah. Sorry I missed your singing. How did it go?"

"Okay, I think."

"What did you think of her, Alan?" Lex was shaking Alan's hand vigorously.

Alan didn't answer the question. "Hello, Lex, good to see you again."

Jessie sighed. "I'll go and give Mom a hand."

Chapter 2

The air already held a touch of frost. The sun was sinking fast behind the purple mountains as though some dead weight was pulling it down. Rangy clouds were etched in a fiery red spread over the western sky. Lonely stands of pines caused long shadows to roll over the bald, soft hills of the Monaro. It had to be the most beautiful sight in the world.

Michael D'Larghi sighed to himself. He'd been born here on the Monaro, and as far as he was concerned, there was nowhere else he wanted to live. He changed up through the gears, grinning widely. The power of the new Kenworth was incredible, all six hundred and fifty horses of it. He shrugged down in the cloud-like seat, enjoying the scent of new leather, and adjusted the mirrors again, fractionally. This truck was so much more luxurious than the last. He was in love. How did they do it? He ratcheted up the volume on his iPod through the Bluetooth button on the steering wheel, set the cruise control and laughed to himself. What were they going to come up with next?

Sunday nights saw him taking the D'Larghi truck to the markets at Homebush in Sydney. This week his load consisted of mostly cabbages and a few pallets of caulis. Then he'd load up the truck with vegetables from the markets to take back to Jindabyne. The trip gave him a chance to talk to the agents and buyers of the produce D'Larghi Enterprises grew from their holdings on the Monaro. He liked to stay in touch with the grass roots of the marketplace. Most people would say it was unnecessary—D'Larghi Enterprises was a large company—but then, they didn't know just how much pleasure he derived from these Sunday night trips, did they? These hours in the truck gave him time to think about the new project he was starting up. Plan, come up with good ideas. The only thing he missed out on was one night's sleep.

He'd done it for years. Ron, who drove this truck the rest of the week, had taken him along from when he was quite small, even as young as six or seven. Ever since Ron had started working for the D'Larghis, really. The excitement of these through-the-night trips was something he'd never forget. He'd chat to Ron for some of the way, sleep, then wake and walk around at the markets, and then sleep all the way home. And it hadn't changed for Michael. He still got a buzz from driving into the Sydney Markets—they were a separate world, a lot of chiacking and laughter, hot gossip and dealing with the best, most experienced traders in the business. Possibly that was one of the benefits of being motherless: he'd been able to escape under the radar and do what he wanted, mostly. His father certainly hadn't been around all that much. Too busy working.

The traffic passed him or fell behind. Sunday night there was usually a lot of ski traffic and quite a few B-doubles similar to his, powering through on their way to the city. Four and a half hours to go and he was fuelled up and had no plans to stop.

He slowed the truck, though, when he came to the bend just before Bredbo. The corner where his mother had died. Her car had rolled three times and slewed round to hit a huge gum tree, head on. She'd been alone in the car. It was coming up to thirty-one years. She'd been younger than he was now. For years, every trip north, his father would stop here; he'd pull over just before the corner. They would sit in the car silently for however long it took. His dad never spoke of his mother, no matter how hard Michael tried to make him. They'd just sit there.

Michael had little tolerance for the word "accident". For him there were no "accidents". Mistakes maybe—but there was always a reason. A cause and effect. He could speculate endlessly: the glare from the late afternoon sun or a sudden loss of concentration; fiddling with the radio. There were no mobile phones thirty years ago. Around ten years ago, he'd gone through the case with a lawyer but he'd found nothing, no cause; no reason for his mother to die. He'd had to let it go because his father was getting too upset.

He pushed down on the accelerator again, cutting off the cruise control, feeling, *needing* the sudden surge of power as the torque cut in. *Leave it alone.* The frustration did him no good. Michael was comfortable in riding boots and soft, worn jeans that snugly fitted his long-legged, six-foot-four frame. A navy blue trucking singlet molded his chest and an old flannelette shirt completed the outfit. The stubble on his chin was twenty-four hours old. He rubbed it.

"A bit different to last night. You wouldn't have recognized me, Frank." He addressed his old driving colleague, lying with his head on his paw on the bed behind him. Frank's only reaction was to open one eye.

"You'd better get down from there. Ron would have a fit if he knew you were on his new bed." Frank gave an exaggerated sigh but didn't move. "He only just tolerates me taking you in his cab at all. You think I'm a soft touch. Don't you know I have fifty terrified employees, who, if I say jump, all ask me how high?" Frank went back to sleep. Michael grinned, and then in a stern voice repeated, "Down. Now."

Frank gathered himself slowly and dropped from the bed to sit next to him. He lazily looked out the window into the darkening sky.

"What do you think of the new girl? The old one was a bit tired, wasn't she? A million clicks on the clock, she was ready for retirement. I had a bit of trouble deciding on the color scheme for the new logo on the curtains. Do you like the black and gold? Not bad, eh? Should cause a bit of a stir when I pull in to Homebush."

Having decided there was nothing of interest out on the highway, Frank curled up on the seat.

"The least you can do is stay awake and keep me company." Michael shook his head. He could break out in song but that usually had Frank joining in with his own version—better to let sleeping dogs lie.

On his own in the truck he loved to sing, but after last night he thought he'd better give singing a miss—for the rest of his life, probably. Who'd have thought Jessie Cranfield could sing like that? That *he* could sing like that.

He had always sung, starting from when he'd been, what, eight? In the choir at mass, then at revues at uni, and even at Scottsford in the US, where he'd done his MBA, they'd shanghaied him into the glee club. It was a great way to meet girls, and anyway, he loved singing. He could sing all right. But last night had been electrifying. And it was a favorite of his: "Someone Like You." He was damn sure he'd never sung as well.

He hadn't realized Jessie's eyes were so blue, like sapphires, and that her voice had deepened over the years to a rich contralto that blended so well with his tenor. That they could do that together—sound like that. Fred's little sister Jessie was all grown up. He'd been surprised. Mostly by the light in those eyes. He hadn't mistaken that, had he?

The challenge in those bright blue eyes.

He flicked his lights at the passing B-double, to clear him for returning to the left lane.

The challenge to which he'd responded, he acknowledged with a grin. Sparks had flown—it was more like a detonation. And more than a few people had noticed. Jessie's fiancé had been furious. He looked like he wanted to punch Michael in the face. That was another reason to be grateful for his height; it tended to make people sit back and think twice before having a go. Meanwhile, Sienna, his girlfriend, had looked a little shaken and, more to the point, hadn't stayed the night. It was a long drive back to Eden for her. And his grandmother had been immediately, warily, suspicious.

He'd better mend some fences. He reached over to the phone and hit Sienna's number.

"Hi, I missed you last night."

"Did you? I'm just serving up tea, Michael." No, she wasn't happy.

"I won't interrupt. It was just a song. A performance, you know, acting the song."

"If that was acting I am a—You can put your acting into a pipe and smoke it."

Michael started to laugh and thought better of it. "Look, next weekend, can I take you out to dinner? Come up for the weekend, or we can go up to Thredbo. There may not be any snow at the moment but you never know. Please, Sienna."

"You know I don't ski." There was a pause. "I'll let you know, Michael."

He was giving up singing, seriously.

*

"I say again, she isn't right for him." Maria D'Larghi ladled out huge servings of fragrant osso bucco into the warmed bowls.

"Now come on, Maria." Ron Fraser got up from the table to hand the food around: one for his wife Renee, one for Maria and one for himself. Then he poured three glasses from the bottle of red wine sitting on the table. He passed one to his wife and put the other down in front of Maria. Picking up his own glass, he toasted, "To good friends. Michael's a big boy. You can't tell a young man these days who he may or may not go out with."

"I am his nonna, and I worry about him. I worry he drives to Sydney every Sunday night; that he has not a good woman waiting for him at home."

"I wouldn't be worrying too much about that." Ron grunted at the swift kick delivered by his wife.

Renee picked up her glass. "Jessie Cranfield is a clever, hardworking girl from a good family. She's got a job in the city, I believe, working for one of the big hospitals. Isn't she an occupational therapist or something? Clare was telling me the other day that Jessie had singing lessons in London when she was there. I'm sorry, but I really enjoyed their performance last night. It was pure magic." Renee looked defensively from her husband to Maria.

"You've been defending Michael for what—ever since we came here? Thirty years?" Ron laughed.

"Well, he really has a wonderful voice."

"You should have heard my Gino sing, Michael takes after him." Maria sighed. "Ah, Sal." Sal D'Larghi, walked in and kissed his mother and sat down. "You missed a good night last night. Our Michael sang beautifully, just like his grandfather."

Sal had showered and changed out of his work clothes. "That's good to hear. It all sounds like wailing cats to me."

"You have no musical bone in your body, Sal. Lucky your son takes after his grandfather." Maria got up to get another plate from the oven.

He accepted a glass of wine. "Thank you, Ron. Sorry I'm late. I just had to check on the tractor, it's using a bit of oil."

"Always for you there is just one more thing to do." Maria turned to the others. "Sienna went home, I know she was upset and I don't blame her." She frowned. "I hope she is okay—that's a long drive at night. Michael shouldn't have allowed it. Her family is a good Italian family, just right for Michael. Sienna is a lovely girl."

"Maybe Ron's right, you shouldn't interfere," Renee said hesitantly. "How do you know Jessie isn't right?"

"Jessie who?" Sal was trying to keep up.

Maria threw up her hands. "Jessie Cranfield. He doesn't even know her. We haven't always agreed where Michael was concerned, Renee, but believe me, I am right." She sat down with a huff. "I told you on Friday that he was singing with the Cranfield girl in a duet. But still you couldn't find the time to come to see your son sing."

Sal stretched out his arm. "No, musical bone, see? It would be wasted on me. I don't know how he finds the time to do this; there are a lot more important things to do."

Renee ignored him and continued talking to Maria. "I know you're his grandmother, Maria, but I assure you, I have been a big part of Michael's life since his mother died and I don't agree that in this day and age if you are Italian you have to marry one. Michael can marry anyone he wishes. And it will be a lucky girl who gets him."

Ron raised his eyes and exchanged glances with Sal—there'd be no stopping them now. His wife and Maria D'Larghi could always manage to disagree about what they thought was right for Michael. Not that they ever swayed him from doing what he wanted. He had to take his hat off to the young fella.

Maria glared at Renee. "Of course Michael can marry who he wants."

"What are we talking about? Jessie Cranfield's family has been here on the land for what? Four or five generations? And—" Renee waved her glass around, "—they would have been migrants too, originally. Michael makes three generations, what's the bleeding difference?"

"But we came out as migrants to work on the Snowy Mountains scheme, we lived in a tent and my Gino sang for weddings to make extra money. If the Cranfields ever lived in a tent they've long forgotten all about it. Girls like Jessie don't look at Italian boys. Or their daddy chases them off."

Sal got up to pour himself more wine.

"That's outdated, Maria. Well, I agree with Renee, if Michael shows an interest in her she'd be a fool not to think about it," Ron said. "I have the utmost regard for your grandson, Maria."

"Not surprising as he's now your boss. And he shares your foolish passion for trucks." Renee laughed. "And aren't we forgetting something? Jessie's engaged, isn't she? Some city boy. This looks delicious, Maria, as usual." She reached over to squeeze her husband's hand. "I love these Sunday night dinners, and having you at home for a night. You can be away the other six, driving that wretched truck, but tonight you're here. Here's to Michael! Thank you and good luck to you, my boy." Renee lifted her glass.

Maria sat and played with the succulent oxtails in her bowl, then paused, looking at Ron, then Renee. "No matter what you think, I am right, Cranfields are Cranfields. They do not change. Michael will be happier with a good Italian girl and Sienna is the right one for him."

Sal refrained from entering the conversation. Renee sniffed and began to eat. Ron suppressed a smile. Maria did like to have the last word.

Chapter 3

Some four hours later, Michael slowed for the city speed limits, driving from the Hume onto the well-lit M7, then merging with the traffic on the M4 and straight into the markets. They were a different type of people, night people. While Sydney slept, big trucks delivered produce from Griffith and the Riverina, from Brisbane and South Australia, all to the markets at Homebush. A huge flotilla of small vans and utes converged on the markets in the small hours of the morning to get their fruit and vegetables; an army of shift workers to get it out to the shops. The rest of Sydney may be sleeping but not the markets—it bustled with a life of its own.

Michael backed into the unloading dock and swung out of the cab, easily undoing the curtains of the tautliner as he walked around his truck.

"Look who's here."

"Bloody hell! Where did that monster come from?"

"Bastard's made of money. Expect he'll be wanting more for the vegetables now to pay for it," a voice growled behind him.

Michael grinned and swung around. "I'd be waiting a long time, Antony, if I thought that was going to work. It doesn't matter what they travel in—my cabbages are the usual top quality." He shook hands with Antony, a pudgy, grizzle-haired Greek merchant, wearing the regulation fluoro vest. He was one of the big buyers at the markets who was always there.

"Go and have a coffee, Michael, I'll see you in a minute. I just check this out first."

Michael handed his paperwork to Antony and wandered over to the cafe, where his coffee was waiting.

He was welcomed by Zara's beaming smile. "Michael, you early tonight?"

"New truck, we made good time."

"You no speed, Michael." She wagged a finger at him.

"You know what my nonna would say about that. No speeding, Zara. Very fast up the hills that's all." He winked at her.

"That's what they all say. You young men do not know what is good for you."

"Antony's coming, could you get him a coffee?"

"That Antony, he drinks tea, I'll get him a tea."

He didn't have to wait too long before Antony sat down with a grunt. "New truck, Michael. I guess there's plenty of work around?"

"Not too bad at the moment. The old one was a bit tired. There's a lot of grain shifting around and Ron likes to keep moving. How are things here?"

"Eh, could be better, could be better. Our life is being made very hard by the supermarket chains. They try to put all little people out of business. They offer contracts to growers, get them to invest more money, then walk away after two or three years. Buy the same thing from overseas. Meanwhile our farmers, they go broke."

"I don't understand why they are so difficult to get along with. You'd think they'd want Aussie produce on tap."

"In a global market they can buy wherever there is a glut. Very cheap. If there is no Aussie food, there is an excuse."

He shrugged. "They can go anywhere they want. They have already destroyed our orange growers. I hear they're burning peach trees now, apples will be next." Antony spat on the ground. "I will see you in a minute. The caulis are good but the cabbages are a disappointment."

Michael grinned. Negotiations had begun.

*

By two, Michael had pulled out onto the M4 and was heading for home. The truck came alive under him and he was almost drunk with the power under the bonnet. The truck was speed limited or he would have had trouble keeping to the 65 mile-per-hour limit. With a light load of vegetables tonight, it flew home. His days of flouting the speed limits were long gone. He needed a license now. Slowly, he'd come to understand keeping the points on his license was a whole lot better than losing them. There were other ways to satisfy his need for thrill taking. Getting this new business project up and running was one. Risky but worth it, if he could pull it off.

He remembered the appointment in the morning with a representative from one of the supermarkets. They were in town doing exactly what Antony had described, trying to sign up crops for the coming year. His secretary had made the appointment. They wouldn't be getting much from him. It was so wrong, this duopoly mentality. Everything in the hands of two big supermarkets.

*

He was home by seven in the morning. The truck was unloaded and fueled up and he handed it over to Ron, who was waiting for him at the office.

"How did it go? Any problems?"

"A pearler, Ron. You'll love it." He ignored Ron's frown at Frank, who was standing quietly beside him. "Flew home and no lights went on that shouldn't."

Ron, small and nuggety, circled the truck, wiping off imaginary mud splashes from the shiny, polished surface with the rag he kept in his pocket for precisely that purpose.

"Caused quite a stir on the CB coming home."

Ron grunted. He never used the CB much but Michael could tell he was pleased, nevertheless. The word was out—D'Larghi's had a new truck.

He looked up at the sign that he'd just had painted in the new colors. Black and gold. D'Larghi Motors. It had been Hamilton Ford for many years. His father had bought the business twenty years ago. And it was Michael's idea to change the name when he came back from the States. His father had taken a deep breath and said, "Whatever you think, Michael." And now his father was going on his second trip to Italy in two years, leaving him in charge. It suited him.

He showered and changed upstairs in the huge apartment he'd recently had renovated, and then went in search of breakfast at Leo's, the early-opening café on the corner. At Leo's, the coffee was good and the croissants crisp and flaky.

By eight thirty he was back at his desk. At nine his first appointment was ushered in.

His receptionist, Mandy, opened the door. "Alan Freeman, Michael." He looked up, surprised, as the man he imme-diately recognized as Jessie's fiancé walked into his office. Maybe "walked" wasn't the right word when you encountered the wave of hostility that entered with him.

Nevertheless, Michael shook hands and pointed Alan to a seat in front of the desk.

"This is a surprise. How are you going? We met the other night." That would teach him for not paying attention to the small print. The name Freeman had meant nothing to him. This was embarrassing.

"I'm in town representing the WGA chain and wondering if you'd be interested in supplying us with vegetables for next season."

Michael couldn't help looking him over. *So, Jessie, this is who you've settled for.* There was no real reason for this sense of competition he was feeling—except it was coming from Alan, too. He wondered how they'd be feeling toward each other when his plan got out, when his chain of fresh vegetable and fruit markets were up and running and he was pitting himself against the big supermarkets. There really was not much point in continuing this discussion.

"How long have you been working for WGA?"

"Three months. I, er, *we*, returned from London in February, just after we got engaged."

And that was making the point. It was like putting Jessie in the room with them. Ridiculous.

"Congratulations, Jessie's a great girl."

"D'Larghi's are one of the biggest growers in the district and I really feel you would benefit from the advantages we offer." Alan pulled a copy of the contract out of his briefcase and handed it over.

Michael flicked through the pages. "The trouble is, I really believe in a marketplace to establish a local value, whether it's low or high. It reflects the true state of affairs of the local scene. Without it, if we were all on contracts, what have you to compare your prices with? How do you set them?"

"Have you thought about contracting just some of your crops, to give you a comparison?"

That was a bit desperate, wasn't it? He shrugged and handed the contract back. "I think not, thank you. Next year, you'll just look at a glut in Brazil and shrug your shoulders and say, 'Well, we can get them for this price now.' And what looked good now is out the window and you're offering us zilch. Good for WGA's shareholders but not so much for the Australian farmer."

Alan didn't hold his gaze.

After Alan had left, Michael walked over to the window. A little red Hyundai i30 was parked on the street. Jessie stood leaning on the car in the late May sunshine, chatting to two women he didn't know. The sunlight filtered through the red- and yellow-leafed trees, striking flames into her hair and lighting up her face as she laughed at something they said. When had she got so ... "beautiful" wasn't the right word—arresting? He watched Alan Freeman walk out and get in the passenger side. Jessie reluctantly disengaged from the two women, waved to them and folded her long legs behind the steering wheel.

Why was he so attracted to her? Nothing he could put his finger on, just the package, he supposed. The little red car drove off and Michael found himself still watching as it rounded the corner out of sight.

*

"How did it go?" Jessie waited until they'd hit the 65 mph sign.

"The bastard wouldn't even listen to me. D'Larghi's living in the dark ages. Well, he'll find himself being left behind. WGA may not be offering him a second chance. I hope the others you suggested are more receptive."

Jessie didn't answer immediately. "Sorry, I'd have thought he was a good bet. Who have you got this afternoon?"

"I thought I'd attack the people in the valley first. Can I take the car after lunch?"

"Sure." She reached over and gave his leg a pat. "They won't all be like Michael."

*

Jessie waved Alan off after lunch, asking again if he was sure he didn't want her to come along and give him directions. She grabbed the keys of the old ute from the hall table. "Just going to see Patti," she yelled out to her mom.

The country looked as parched and as bald as a badger, as it usually did in May, but her dad had been saying the season was pretty good. The Monaro was misleading that way; the animals bred here were big and tough with great constitution but you had to wonder how they got their nourishment. Her family ran black Angus cattle, and had done for thirty years—before that it had been Herefords. She'd only known the black cattle. But the pictures on the wall in the study were proof that they'd been red and white at some stage. There'd been sheep too, photos of magnificent woolly animals covered in champion ribbons, but the sheep were gone before she was born. Old Lachlan Cranfield, her great-great-grandfather, had been a cattleman, tough and hard, by all accounts. Jessie had been told he'd kicked out his eldest daughter when she'd got pregnant to one of the men who worked on the station. He'd disowned her—never set eyes on her again. But her great-great-grandmother, Susan, had planted five oak trees: one for her daughter and four for the grandchildren she'd never seen. The trees were now huge and stood near the entrance; they were the reason the farm was called Five Oaks. She wasn't sure when that had happened. But it was a great story and each time she passed by them, she thought to herself that Susan had had the last word.

The Cranfield history was a maze—she had no idea how many of the stories were true, or where they fitted chronologically, but they were ingrained in her. Putting people into the right generation was so confusing because she had no idea of dates or which generation the story belonged to. Was it her grandfather or her great-grandfather who'd planted these pine-tree windbreaks? The pines had to be over a hundred years old. No matter, they were part of the place—just as she was.

The oaks at the gate had turned brown and the leaves crunched under her wheels as she turned onto the main road. She couldn't help regretting that she'd insisted Alan went to see Michael D'Larghi. She hadn't expected his total refusal to the WGA deal. Surely farmers needed a break? What with the drought that didn't ever seem to end and animals dying like flies, followed by flooding rains that washed the pasture and the crops away, who would ever be a farmer? She shook her head. Even if she'd wanted to, she was not being given the chance. Fred was the farmer—he was getting the property. It was written in indelible ink.

These WGA contracts sounded to her like a wonderful opportunity for people on the land, to give them some certainty. You sure as hell didn't get it on a year-by-year basis. Prices fluctuated; cropping was a huge gamble. She'd lived with it all her life. Kings one year and blowing the overdraft the next. And the costs were unbelievable—they just went up and up. She'd suggested Michael to Alan as one of the leading growers in the district. She'd thought that if he went with it, the others would be certain to follow. Unfortunately it hadn't worked out that way. A bad choice. And it had been the last thing on her mind that they'd be paired together on the stage.

Jessie turned in the Sinclair's gate. Patti, Paul and David were virtually next door, if you didn't count the little soldier-settler's block in between. And the country didn't look too bad here either. Thank heavens the drought seemed to be gone—for the moment.

"Well, hello stranger." Patti Sinclair put down her laundry basket filled with freshly folded clothes and came over to the car. "You've grown," she said as Jessie got out of the car.

Patti was still as diminutive as ever and the cherubic face was unchanged. Jessie topped her by a foot. They hugged and laughed at the old joke.

"Very funny, you don't have to do that any more—I finished growing twelve years ago. And you know it, because you used to measure me when you babysat."

"Ah. So I did." Patti laughed delightedly. "How are you, Jessie? It is so good to see you. I can't believe you're here already." Patti picked up the basket and they walked toward the kitchen. Jessie opened the screen door for her.

"Why did you measure me all the time?"

"You were trying desperately to get taller and you never believed your dad when he said you hadn't grown, or if he said you had, you disputed by how much."

"How peculiar. I must have been a bit strange. Still, I felt as if I knew your house and Olly's better than my own, growing up."

"Very odd child but I loved you all the same." Patti laughed again and put the basket down on the kitchen table. "I hear Olly's moving into a retirement village."

"No, really? I must go and see her. They lived at Five Oaks for so long they would only have been in the house for a couple of years. Where's David?"

"School. He'll be back shortly. He'll be so glad to see you in the flesh instead of on the screen. Skyping is all well and good but it doesn't compare with the real thing. Which reminds me—when are we going to meet Alan in the flesh?"

"Tomorrow. He's gone to a couple of appointments this afternoon but he's coming to the shindig." Jessie fished a model horse trailer, complete with two horses, out of her bag. "I brought David this. Is he still mad about horses?"

"My beautiful son will love you to bits."

"Isn't it strange? You were my babysitter when I was growing up and then I got to be David's. I've missed him these last three years."

"And he's missed you. We have always had a pretty special relationship, you and I, despite the ten years between us. You were eighteen when David was born and you two get on fabulously. Strange, isn't it?"

"How've you been? Really?"

"Some days are better than others. It's great to see you again. David talks about you all the time."

"Well, I have David to thank for my career choice." Jessie laughed and picked up a photo of David off the bookshelf behind her. "How's school going?" Jessie frowned and looked over at Patti, who was fidgeting with the kettle.

"He loves it, most days. Some days are hard when he seems to know he is different and he can't understand why the others won't play with him or he can't play in the cricket team or something." Patti grimaced. "Mostly it's good," she said more firmly.

There was a short horn blast outside. "Oh, it's three already. There he is. He always insists that he gets to blow the horn to tell me he's home. Come on."

They went to out on the steps and Jessie watched as David was helped out of the little bus by a small, middle-aged woman. He lumbered across the back lawn, a big smile on his face, swinging his backpack. Jessie didn't think David could look happier until he suddenly caught sight of her and broke into a run.

"Jessie!"

She loved the way his face lit up. She ran down the steps to meet him and grunted as they hugged. "You're enormous! You can't have got this big. On my laptop you're only this size." She released him and made a square with her hands around his face. Patti took his backpack in one hand, then she and Jessie swung him up the steps and into the kitchen.

"I didn't know you were coming." He settled himself into a chair at the table.

"I wanted it to be a surprise. Look, I got this for you in England. There are lots of horse trailers over there."

"It's very good. Just like ours only it has windows at the side." Patti handed him a big glass of milk, which he started on eagerly. "And the horses stand across, like these ones."

"Thank you, Jessie." He put the horses and trailer down politely on the table.

Jessie felt a little disappointed that he wasn't more excited about his gift. It was only small but he loved his horse and trailer collection. He had hundreds of them. Usually horses and vehicles were a huge hit with him.

"Why don't you go and get the present Uncle Sandy got you for Christmas. To show Jessie." David's face lit up as he clambered obediently down from the table.

"Patti, he's growing up. He's changed so much."

"Kids do that. Even Down's children."

"Oh, I didn't mean it like that."

"I know. Sorry, sometimes I—the condescending, well-meaning, *pity*—just gets to me."

"I wouldn't do that."

"Of course you wouldn't. You always say what you think and I love you for it." Patti put her arm around Jessie and gave her a quick hug. "Don't mind me. Just having a bad day. If you hadn't been here when he was born, I'm not sure how I'd have got through it. Paul was so useless. Really." Patti put some crumpets in the toaster. "Now, I'm hearing amazing things about your performance last Saturday."

Jessie groaned. "Not you too. Honestly, I don't know why everyone is putting this sexual interpretation on it."

"Interesting reply." Patti looked up. "I was only referring to the singing." Then she smiled. "Come on. I'm the one who knows more than anyone else. I know you were besotted with Mr D'Larghi when you were what, thirteen?" Patti buttered the three hot crumpets then spread them with honey.

"And he was twenty-two and just back from studying in the States. He never even spoke to me. It was only because Dad was always holding him up to Fred for years as the bad boy that he got this glittering reputation. That was enough for me. Anyway, what thirteen year old wouldn't have thought he was gorgeous?"

"And now. What does the average twenty-six year old think of him?"

Jessie shrugged. "Absolutely nothing out of the ordinary. I wonder what the fuss was all about."

"It's me you're talking to, honey. And I'm well aware of what the average thirty-six year old is thinking."

"Jessie." David stood at the door, his arms filled with his whole complement of superhero figures.

"Wow, David! Look at that. Oh boy, am I out of date." Jessie sank to the floor in front of him. "Let me help." She took up an armful of toys and put them on the table. "You've got so many. Who are they? I don't even know this one."

"That's Iron Man. Mom says I'll need to move out into the shed if I get any more. I won't fit." He chuckled.

"Still have your tea black?" Jessie asked Patti, as she got up to turn off the whistling kettle.

"Please. I'll just get this biscuit mixture ready. I'm taking my usual ton of Anzacs to the thing tomorrow. You're all set, aren't you?"

"Patti, you should have told me." Jessie gestured to the spread of figures over the table.

"Well, it's a fairly recent development. Don't worry, I have to admit it took me a little by surprise. So Belinda's been keeping you informed about her baby."

"Yes, I'm dying to talk to you about it properly. Alan's check is signed, so he's all ready."

"I can't wait to meet the boy. You know the engagement isn't official until I give the thumbs up. Will you have time to help me with the riding part?"

"Of course, I've missed it so much, the riding for disabled, and the kids."

"Good. Belinda wants us there at eleven."

"I can't believe I got this week off. There are only three OTs working at the moment, and as I hardly had any leave due, I had to beg a couple of favors. But getting Alan down here to stay and meet everyone was such a great opportunity, plus helping Belinda out and being able to sing—you know me, I can never turn down an invitation to get on that stage." Jessie wandered over to the bowl of cookie mix and helped herself.

"Yum. I'm finding everything so incredibly nostalgic—you make the best biscuits. I didn't know how much I'd missed home till I drove in past those oaks at our front gate. I know it hasn't been all that long since I was home but it's funny how the country grabs you. What do they say? 'Something in the air?' I'll always feel that I'm a Monaro girl."

"Tough and resilient. You can marry and settle somewhere else but you'll always be part of this place."

"How would you know? You've never left. There's a big world out there."

"My world's here. I'm happy. But you'll be happy anywhere, Jessie. You throw yourself into things. I'm just saying that it's one thing you can never change."

*

"Oh, Mom, this is so good." Jessie munched on her mother's peanut slice, still warm from the oven. She had joined her parents at the kitchen table for her second cuppa of the afternoon. "I don't understand farmers."

"If you don't, pity help anyone else try to." Clare sat opposite, in her comfortable gardening clothes. Lex sat at the end, engrossed in the local paper. Fred had gone home early—Sonya had SOSed for help with the twins—and Alan, as yet, hadn't returned. Jessie hoped he hadn't got lost. Along with mobile phones, the GPS was no use in a lot of places around here.

"They all want a contract," she said, "they *say* they want a contract but they have unrealistic views on how much money their cabbage or lettuce are worth. Top dollar is what they want and they won't budge. That Michael D'Larghi is unbelievable. Alan said he wouldn't even consider it."

"It wouldn't surprise me," her father muttered

"You sang so beautifully the other night, Jessie. I was so proud of you." Her mother pointed at the plate.

"It's a lovely song." Jessie shook her head and looked out the window, down to the bottom of the garden, a scene both poignant and familiar. The garden became paddock at the other side of the small creek that meandered through before heading south. They pumped water for the house up from it—when it ran.

It had been her mother's idea to incorporate the creek into the garden. She'd planted a wild kind of water garden filled with winter roses and blue aggies that, as a child, Jessie had used for wands if she was playing fairies and wizards, or a whacking stick for her more adventurous games. The garden was covered in white violets in spring. Her mother had somehow convinced her father to bring in some huge flat stones where you could stand on and look into the water. Or you could walk across the creek, if it was behaving.

It was so peaceful with the little blue wrens twittering and hopping about in the brown, wintery beds and looking at that was much better than thinking about her duet with Michael. Alan had still been furious with him this morning. She stood. "Are you coming tomorrow?"

"No, I'm sorry, I have a doctor's appointment in town that I've been waiting for for ages. Where's Belinda up to now?"

"They're announcing the start-up for her project—potting and growing seedlings. It's training the kids for a job after they've left school, all done in conjunction with TAFE. I've seen something similar in London. It's a brilliant idea, and I talked Alan into going to it as well. WGA's written a check. Good promotion." She grinned at her parents.

"Remind me to give you one too, dear, before you go."

Jessie took her cup to the sink. "I think I'll just go out to see my friends."

Her parents knew full well who she was referring to. "Give them a bit of hay from the shed, will you?" her father called after her, putting down his phone for a moment.

With her arms full of hay, she found her two best friends right down at the bottom of their paddock: Dolly, her first pony, small and sturdy, with a wicked look in her eye and a mind of her own, had to be twenty-five years old; and Savior, a retired racehorse that she'd loved to ride both at home and in the local shows, until she'd left school. They trotted up towards her, nickering softly in welcome and Savior performed his usual dance of excitement, pigrooting a couple of times to show how pleased he was to see her. Or probably it was the hay.

"You haven't forgotten me, guys, have you?" Jessie buried her head in Savior's warm neck, then she stood and watched them as they nuzzled and tore at the hay. "Well, fellas, are you ready for your big day out? Tomorrow's the day. You'd better be on your best behavior. I think I'll take you out for a little ride and quieten you down a bit. Not to mention seeing if I can remember how." She laughed.

With only a bridle and her old mounting block still where it always was, she climbed on Savior's back and thought they'd just ride up and down the paddock. Then she changed her mind, leaning down to open the gate and gripping with her knees as she felt Savior tense under her.

"Okay, guys, let's go." And they started cantering along the dirt track, onto the silvery-grassed treeless plain, Dolly following behind, her legs not quite long enough to keep up.

Oh, she'd missed this so much. God, it was so beautiful—the air was crystal clear and the mountains in the distance like a mass of tumbled building blocks with patches of snow already on the tops. Coming down this week was a lovely excuse to have a little time at home. There hadn't been an opportunity to get here since their return from London over two months ago.

She was laughing helplessly when they pulled up. Savior had started trotting on the way back and she couldn't stop him. Not the best stride for her bareback state. She slid off.

"You horror!"

He reached around behind her and nudged her back.

"Hey, watch it. You want a scratch, don't you?" She turned, laughing, and obligingly rubbed the horse's velvety nose and then up to behind his ears, quickly unbuckling the bridle and slipping it off.

Tomorrow was more than just riding for the disabled, which she'd been involved in since Patti got started around five years ago. The Riding for the Disabled group was only there for show, really, and to give the kids a ride. She smiled. She'd always lent her horses, even if she couldn't be there—which was more often than not. And she was looking forward to it—they always had such a ball. Just to see the looks on the kids' faces and the connection they had with the ponies was simply beautiful.

On the way back to the house she passed her mother on her knees in her garden. She wore gardening gloves and an old felt hat, a very familiar sight. "Should you be doing this?"

"I'm not dead yet. I'll let you know when I'm past it," her mother told her with some asperity. "Anyway I still enjoy it, that's the main thing. What's it like being an occupational therapist in Sydney?"

"Pretty good, I suppose."

"But ..."

"Hospitals are the same no matter where you are. Huge, bureaucratic nightmares where you push and push and don't get anywhere and the patients you've worked so hard on just up and disappear."

"Oh, dear. That sounds pretty grim." Her mother sat back on her heels and watched her closely. "Not like you either."

"I'm a little flat, I guess." She poked at a plant she was pretty sure was a weed.

"You like the job, though?" As always, her mother's statements had a question mark at the end.

"Always. Absolutely. It's a dream job. An OT I was lucky to get it, with all the redundancies in the health sector these days. It's always difficult starting somewhere new until everyone gets to know you."

"Do what they're told, you mean."

"Mom, I've changed, I'm more mature—I've learned patience. It's just that—" She stopped.

"That?"

"I'm not twenty-one any more." She looked at her mother when she heard her snort. "I know I'm only twenty-six, but I want more control. I want to see what I'm achieving. Honestly, hospitals are not good places. Necessary evils. The whole thing about what I do is to help people live their lives better than they could before. Simple. I want to see it happen and then follow it through. That's why this project sounded so good when Belinda told me about it. There couldn't be a more perfect person to get it up and running either."

"I don't know. With that extra degree you got in London you are very highly qualified now. Hey, that's a forget-me-not, you can leave them there."

Jessie moved on to a more grassy-looking plant—if she stuck to those she shouldn't get into trouble. "You know, I don't think I was entirely ready to come back to Australia. Alan got the job he'd been angling for and I know it was right for him, but London was such an amazing place." She gestured vaguely with another weed in her hand.

"Here." Her mother pointed to a bucket that was slowly filling with weeds.

"Maybe I was putting off making the decision to settle down. Living in London was so uncomplicated." The weed Jessie was vigorously pulling suddenly came out of the ground with a whoosh and she fell backward, landing on her bottom. They both laughed.

"No one expected anything permanent of you. We were all just there for a good time—what we could get out of it. Zip here, zip there ... I had a fabulous job, but we spent all our money. There were concerts and plays galore and everyone was ready to dash off somewhere for the weekend. We could go anywhere at the drop of a hat: the Greek Islands; the Turkish coast; Croatia; a weekend on the Black Sea." She gave a little sigh. "Here, all Alan's friends are pregnant or have a toddler, my friends are still overseas and footloose and fancy-free, and there are not quite the same choices. I'm just not ready for it all. I still have this wonderlust. I want to go places and see stuff. Problem is, I never really saw myself settling down in the city."

"Well, you never saw yourself as settling down in the country either—you couldn't wait to get away. It sounds to me like you're having a problem settling down anywhere. Perhaps you're *not* ready, Jessie. So far you've told me you don't see yourself settling down," her mother said gently, "so do you really see the rainbow ending up at Alan's feet?"

"I did. I *used* to. No, of course I do."

"Have you thought about setting a date?"

"No, Alan thinks we should get a house first."

Her mother frowned. "You know we'd be giving you a wedding."

"No, Mom, you do it differently now. We'll be paying for the wedding. Some help would be appreciated, but honestly, we will be doing the wedding."

"I'm not sure how your father will take that news. It's up to you, of course, but I've always wanted to send you off from here. Have a wedding in the garden."

"Thank you, but I just haven't talked it out with Alan yet." To be honest, she hadn't even thought about it. Kept putting it off.

Jessie walked back up to the house feeling restless and wishing Alan would return. She found a pair of old gardening gloves on the back verandah and went back to help her mother.

Chapter 4

This event was a whole lot bigger than she had expected. She looked around the showground in amazement. It was more like a fair. So many people had turned up and it was only a Tuesday. No doubt about it, community spirit was always strong here. All the primary schools in town must have got the morning off. There were children with balloons; parents with their kids in strollers: stalls selling cupcakes; barbecues cooking sausage sandwiches; beautiful handcrafts that people had donated. Marge's quilters' stall looked very colorful.

Alan helped her lead her horses off the float. Walking down Bond Street in London, Alan looked confident and powerful. Nervously skirting horse droppings at the showground, he did lose that bit of gloss. But then, he'd never been around horses much so it was good of him to help. Savior pranced a little as he skittered down the ramp, with Alan holding on tightly. Jessie followed with Dolly, always the more headstrong of the two, and then led the way to the small area roped off for the riding. There was already a line of children with excited faces. One lone horse trudged around in a small circle, led by Patti Sinclair.

"Come and meet Patti," Jessie said to Alan.

"Ah, why I don't I come back in half an hour or so? I need to talk to the organizers and see if they want me to speak; check out the order so I know what I'm doing." Alan was looking at his watch and jumped when Savior nudged him from behind. "Can you take Savior?"

"Sure, I'll be fine." Jessie took the reins and kissed Alan on the cheek. "Good luck." She looked down at the straggly line of children. "Don't worry, kids, I'll have you up here very soon. Hi, Patti, don't suppose there's another hand to help lead around is there? I've brought both my darlings."

"Hello, Jessie! Long time, no see." Patti grinned.

Jessie laughed at her and made a face. Twice in two days *was* pretty amazing.

"I'll send for help, will I?" said Patti.

"Thanks." Tying Savior up to a tree, she made sure the horse was well away from the line of children and went to get the saddles.

"Hello there, would you like a ride?" She looked down at a sturdy little boy in a blue baseball cap who was jumping up and down with excitement. "Hey, quiet down, you'll scare old Dolly here. We don't want that, do we?" She smiled as the child immediately stilled. The kids would do anything she said, they loved riding so much.

"What's your name?" she asked, lifting him up onto the horse. He was heavier than he looked. The joy on his face was unmistakable.

"Sam."

"Sam, this is Dolly." She adjusted the straps and off she went, leading Dolly and following Patti around the track.

She glanced at the next child in line when she returned with Sam and Dolly. He was a fair bit heavier than the last.

"Can I help?"

Jessie looked up. And up. Michael D'Larghi stood there in chinos and a leather jacket.

"Hello Michael," she said, swallowing her surprise. "Are you sure?"

Michael's answer was to lean down and lift the little boy, easily, up on to Dolly's back.

"Um, thanks."

"You have a spare horse, I was told. Can I lead one 'round for you?" His dark eyes were amused.

"That would be wonderful." She paused for a moment, not sure whether to question him on his qualifications. The boy started kicking Dolly, annoyed at the hold up. "Hang on, honey." She turned to Michael. "If you could take Savior over there, he's easier to manage than this brute. Dolly has a mind of her own."

She watched carefully out of the corner of her eye to see if he could manage all right. Being calm and confident was a definite advantage. She watched him smile at a little girl in a wheelchair as he gathered her up and placed her carefully on the horse. Savior, the turncoat, already had a look of total adoration on his face as he nuzzled Michael's coat pocket. Michael didn't seem to mind. The little girl's mother was advising him anxiously how to hold her. Michael listened patiently. He was doing fine.

"So what are you doing here?" she asked him when she returned and was waiting for her next charge to be unstrapped from her wheelchair.

"We're one of the sponsors. I've brought a check."

"Good for you." She smiled. "It's a wonderful project." She didn't think she'd tell him about the WGA check in Alan's pocket. So how much was D'Larghi's giving, she wondered?

Alan appeared out of the crowd and immediately began eyeing Michael and her off suspiciously. Luckily Patti had finished her round and joined them.

"Well, Alan, it's lovely to meet you at last. Patti Sinclair." She draped the reins over one arm as she leaned forward to kiss him on both cheeks.

"Patti, we've met—over the internet. But it's good to finally meet you in person."

Michael and Alan briefly shook hands. Patti hesitated. "You two know each other?" She looked from one to the other as the silence lengthened. She cleared her throat. "Well, come on, we can't stop. We'll talk later." She gestured to the line of children and parents that was steadily growing.

The strangest hour followed. Alan, arms folded and belligerently watching from the side, was not offering to help, while Michael and Jessie followed each other round the track. She was impressed with Michael, who had Savior perfectly under control, not that he was ever a problem at Riding for the Disabled. She could feel Michael's eyes on her—and if Patti winked at her again or rolled her eyes one more time, she would personally kill her.

*

Later, listening to the speeches, Jessie stood behind the crowd of people, her back against a tree, with Alan and Patti standing beside her. Belinda spoke about how the land had been leased to the charity by the council, and that they were planning to start building sheds soon for the launch in a few months' time, hopefully. Then Alan was called to the stage. Amid the applause, he walked forward to a beaming Belinda, handed over a check and received her delighted thanks and hugs.

"We would especially like to thank WGA for their very generous donation of twenty thousand dollars to get everything started. And we have just heard that D'Larghi Enterprises are matching it and raising it by five. Thank you, Michael, so much." There were tears in Belinda's eyes as she hugged Michael D'Larghi, who had come up behind her to join the party on the makeshift platform. The clapping escalated.

"We have to support the community we live and work in. This is a wonderful project to help people help themselves," Michael said into the microphone.

Alan shook hands with Michael, but he didn't look all that pleased. WGA had been outmaneuvered.

"Times have changed," Patti whispered to her.

"What do you mean?"

"A little while ago, that twenty-five thousand would have been cash."

Jessie looked at her friend.

"D'Larghi's deal in cash, you know, always have. They are such show-offs."

"No, they're not, it's just the way they do business."

The Italian community in town had always been strong, ever since the fifties—a by-product of the Snowy Hydro-electric Scheme. They'd formed part of the thousands of migrants employed to build the dam who settled in Cooma. What Jessie did know was that they had all worked incredibly hard and saved their money. They may have avoided a little tax by dealing in cash, but what was wrong with that? What was the difference to the complicated trusts her father had set up? She'd be surprised if the aim of those hadn't been to avoid paying tax, or at least to *minimize* it.

Patti and Jessie walked back to the horses to begin loading them onto the trailers.

*

"Hello, Patti, Jessie, can I give you a hand with anything?"

Michael just couldn't help himself. *Leave her alone.* He'd tried. Jessie Cranfield was wearing a soft, cherry-red jumper over her skin-tight riding pants and she looked fantastic. Good enough to eat. Following her as she walked her sturdy little pony around had been quite disconcerting—her shapely behind and long legs and, God help him, why did she have to wear that jumper? He'd have liked to bury himself in its fuzzy softness. He'd had difficulty concentrating on all the things he should have been concentrating on.

"No thanks," said Jessie.

"Yes, that would be great," Patti said at the same time, looking grateful. "The saddles have to go in the boot, thank you, Michael."

He was so aware of Jessie watching as he lifted the saddles. Alan Freeman was suddenly beside him. As Michael lifted up a saddle, so did Alan. He felt like flexing his muscles for her, beating his chest, anything to impress her. It was ridiculous. He hadn't reacted to a woman like this since he was fifteen. Michael told himself this was not the way to impress Jessie Cranfield. Why on earth did he want to? She was so obviously unimpressed. And her fiancé had been giving him dark looks all day.

Patti handed him her pony's reins. "I didn't know you could handle ponies, Michael."

"Dad's always had a couple of horses around for mustering in the high country. I have to admit I'm more used to harnessing mechanical horsepower."

They both watched as Jessie struggled with the back of her trailer. Seeing the look on Michael's face, Patti laughed. "I don't think there's any point helping over there."

Alan helped pull out the bolt Jessie had been having difficulty with and the ramp came down.

Jessie came over to Michael. "Thank you very much for all your help." She gave him a look that was anything but grateful.

"Glad to have been of some use. Anything wrong?"

"Just wondering why you had to make your check more than WGA's."

"It's a great project, don't you think?"

He felt Jessie's eye on him as he tried to pull the pony onto Patti's trailer. And then she gave it a swipe on the rump to make it move.

Chapter 5

With her charges safely stowed in the trailer, Jessie climbed into the old Landcruiser and placed her phone beside her. Alan was not saying much. Was it really because of the singing the other night? He couldn't seriously still be jealous. It was just a song, after all. Was he annoyed at the way Michael seemed to be appearing all the time? Or was it that D'larghi Enterprises had donated more and stolen a bit of WGA's thunder?

"Could you turn up the heating?" Alan crossed his arms.

Jessie laughed at him. "You should have brought a jacket. I thought living in England would have prepared you for our cold weather."

"I was only there one winter and everyone seems to enjoy it, the excitement of snow and the short days."

"And the pub was warm."

"True." Alan grinned. "The pub was warm and the food predictable but good."

"In other words, you hardly ever left it to go outside and experience the cold."

"Probably not."

Jessie shook her head. The westerly wind was getting stronger and it was definitely colder. The temperature had just dropped to single figures, she was sure. It was almost five and the daylight was disappearing fast.

"In a month's time, it will be dark at this time."

"At least it will only be a couple of months instead of half the year before it starts getting light again."

"Do you miss England? Do you want to go back?" Jessie couldn't help sounding a little wistful.

"I was pretty chuffed when they offered me this job, Jessie. It's not the sort of thing you turn down." He reached out his hand to pat her thigh. "And now I've got you—well, it's the cream on the top." He paused. "I'm sorry, Jessie, I've behaved like a bloody fool. Forgive me. D'Larghi threw me into a spin. I don't know what came over me."

Jessie sighed. "Alan Freeman, I could hit you but I'd probably end up kissing you and we'd run off the road. I was wondering where *my* Alan had gone to. Of course I forgive you. I'm sorry your first visit home got off to such a wobbly start." She swerved to miss a pothole in the road and the trailer swung around a little. "Sorry, it's a while since I've driven a trailer. I'd better concentrate."

Alan sat back and looked out the window.

Communication. That was what relationships were all about. And that was hard when they hadn't been seeing all that much of each other lately. They both worked late and Alan was often away for a few days at a time.

She stole a look across the seat. It was his cheeky, bronzed-Aussie face that had attracted her in the first place. It was funny how she'd clung to anything Australian when she was away. They'd met in London, at a badminton club of all places, and they'd been paired up together as "The Aussies" to take on the rest. Neither of them had played before and it had been hysterical. That little ball flew and feathered, then would suddenly drop. It took a little while to get a handle on it. But it wasn't long before she realized losing wasn't an option: inexperienced as they were, Alan played to win. And if she was honest, the same applied to her. They high-fived at the end of the match and Alan had said, "I'm buying you dinner."

The phone rang, and then went dead. Reception was always bad along this part of the road.

"They'll ring back. I think it's Mom." She checked the number. The wind was now buffeting the trailer behind her. The sooner they got home the better.

"I can't believe you can't get reception—oh, hang on, it's on." Alan buried himself in the world of text messages on his phone.

It had been so lovely to meet someone from home and they'd paired up quickly. Maybe she'd missed home and Australia more than she'd thought. Alan had proposed on Australia Day, at a lovely pub in Herefordshire, with snow drifts four-foot deep outside and a beautiful fire inside and holly berries on the mantlepiece. He was a very thoughtful, beautiful, person. What was her mother talking about rainbows for? Why would she think that Alan was the pot of gold? She didn't like looking at it that way at all.

She pulled up at the gate to the little paddock her friends called home and went around to let down the ramp. Her mother appeared out of the dark with a torch.

"Thought you might like some light. It's freezing out here." Clare shivered, pulling her cardigan round her.

"I've got some calls to make and, if it's all right, I'll have to use the phone in the house," Alan said. "Two people have canceled for tomorrow." He made it sound as if it was Jessie's fault. "Can I help?"

Jessie noticed Alan was shivering too. "No thanks, Mom and I can do it. Go and get warm."

Alan disappeared and her mother got in.

"He doesn't seem very happy."

"No." Jessie didn't feel like elaborating. They pulled up at the horse paddock gates.

"I'll get Dolly out first. Come on, girl, we're home now, carefully does it. Now you, Savior, not that I'm talking to you, you traitor. Why did you have to be so nice to him?"

"Who? What are you talking about? Hurry, darling, I am getting very cold."

"Must be snow on the mountains tonight. I'll just put the Landcruiser in the shed. Get in quickly." Jessie drove her mother back to the shed and parked.

"I wouldn't be surprised—they're forecasting snow. Did you have a nice day?"

"Yes. Those kids are amazing. When kids want to do something they can be little angels, can't they? And they *really* love riding. They commune with the horse in some way. And Savior, he's like a lamb with them. Really gentle."

"Did Alan enjoy it?"

"Well, I think so, until Michael D'Larghi gave Belinda a check bigger than WGA's."

"Oh dear. Is that the problem? You need to divert his thoughts from Michael. Why don't you ask some friends over tomorrow night? The Sinclairs and Fred and Sonya. Belinda, of course. Are you staying for the weekend? You could go up to the lodge for a couple of nights. There's bound to be more snow in the next couple of days. It should be perfect up on the mountains."

*

Michael got up from the computer and went to the bar fridge to take out a beer. It was time to go home. He'd send Sienna flowers tomorrow. Funny, she hadn't ever made a fuss like this before; she'd always been so easy to get along with. But she was good company and he didn't want her hurt with this singing business. Everything was a little more complicated now as he was trying to entice Sienna's brother Johnno Fellini, with his knowledge of the fishing industry, into his market venture. He really didn't need to rock the boat. Sienna had finally agreed to come skiing this weekend. He had still to face his grandmother about the singing debacle and with all the fuss everyone else was making, he didn't suppose he'd get off lightly from her. *Jessie Cranfield, you have a lot to answer for.*

He picked up his keys and went to turn off the computer. The apartment above D'Larghi Motors that Ron and company guests used when it was necessary, and that he'd just spent a fortune renovating, was great, but officially, home was still the farm. Nonna's sole mission in life was feeding him and his father so he hadn't had the heart to move out altogether. But if his grandmother made one more comment about how it was time he settled down, he might change his mind. When he'd got back from the States, he'd insisted on moving into the annex his grandparents had built on to the house when his grandfather was sick and they'd needed a full-time nurse. It gave him a little autonomy.

They said you could live to work or you could work to live, but in his family the difference was pretty negligible.

He put the empty bottle in the rubbish and headed for the door. It was annoying to be so distracted by Jessie Cranfield. She had no right to take up so much time in his thoughts. *Go back to Sydney, Jessie girl. Go back with your fiancé to your life.*

He strode past Frank, curled up on the mat outside the door. "Come on, Frank, hop in." The dog got up, stretched and slowly followed him out.

Michael drove over the beautiful, fertile flats along the Murrimbidgee River that were the beginning of the D'Larghi estate. The sprawling house Gino and Maria had bought in the seventies was nestled halfway up the hill. Ron and Renee Fraser now lived in the big brick house, only five hundred yards away, that his parents had built when they were first married. His father hadn't wanted to live in it after his mother died

"Hello Nonna, sorry I'm late." He was in the door shaking off the cold and firmly closing out that wild westerly. Frank walked in beside him.

"Your father and I have eaten. Come and sit down, I will feed you."

Here it came—the interrogation. He went to wash up and then sat at the table. For the second time that day, he was feeling fifteen again. Damn Jessie Cranfield.

He'd better get in quickly. "Sienna is coming skiing with me this weekend."

"That is a very good thing, Michael." His grandmother gave a little satisfied nod and he relaxed. With luck, he could be off the hook.

His father, Sal, his finger marking the page in the newspaper he was reading, came and joined him, accompanied by a bout of coughing. His father was looking a little older, his hair as thick as ever but quite silver. He'd always been a good-looking man, albeit with a short temper. There was no point in asking him if he was well—he would never talk about his health. Tough old bastard. It was probably the smoking. Michael was well aware Sal still smoked when out of sight of his mother, who would give him a truly thorough dressing down if she caught him at it.

"Anything interesting?" Michael asked, nodding to the paper in his father's hands.

"Cattle prices are down again." He shook his paper in frustration. "And they import beef from the USA. I don't understand—they let the multinationals walk all over us."

"Heard the same thing at the markets the other night. Oranges coming in from Brazil and cabbages from California. There's no such thing as free trade. We just let subsidized agriculture from overseas come right on in to compete with our unsubsidized crops. Unfortunately, when we want to do the same in return, if there isn't a tariff, they chuck an excise duty, or something similar, on our goods. My markets will only sell Australian grown and Australian made."

Sal groaned in frustration. "We grow most things here or close by—the best fruit and vegetables from the Riverina, the most tender meat, trout from the Snowy and we could bring up the fish from Eden. Cheese from Bega."

Michael laughed. "I know. That's the plan. It's the bureaucracy that's so difficult to deal with. But it hasn't beaten me yet."

"You're right, Michael. You persevere and you will win. What's the latest on the project? Mamma, can I have another coffee? "

"Pretty good. No major problems. It's a bit like an obstacle race—you don't know what they're going to throw at you next. I'm coming up against the panel from the state government soon. When do you leave?"

"Tomorrow, I fly into Rome on Friday, with a stopover in Bangkok."

"How long will you be away?"

"A month." He clapped Michael on the shoulder. "You think you can manage?"

"Yes, I can manage. You go and have a good trip, and don't worry."

Sal had been a workaholic forever; he'd been the one to build up the D'Larghi empire to what it was today, but he'd begun to take these trips back to Italy. Maybe he was beginning to slow down a little. Step back. This project was Michael's, and his alone.

*

"To Alan and Jessie. Long life and every happiness." Her father finished the few words he'd put together for the occasion.

Jessie raised her glass again, smiling broadly. These were the best friends she had. Circling the table were her parents, Sonya and Fred, her brother and sister-in-law, Patti and Paul from next door and her oldest friend in the world, Belinda.

Fred filled the glasses again and stood. "Another toast," he said, and Jessie groaned. "I just feel I should warn you, Alan, my sister is beautiful and good natured—mostly—but watch the temper."

"That's it, brother, you are finished. You may now go home."

"But Jessie love, I *am* home." Fred grinned at her. He'd probably had enough alcohol. But Jessie couldn't help laughing at him. "Temper's a bit of a Cranfield thing, but there's one more thing, though—Jessie won't tell a lie. I've never known her to lie, ever. Quite amazing, really. You're a lucky bastard, Alan. She's a loyal little thing."

"I'm not anyone's little thing, Fred." Jessie gritted her teeth, "Mom, I think we need the next course." She started to get up but her mother pushed her down again and she and Sonya disappeared into the kitchen.

"I can't believe you've been working on the Growcare project for three years, Belinda," Jessie said.

"Yep, three years, this November. It's very hard to get people to acknowledge that, first of all, kids with disabilities grow up, and that they need training and a life after school. They just don't hear you."

"I take my hat off to you, it's a wonderful idea." Jessie played with her glass, moving it in little circles. "I wish I could be doing something as useful."

"Well, the offer's open—I'll be needing someone soon, if things start to happen. Wouldn't it be fantastic if you could …" Belinda sighed.

"Unlikely though, we'll be based in Sydney for the next few years. Actually, you never know with my company," Alan said.

"I know, I was only fantasizing. That was an amazing amount of money we got yesterday."

"So how much did you end up with?' Patti asked.

"Sixty-eight thousand. *Wonderful.* And thanks to you, Alan, and WGA. It's a fantastic start but we need more. Rotary came up with five and the Associated Agents collected lots of donated stock at the yards and sold them for us. They came up with ten thousand. The federal government think they can match that but we have to apply."

"I'm always impressed with the incredible generosity of this place. And the D'Larghis are amazing."

"That's Michael's doing, he never stops," Paul said. "I hear he's got some new idea going. A fresh vegetable shop—or chain of them, I should say."

"I can't imagine that will be very successful," Alan said dismissively, sitting back in his chair.

Patti piped up. "What do you mean? Everything the D'Larghis touch is successful."

"Just that he might be out of his league this time. I'm sure he knows his business very well." Alan changed the subject. "This is very good, Clare, the meat is beautifully tender."

Her mother dimpled with pride. "It's one of ours. Lex gets someone in to kill one of our steers every now and again. I can't quite understand how life gets busier and busier even though we're doing less and less—of what we used to do. I'll be looking forward to retiring."

"What's this? I hadn't heard. What do you think you're going to do?" Jessie interrupted.

"Only joking, my darling. You know your father won't retire. Why don't you and Alan go to the lodge this weekend? There's been a couple of inches already and it'll be light, but there might be some snow up on the top. It's always good before the season starts and the people get there."

"Yes! Alan, it would be lovely. We've had a share in one of the old lodges up there for years. Patti and Paul, how about you?"

"We've got my mother coming this weekend, sorry."

"That's a pity. Belinda, Fred?"

But they all had excuses. No matter, she and Alan would have fun.

*

Alan walked into the bathroom in his pyjamas. "Listen, Jessie, I can't come skiing this weekend."

"Why not?" Jessie stopped brushing her teeth.

"I want to get back."

"Missing the city already are you?" she teased.

"Seriously. Why don't we go back on Friday morning?"

"You've got no idea how beautiful the mountains are. I want to show you our lodge, you'll love it."

"I haven't got the time, babe. Why don't you put me on the plane and drive back when you're ready?"

"It won't be the same without you. I won't go by myself." Jessie was disappointed. There was no real reason he couldn't come that she could think of.

Chapter 6

Michael first saw Jessie Cranfield in the parking lot at Thredbo. It was snowing lightly, powdery, large flakes. He watched her pull the skis off the top of her little red car, looking gorgeous in the pale blue puff parka and matching beanie. She bent and picked up her backpack, slung the skis over her shoulder and walked away. Neat and efficient, which didn't surprise him.

Great. As if he hadn't had enough trouble getting her out of his thoughts since Tuesday.

He unclipped the two pairs of skis on top of the car and opened the boot. "Is this all you brought?" He smiled as he pulled out a bulging bag.

Sienna frowned up at him. "I have been very careful. Everything in one bag. I had no idea what I would need, so I had to fit in a lot. I haven't done this before." She picked up a pair of boots. "These boots are heavy."

"Here give them to me." He closed the trunk and locked the car. Click. "Let's go." In the opposite direction taken by Jessie, thankfully.

"So are you going to teach me how to ski?" Sienna asked, as they started the walk up to the village.

"Yes, there's not enough time to get lessons, but I can get you started."

"Where did you learn?"

"In the US. One of my mates took me under his wing and we went skiing all through the winter."

"You never came up here?"

"Oh, no." Michael laughed. "There was never time for such self-indulgence."

"What's it like, apart from being cold and scary?"

Michael stopped. "First, you won't notice the cold. Secondly, there's nothing like it, I promise you. It's going to be fun. And I am here to keep you warm."

Sienna held her arm out and watched the snowflakes catch on her coat sleeve and then melt. "What magic stuff. It's so pretty. It's not all that far from home but it's another world, isn't it?"

"Come on." Michael pulled her along. "I've booked an apartment. We'll unpack and find some food, and then the fun begins."

*

From the back of the noisy bar, Jessie watched Michael D'Larghi sitting and talking to a girl wearing a smart black and white jacket with a faux fur collar; she had long brown hair and big brown eyes. Jessie wasn't sure, but it looked like the girl he'd been with last Saturday night. What was he doing here? Cranfields had been coming here for years. Never had she seen Michael D'Larghi here before.

He looked comfortable. He was talking to a few other people, laughing. They were drinking from a bottle of red. She was extra sorry that she hadn't been able to talk Alan into coming with her. She'd tried but he'd stayed adamant. He'd caught the plane back to Sydney early this morning.

She nearly hadn't come—but she simply couldn't resist when she'd heard the report of two inches of fresh snow falling on the mountains.

What was she doing watching Michael D'Larghi like this? *Voyeur.* She put her drink down and tried to slip out quietly.

"Hey, Jessie!" a female voice boomed.

Oh no. Half the people around her turned and looked.

"Hello, Sandy." She recognized an old skiing mate. Sandy was a ski instructor who spent the northern winter in Europe or Japan and the Australian winter here. She was sitting with a group of people who all looked vaguely familiar.

"Come and have a drink. I didn't know you were back." Sandy's eagle eyes spotted Jessie's ring. "You're engaged! You sneak. Where is the brave man?"

"In Sydney. Pressures of work."

"That would be right. Having to keep you in the manner to which you were born, eh? Poor man."

"Thanks, Sandy." Jessie rolled her eyes. "How's the season going?"

"Snow, baby, there's snow on the ground and it's snowing and there's more snow coming and We. Are. Celebrating." She grabbed Jessie and gave her a big kiss.

"Good. I'm glad to hear it. See you tomorrow."

"No! They're just starting the karaoke, you can't go before we do our song."

Jessie groaned. They'd sung "I Will Survive" together in this same bar more times than she'd like to remember—actually, probably more times than she *could* remember.

"Sandy, no. I'm going."

"Who do you have to get home to? Fiancé's working! Come and sing with Sandy."

By this time, Sandy had her in a headlock and was dragging her down through the crush of people to the tiny space where the microphones were being set up.

"Look who's here, karaoke queen of the mountains."

"Shhh, Sandy." Jessie looked up and saw Michael laughing at her. She smiled back rather weakly. There was no way out of this one.

Microphone in her hand, the music started and luckily people weren't quietening down at all. Maybe she could get away with just the one song before some drunken fool wanted to come and take over.

But after the first few bars, the crowd grew quiet. And soon she and Sandy remembered their old moves and had their audience singing along. Michael drew her gaze; he was smiling and turned to his girl to make a comment.

Was that jealousy? That feeling that she'd like to scratch that girl's eyes out. *Eew.* She threw herself into the music—now even Sandy had stopped and was watching her open-mouthed. At least she had Michael's full attention again.

"That was some singing, baby. You've improved a whole lot," Sandy said over the enthusiastic response. She had, the singing lessons had helped her considerably. Little things like going up and down scales and improving her breathing. She held out the microphone helplessly to anyone, someone who'd relieve her. Out of the corner of her eye she saw Michael being urged and pushed out toward the tiny space. But the audience was not letting her go. Damn. The girl sitting beside Michael looked stiff and unhappy.

"'Someone Like You!'" a voice from the crowd yelled out. They must have heard it the other night. Hell, no. She looked anxiously at Michael but it was impossible to read his face. Then he gave her a wink. He scrolled down a few songs and picked one. She didn't know what it was but she recognized the music once it started.

And it happened again. Goosebumps and tingling and a thumping heart and feeling that she was so in tune with his voice she could go anywhere. Do anything. Damn.

Chapter 7

The eastern-facing slopes had lost their light pretty early. Jessie had decided to ski all day and then go home. Tomorrow she'd be safely back in Sydney. She didn't want to run into Michael again. Looking around, she realized there wasn't a lot of snow on the ground yet this season, despite Sandy's claims to the contrary. The snow machines were out in force and there was a decent run down Crackenback. But a couple of the runs weren't open yet, which made running into Michael a possibility.

But not all that likely. She'd glimpsed him on Friday Flat, the beginners' slope, mucking about with his girl. Probably neither of them could ski, they were just up here for a good time. *Good luck to them.* The season hadn't properly opened and wasn't due to, not for a couple of weeks. Even at the lodge there was only one other couple, and she didn't know them. She pretty well had the Black Diamond run to herself. She adjusted her goggles and pushed off down the hill.

Skiing was one of her passions. She'd learned to ski before she could walk. She loved it up here—there was something about the clarity of the air and the delicious pine scent and the quiet. Sounds took on a different quality when all you could hear was the drip of icicles melting on to snow. When you could see your breath and hear it at the same time. The slippery-slide crunch of skis over the snow. The single warble of a magpie.

And no one else around.

When she got to the bottom she was puffing slightly and couldn't help laughing. She was definitely not fit. In Europe she'd favored the hiking jaunts rather than the built-up ski resorts that were almost like little cities crammed full of people in glamorous ski gear. What she'd loved was putting on a backpack and walking the Lakes district, stopping where she liked, talking to the people she met along the way. The British left you alone; they'd answer, perfectly politely, if you asked them something, but there was an unwritten agreement that was as far as it went. You had to be a bit more cautious with fellow tourists—they were usually on for a bit of a chat. The scenery was magnificent and there was always a warm pub around the corner.

Alan had only accompanied her once on her wanderings. It had been just before they'd left; she'd been dying to go to Northumberland to walk the Hadrian's Wall track. It was full of tumbledown Roman forts and baths and history but he'd been so alarmed by not having his phone or laptop in his grip, let alone a set of car keys, it hadn't been the most relaxing of times. Then it had snowed and they'd had to abandon their holiday.

One more run before she packed up. She looked up the mountain, which now had long shadows rolling down the steep face, and went to climb back on the lift.

She was halfway down before she sensed someone behind her. Looking back, she thought she glimpsed a figure but wasn't sure. She picked up pace, giving an extra push with her poles at the next turn. Then someone was passing her, a very tall someone. Was it? Goggles and head gear and thick parkas didn't allow for easy identification, but the sheer size of him alone made her think it was Michael. This person could ski, she discovered, as she picked up her pace. He was alone—no one else was coming up behind her.

She remembered there was a little shortcut through the pines, as long as the snow was thick enough. She couldn't contain a little bubble of laughter as she cut in front of the skier for the next turn. He was very close behind and as they got to the bottom, he edged his skis in front as they pulled up with a swish.

"I won." Michael pushed his goggles back, laughing and leaning on his pole, his olive skin glowing with the exercise and the cold.

"I didn't know it was a race."

"Do you want to? I'll race you from the top."

"Sure, if you're certain you want to take me on." She just couldn't take the challenge out of her voice, could she?

They got the lift up together; Jessie a little lost for words. Michael had no problem, he talked about skiing in the States and getting caught in snowstorms and how he loved snow-boarding. She was finding it a little difficult to concentrate. It had been a while since she'd raced down this Black Diamond slope. She'd give him a run for his money anyway.

As they stood poised at the top, she grinned at him and positioned her goggles.

"Ready?" he asked.

"Go!" she answered. She pushed off a fraction in front and paralleled down the first steep slope. He was still following when they got to the belt of pines she'd cut through before. It wouldn't work this time because he was right behind her. There was a little hillock she'd avoided before, she would jump over it. She was airborne before she realized there wasn't much snow below it. She tried to twist in midair to get to the snow drift on one side.

A spill on the ski slopes was always spectacular and this was a beauty. She landed in the snow drift, lost her poles, and one ski caught and her leg was twisted underneath her.

"Jessie! Jessie, are you all right?"

Michael was bending over her and brushing snow away from her face. Her leg hurt as she straightened it out. Foot, she thought, narrowing it down to her right ankle.

"Will you let go? I'm fine." She struggled to sit up and looked around for her poles. Neither was within reach. She winced.

"What's wrong?" Michael squatted down beside her, having divested himself of his skis.

"My right ankle, I think. I've done it before."

Michael looked at her boot and prodded around gently. "How about I help you walk?"

She wished he hadn't. He was so close she could hardly breathe and she didn't think it had anything to do with the spill. Her legs had no strength and if he let go, she would definitely fall over. He smelled good and he was so strong. She felt dizzy; she must have banged her head.

"Put your arms around my neck."

Obediently, she did as she was told and noticed a look of unease sweeping across his face. He took more of her weight.

"I don't want to leave you at this time of night. If you get up behind me and put your feet on my skis we might be able to make it if we go slowly. Wait till I put my skis on. Hang on."

But he'd let go and, without his support, she was falling. He grabbed her and pulled her toward him. This time their faces were very close and his lips looked warm and firm. She closed her eyes and willed herself to stop thinking about his mouth. She put her arms up to push him away and tried to put weight on her foot. No that wasn't going to work. She had to get him away from her, quickly. She'd never wanted to kiss someone so badly. This was lust. She breathed out. Pure, unadorned lust. She wanted his tongue sliding into her mouth, their breath clouding around them. Stop it.

*

He struggled to control himself. She was soft and warm and he bet she tasted so good.

He just couldn't not kiss her. But he couldn't kiss her either. He reached down and recovered her beanie, brushed off the snow and pulled it onto her head. Jessie started to laugh.

"What's so funny?"

"That'll teach me for showing off."

"I don't know, it was like you just dropped out of the sky, a lovely present." He smiled.

"Don't be ridiculous." But she looked shy all of a sudden.

Her face was so close, she trembled a little and he put his arms round her to steady her. Or that was his excuse.

He couldn't take his eyes off her mouth. He thought she would taste of gelato. Why did she always bring food and drink to mind? The other day she wore that cherry-colored jumper and the night they sang together, when he felt a fizz, like he'd been drinking champagne. The world disappeared, the snow, the cold, the mountain side. It was just this woman in his arms and her mouth. Their breath mingled. Jessie was incredible. But she was engaged. To be married. To someone else. Hell. He put some space between them and rested his head on top of hers while he tried to get his breathing back to normal.

"Sorry."

"Why?" she whispered.

"I wanted to kiss you."

"I wanted you to kiss me." She took a breath. "Could you tell?"

No he hadn't. He'd thought it was just him.

Jessie's manner became brusque. "Forget it. I'm sorry too."
She didn't look sorry.

"Now how am I going to get down the mountain? Are you
sure you can take me? Phones don't work up here."

The trip down seemed to take forever and was still over
far too soon. He was so conscious of Jessie's arms round his
waist, her face, her warm body pressed against his back, holding him tightly, as they waltzed slowly down the mountain
together. He tried to redirect his thoughts.

"When did you do your ankle before?"

"I was twelve, I went in the races here—my first ones at
high school. I was laid up and missed two weeks of school.
That was all right but then I couldn't play any sport for the
rest of the term, so I was mad as hell. Ouch." They'd gone
over a bump.

"Sorry." He flexed his knees to take more of the weight, trying
to relieve the pressure on her ankle. "I've never broken anything."

"Not even when you were learning to ski in the States?"
Jessie's sharp intake of breath told him he should slow down
some more.

"I got a basketball scholarship—I had to be careful to not
get hurt."

"Do you play basketball?"

"Not any more, I wasn't tall enough."

"Yeah, right. How tall are you—how tall do you have to
be? I mean you look tall enough to me," Jessie mumbled into
his back. She sounded embarrassed.

Michael grinned and pulled her arms tighter round him. It
was funny being so close and not being able to see her face.

"Six-four, and I could have done with a couple more
inches, easy. Watch out for this bump." He slowed down
again. "I was introduced to skiing in the north of New York
State. It was really beautiful. A mate of mine's family had a
log cabin where you could get snowed in for weeks. At least,

that was what I was told, but unfortunately it didn't happen to me."

At last the village came into view. The ski lift, a few late skiers, he should have been relieved. They skied right up to the first aid hut. Jessie carefully stepped off his skis, supporting herself against the wall.

"Wait there." He unclipped his skis, then took his gloves off and lifted her in his arms.

"Don't! Put me down, you oaf." Jessie was laughing.

"No way, I have to complete my Sir Galahad act and get you safely inside. Don't struggle—you're heavier than you look." He was laughing, too. By this time they were attracting attention. There was no sign of Sienna, thank God; she should be back at the apartment showering and getting warm. Reluctantly he put his bundle down, and helped her into a chair.

"Thanks, Galahad. All safely ensconced." She turned to the first aid assistant. "Hello, I'm Jessie Cranfield and I've hurt my ankle. The right one." She smiled her thanks at him briefly. That was it. And he had to turn and leave her.

Chapter 8

Jessie sat in the red plastic chair Michael had deposited her in and watched him walk out the door, pick up his skis and thread his way through the groups of lingering skiers. Already the light was fading. His height and athletic gait distinguished him from the rest.

She grimaced. Was it the cold, the ankle or the almost-kiss that had her trembling like a leaf? She felt like smacking herself. Michael had been just as bad. His girl was just a few yards away, not that distance had anything to do with it.

Oh, Alan. She had been so tempted. If she could barely resist the first guy who came along, it didn't bode well for their marriage.

The peculiar thing was that this lack of control wasn't in character. She knew how to step back, pull away—all right, she laughed to herself, maybe the stepping was the problem—before things went that far. She sighed and started to unclip her boot.

Sandy noticed her on her way through to the instructor's office. "Jessie, what are you doing here?"

"Um, had a bit of a spill, I'm waiting for the first aid, cookie."

"What have you done?" Sandy was on her knees and feeling around Jessie's leg although not that much was showing above the boot. It hurt too much to put it on to the ground, that much she knew.

"I think we'll take this boot off before you swell up too much and we have to cut it off."

"Gee, thanks. You were always one for the understatement." Jessie couldn't help wincing as the boot came off. "Could you send someone up to get my skis? They're about a quarter of the way up."

"How did you get down?"

"A friend."

*

Strapped, bandaged and crutches firmly ensconsed under her armpits, Jessie walked out the door followed by Sandy and met Michael, carrying two bags, followed by the girl, the one who'd been in the bar.

"Hi, how's the ankle?"

"Sprained."

"Lucky it's not worse. What are your plans?"

Jessie hadn't decided what she was going to do. "Probably stay the night and drive back tomorrow."

"That's not wise—it's your right foot. Sienna and I are leaving now, could we give you a lift?"

"No thanks, I'll be fine." No way was she going to get any more involved with Michael D'Larghi. Not under any circumstances. Two hours in a car, with him—no way.

"It's no trouble at all, is it, Sienna?" Michael fixed her with brown eyes that had hardened, suddenly flinty and sharp. And here she'd been thinking they were velvety pools.

"No," Jessie said firmly. "I mean, that is really thoughtful, but really, I'm not interrupting your weekend." She glanced at the pretty girl standing next to Michael. The girl who wasn't saying, "But you obviously are."

"That's okay. Jessie, this is Sienna. We were leaving anyway. What I thought—do you mind if she drives your car and I'll put you in mine?" He smiled. "You can stretch out. There's more room in my car for that leg than in yours."

How did he know what she drove? She looked at the girl. "Hello Sienna, talk some sense into him, will you?"

Sienna smiled and gave a little shrug, "There's no budging him once he's made up his mind. We'll be happy to help you—you shouldn't drive with that leg."

'I'll be fine tomorrow."

"Don't be ridiculous. Where are you staying? Sienna, could you get Jessie a coffee from the cafe while I get her bag? Is there someone where you are staying who can pack your things for me?"

"I don't think so, thank you, Michael." Jessie was feeling angrier. Stupid, a stupid fall and a stupid situation and now it was getting worse than stupid. And then she realized—her bag *was* packed, all Michael had to do was unlock the lodge and pick up her bag and her handbag.

"How about you give me your keys and I'll be right back?"

Jessie fished for her keys in her pocket and handed them over. She wished she could have done it a little more graciously but honestly, what a high-handed bastard. She hadn't even said yes.

Then she watched Sienna make her way over to the café.

"Well, well, Michael D'Larghi, he's your knight in shining armor," said Sandy. "I thought something was going on between you two when you were singing on Friday night." She squatted down and poked at Jessie's ankle.

"Ow. Leave it alone. There is nothing, and I mean *nothing* between us. When did you meet him?"

"He started coming up a couple of years ago. Great skier. That doesn't look too bad, my girl. Keep off it for a week or so."

"Ha, very funny. I'll just take an anti-inflammatory. My job requires walking—a lot of walking."

"Just warning you, it's not good for it." Sandy straightened. "Guess that means I won't be seeing you any time soon, will I?"

"Don't give me any more good news or I will falter under the weight of it all."

Sandy winked. "Enjoy the trip home." Jessie watched her disappear down the hallway.

"Here you are." It was Sienna, standing beside her with two coffees. "Does it hurt much?"

"No, I'm all drugged up and strapping helps, thanks. It's just putting weight on it." Jessie took her coffee. "Where are you from, Sienna?"

"Eden. My family's in fishing and has been for a hundred years."

Jessie laughed. "Mine's the same, only it's cattle. This is very kind of you both. I hate to put you out."

"There's no discussion, honestly. Once Michael makes his mind up there's no moving him. And really, I'd had enough snow and ice. I hear the weather is closing in too, so it might be a good time to go. This is my first time up to the mountains. It must be incredible when everything is covered with snow."

Jessie looked out the window. The light was fading fast but thick, white clouds were forming. It could easily snow. How horrible this guilt was. Couldn't Sienna see the neon light marking "cheater" on Jessie's forehead? Even if nothing actually happened. The girl seemed so nice, and she and Michael had nearly kissed.

She could hardly bear to look her in the eye.

Belted up in Michael's car, Jessie didn't feel any happier. Everything had happened like clockwork. Michael had organized a little quad bike to get her to the car park. Sienna had been really lovely. And she'd felt such a bastard.

Michael slowly backed out and turned to wait for Sienna, in Jessie's car, to catch up with him.

"Sienna is a great girl. Have you been going out long?"

"Yes, she is and, yes, about a year. How long have you been engaged?"

"About four months. I met Alan in the UK." She turned and faced him. "I'm not sure what happened up on the mountain but I think we should put it behind us."

"Nothing happened. Not really."

No, but it almost did. Does that constitute a crime or not? Jessie wondered. She sure felt bad, if that was any consolation. "Are you going to tell Sienna?"

"There was no doubt in my mind I wanted to, so yes, Sienna needs to know."

This conversation about a kiss they'd never had was driving her insane. Already she was hot and bothered and they weren't even out of the car park. Just thinking about kissing him, unzipping his coat and running her hands up his silken skin underneath. *Hey, girl.* This was not how it was going to pan out.

"I still want to." He glanced at her and he looked perfectly serious.

And so did she.

"It's not going to happen, Michael."

Chapter 9

"We can't help what's happening," Michael said. He drove like a racing driver, decisively and using the power of his big car. His large hands held the wheel lightly but firmly.

"We can all take responsibility for our actions." She sounded like a prim kindergarten teacher.

"Yes." He looked at her again quickly. "That's why we tell Sienna and Alan that things have changed."

"Things have changed?" She looked at him blankly. This was happening very quickly.

Michael laughed. "Oh yes. Very definitely changed. I feel very strongly that I would like to pursue my," he paused, "my involvement with you. You must feel this attraction between us." He turned sideways to look at her.

She could feel the redness spreading across her cheeks and right down her neck. He wasn't even touching her. His excitement was infectious. He made everything sound so simple. He was right—it had changed. Everything was upside down. And she was very attracted to him. She looked straight ahead into the dark, willing the heat away.

She could ring Alan and say, "I've met someone else, I need some time." No, she would go and see him, tomorrow,

Sunday, when he wasn't working. How could she get to Sydney? Her parents wouldn't let her drive. Lord, she was jumping ahead of things. What was she thinking?

Michael had been quiet for a couple of minutes, probably thinking out his own plan. Maybe he did this all the time. Had all the right moves.

"I wish I knew the hell what I was going to say," he said finally.

Then again, maybe he didn't.

"I don't." Her laugh was nervous. Michael reached over and took her hand.

"It will be okay, there is something very right about this."

Here in the car with Michael, just the two of them, just for a minute, she thought so too. All the same, it was a bit like taking a step into midair—a strange, weird freefall. The decision would change the rest of her life. The world faded away. Worries about the future, her job; what she wanted to do with her life. Alan. She looked at their joined hands. His long brown fingers intertwined with hers. Her thumb found roughened bits on his palm and she stroked them.

Reluctantly she disentangled her fingers. *Stupid, stupid, stupid.* How on earth could she have possibly thought it would work—be so irresponsible? She would end up hating herself—or him. She couldn't help fiddling with her ring. Michael noticed.

"Take it off." It wasn't an order, just a suggestion.

"No. This is not going to work. You and me. I love Alan." She meant it.

There was silence in the car while they wound their way out of the Kosciuszko National Park. The headlights picked up the hump of a dead kangaroo in the middle of the road. Michael carefully went around it and pushed a button on his phone.

Sienna answered immediately. "Hello, Michael." Her voice came through the loudspeaker. It was so clear it startled Jessie. Jolted her back to thinking more clearly.

"Dead kangaroo up ahead."

"Thanks, I see it."

"It's wrong. To be so impulsive. We've only just met."

"I beg to differ." Michael smiled. "Anyway, what makes putting it off any better?"

"We're not giving what we are committed to a chance. Alan and Sienna deserve better from us. To walk out at the first hurdle is immoral. I won't do it, Michael."

"Are you going to deny what has happened, *is happening* between us? Can you push it aside? Make it go away? Pretend it isn't there at all?"

"I don't have to give in to temptation the first time it rears up at me. I'm stronger than that."

Michael started to laugh softly. "Is this a challenge? I could spend the next ten years throwing more temptations at you, or as long as it takes. I wouldn't do that if I were you. Actually, that's exactly what you were doing from the first minute we went up on stage together. I didn't imagine that look in your eyes."

Jessie shook her head and looked down. She wanted to say he'd been mistaken. But it was true. "Yes, perhaps. I also wanted to prove that I could match you. Your reputation pre-ceded you—everyone knows you're a great singer." Then she turned to him. "We're not going to hurt them."

She let the quiet in the car settle over her again, lost in her own thoughts. She simply couldn't do this to Alan. She loved him. A real love, not this wicked surge of lust that threatened to take away her sanity.

They hadn't been seeing each other for very long before she'd known she was in love. They fit so well together; he was a great mate and they had a lot in common. When Alan got the job back here, he'd said immediately, "Hey, let's get engaged! Come back with me." She hadn't been really ready to leave but she had to go home sometime. Alan had risen quickly on the corporate ladder—he was ambitious and competitive; qualities she had no problem with. To be truthful, though, he hadn't been all that relaxed this week at Five Oaks with her family. Trying too hard is how she'd describe it. Who knows—she might have been the same with his family, if she'd ever been to stay with them.

She let her thoughts go a bit further. How would her family take it? Michael instead of Alan. She studied Michael's profile. Sensing her gaze, he turned quickly, looked at her and smiled. And it was suddenly hard to breathe. Looking out of the window, she saw the thick bank of trees lining the road, their leaves dripping with moisture. Fog was coming in, weaving around the yellow road signs and reducing the headlights coming toward them to thin pinpricks of light. Eerie. She shivered.

"Cold?"

"No."

"I remember at school you used to wear your hair in two ponytails."

"You were in Fred's year, nine years older—as if you would ever have known I existed."

"Tough and independent. Always competing with your brother and pushing his patience to the limit," he teased. "I remember."

Jessie laughed. "I so hated being a girl. I wanted ..."

"Wanted what?"

"I don't know, maybe the freedom that comes with being a boy. I wanted it all. Couldn't wait to do all the things Dad used to let Fred do: camp out; go shooting. I had to be twelve before I was allowed to drive and Fred was driving when he was *eight*. I was frustrated. I guess by being annoying, I got to be noticed."

"You were noticed."

"For all the wrong reasons. Being pushy and tough and annoying." She laughed and then took a breath. "I mean it, Michael. We stop now. I don't think I have anything to apologize for and neither do you."

*

Michael didn't know what to say. He knew what he *wanted* to say: *I'm sorry, Jessie girl, this is not quite finished.* Just her presence in the car was making him horny. This was probably not the time to press the point. He was patient—content to lose the odd battle as long as he won the war. The question he had to answer was why was he so certain about it all? He settled down to the driving, eating up the smooth bitumen, rounding the long curves. Maybe he should stand back for a while. Her eyes were black in the darkness of the car and he couldn't read them.

Now the fog had lifted and they were making good time. It was nearly eleven when they turned into Five Oaks' entrance. The headlights lit up the sign. It looked a bit faded and in need of a repaint. He drove under a stand of huge trees, almost leafless now, and through sweeping lawns up to the house—a sprawling white homestead, with a long, wide verandah closed in by glass at one end.

The light went on as Michael pulled up. Mr Cranfield came out through the front door.

"Your father is keen. You rang them?"

"Yes, I rang before we left. I—thank you for rescuing me this afternoon and for the lift. I—I'm sorry."

Michael looked at her. In the car's interior light her eyes had returned to their bright blue but they were guarded. "I'm sorry too. Give me a ring if you change your mind, Jessie."

He watched her swallow but she just looked at him with those eyes, enormous in the paleness of her face. It had been quite a traumatic afternoon. Maybe it was all a bit of a shock. Give her time.

Twin lights lit them from behind. Sienna got out of Jessie's car and Jessie opened her door and he had no choice but to go and help her out.

He handed Jessie her crutches.

"Dad, this is Michael D'Larghi and Sienna Fellini. They've been so kind to drive me home."

"Michael and Sienna, I appreciate this. It was very good of you."

Jessie's father sounded very formal. He didn't say any more or make a move to shake hands. Michael went round to get her bag from the backseat. It was easy to pick up on Mr Cranfield's stiff and unfriendly demeanor. Why, he had no idea. It was almost as if he had the shotgun out and was waiting to defend his daughter's honor, like in the old movies.

"Come inside, Jessie, it's late."

"Dad," she said. Jessie obviously didn't understand either.

She waited at the front door until Michael put Sienna into his car and walked back to the driver's side. She looked at him and gave him a little wave. He gave her a quick smile. He didn't put the car into gear until Jessie limped inside and Mr Cranfield closed the door behind them.

Chapter 10

The taxi drove off, leaving Jessie, her crutches and her small bag on the pavement. Her mother had driven her to Cooma airport and, one and a half hours later, here she was. Her father had disappeared after breakfast and they hadn't seen him all day. She'd had no idea where he'd got to until he'd turned up to say goodbye.

She looked up at the apartment she shared with Alan on the fifth floor. The lights were on. Despite her key getting the wobbles she was soon in, hobbling down the hall and into the elevator, then pressing the button for the fifth floor. Another key into the front door and she was inside.

"Hello." Alan leaped up from the sofa. "Why didn't you tell me you were here? You didn't tell me which plane." He looked at her crutches and bandaged ankle and took her bag from her. "Wounded. Poor little Bambi."

She hated when he called her Bambi. A shy little deer she was not.

"Come and sit down. I'm glad you didn't drive. I agreed with your parents over that. Did you get a taxi?" He leaned in and kissed her on the cheek.

Jessie sank down into the large white leather chair they'd bought a week ago and propped the crutches against the wall, where they promptly fell over.

"Damn." She burst into tears.

Alan reached over and picked them up. "Hey, don't." He sat on the arm and looked at her anxiously. "Come on, stop crying. What's the matter?"

"It's been a terrible couple of days. Mom and Dad wouldn't let me drive. I've been arguing with Mom for the last twenty-four hours. Ever since I got home from the lodge. Oh damn, it's not home any more, *this* is home. I'm so glad to be here with you. Hold me, Alan, hold me very tightly and tell me you love me and—" She was half up, balancing on one leg and his arms were around her. She buried her face in his shoulder.

"You think you've had a bad time. What about me? I was the one who had to sit and listen to you singing your heart out to D'Larghi—in front of the whole town. I couldn't take it any more, I had to come home. You've got to promise me you'll never see him again. No more singing."

Jessie worried at her lip. "I promise, I did up at Thredbo but that was the last time."

"What did you do up at Thredbo?" Alan pulled back slightly to look at her.

"Michael. We sang in the bar at Thredbo but I'll never do it again."

"What was he doing there? You said you were going up by yourself."

"I did. He was there." Jessie closed her eyes. "I had no idea, honest, that he would be there. He was with Sienna, his girlfriend."

"Right, so you sang together again, did you?"

Jessie nodded. "Then he was there when I fell over and he brought me down the mountain."

"So he saved your life—anything else I need to know about?" Alan was getting angry.

"I almost kissed him." She honestly hadn't been about to say that.

Suspicion narrowed his eyes.

"So where was Sienna when you *almost* kissed? She just stood there when he held you?" Alan sounded as if this wasn't making a whole lot of sense. His arms dropped away. She had to hold on to him to keep her balance.

"No, she wasn't there then. We were halfway down the mountain. I'm sorry. But it doesn't mean anything. It's over."

"What's over, exactly?" Alan was looking at her strangely.

"I just felt so guilty, I had to tell you. We mustn't have secrets, Alan, but it doesn't matter because … it just doesn't matter," she finished lamely.

"Well, that's good then. You feel a lot better getting that off your chest, and I feel a whole lot worse."

No, she didn't feel better—it felt like a huge rock lay between them, lumpy and heavy and immoveable. It might go away, if she left it alone, gave it time. She imagined it dissolving into grains of sand. It had to. *Hang in there, Jessie.*

"I think we should have a drink," she said.

"How do you think I feel? How would you feel if I'd just come and said I'd almost cheated on you? Hey?" He shouted and she fell back into the chair.

"I didn't cheat."

"Don't give me that." He was shaking with anger and Jessie felt the first stirring of fear. This was a side of Alan she'd never seen before. She didn't reply.

"What did you say, 'I almost kissed him?' That's pretty revealing, isn't it? Why? Tell me that. A little experiment? I'm away for a few days and you're ready to party? Damn, you felt like a kiss and he was handy?"

"No!" Jessie couldn't help a nervous laugh. It hadn't been like that at all.

"It's not a laughing matter." He picked up Jessie's crutches and threw them across the room. They whacked into the wall. Jessie sat, shocked, not knowing what to do.

"I think I'll go for a walk. I'll be back, sometime." And he was gone.

Jessie let out a breath. She really hadn't thought it would be this awful.

She couldn't blame him for getting so angry. Alan was right. He'd only been gone a day and she had felt this incredible desire to kiss another man.

*

Her phone was ringing. How long had she been sitting there? Jessie fished for her phone in her coat pocket. She hadn't even taken it off.

"Hello, Mom. Yes, I'm home. Everything's fine, love to you both. Yeah, we'll talk tomorrow."

She stood up slowly and hobbled over to the crutches. They hadn't had a fight before. She should be used to temper tantrums, her dad had plenty, but they didn't ever descend into throwing things across the room.

It wasn't Alan's fault. What a terrible hash she'd made of everything.

Swinging into the kitchen, she heard the front door opening behind her and turned.

"Sorry, Jessie." It was Alan. "I lost it, big time. D'Larghi brings out the worst in me. Let's forget it."

He came up and put his arms round her from behind, resting his chin on her shoulder. "Let's go to bed."

He jumped into bed quite enthusiastically—it was as though the last hour hadn't happened. She was the one who had to turn away.

"Ouch! My ankle is still quite sore."

Alan hesitated. "Oh, of course. You get some rest." He kissed her on the top of her head and rolled away.

It was impossible to get to sleep. She felt like like she was twisting in the air when she saw there was no snow. Falling into the icy snow drift. Michael pulling her up. Michael's hands on the steering wheel.

"Alan, are you awake?"

"Mm."

"I think we should go and visit your parents soon. I've only met them the once."

"Yes, well, we'll sort something out soon."

"They're not that far, the Central Coast. Let's organize it. What did you think of Five Oaks? What do you think of my parents?"

"Lovely people. I like their daughter better. I understand you a little better now, I think. What did they think of me? It was an intense few days." He yawned. "A week I wouldn't like to repeat. How about we wait for a while before we broach it with my parents? Anyway, I need time to line up all my old girlfriends to make you jealous."

"Very funny." She punched him lightly. "He was not my boyfriend, okay? Sleep tight, I love you, Alan."

"I love you, Jessie, so much."

It was a while before she fell asleep, Alan, apparently, had no such problem, as she felt him almost instantly relaxing into sleep beside her.

*

"You should stay at home today. Put your foot up." Alan poked his head round the bathroom door, patting his face with a towel.

"No, there's far too much to do at work and I've already had a week off. There are plenty of wheelchairs if I want one,"

Jessie muttered. She was on her knees, trying to work out what shoes she should wear.

"Well, get a taxi. I've got to run, I'm late. See you tonight."

Jessie looked up briefly from her position on the floor. Alan bent down and kissed her. His lips were cool and minty. Staying at home was not an option. Anyway, she had a feeling they had some interns for a couple of weeks—they could do the running around. And she had to be there to see Mr Flinders before he went home, and talk to the son about trying to organize some special cutlery he could use, talk to him about the house. There might be something else she could get for him too. She was worried about Mr Flinders; he was such an independent old man. The stroke had knocked him around badly, but he was refusing to help himself and so far she hadn't been able to talk to the son. She was sure he was going home today.

Which shoes for heaven's sake? One trainer would have to do with her black pants and she'd leave the bandaged foot with just a sock, for now.

*

The shower was not working its magic this Monday morning. Michael's Sunday-night drive to Sydney usually fueled him up and he started the week full of energy, on a high. Instead, all he had done was worry about Jessie Cranfield. He wondered again if she'd managed to get back all right. He hoped to heaven she hadn't decided to drive. He'd wanted to ring her but he knew that was a total no-no. *Don't even think about it.* He saw Ron's car pull up in the yard and went downstairs.

"Good morning, boss." Ron gave him a grin and handed him a coffee and one of the warm, just-out-of-the-oven strudels he loved from the café down the road. "They said you hadn't been in yet, so I brought you one."

"Thanks, Ron."

"Everything go all right?"

"Yep. She went like a bird. Here are the trips for the next few days. Potatoes out of the south and they're going to Brisbane. Three loads. It's a shame they have to go so far away." He looked at the papers in his hands. "Yep, they're going to be exported. So they go to the docks in Brisbane. You've done it plenty of times."

"Sure, boss." Ron was going round the truck, wiping away his imaginary splashes and, as usual, kicking the tyres. Ron did like his unit in pristine condition before he set off. He got his cooler out of the car and transfered it to the cab of the truck.

"I've got a lot of meetings this week," said Michael. "Trying to get this new project up and running."

Ron leaned back against the truck, his arms folded. "And exactly where are you up to?"

"Good question. There's so much regulation. Consulting with all the departments, checking we're not disturbing the environment. You know, the big supermarkets, they move in to a town, particularly in the country, and within two to three years the local vegetable shop has gone. Why don't they call for that impact study? We're not talking about saving frogs or lizards here, we're talking about real people." He handed the papers back to Ron.

"Now, if we can get big enough, buying in bulk, with a chain of shops, going right down south to Eden and Merimbula, we can take them on. There's a market out there for fresh produce that hasn't had to travel hundreds of miles to get to the people around here. I'm sick of the way the supermarkets ride roughshod over everyone.

Ron finished his coffee and put the cup in the bin. "Well, good luck, boss. Rather you than me. See you around about Thursday." He climbed into the truck and wound down the window. The engine roared into life and Ron left it idling while he completed the complicated log book and trip sheets he had to fill out before he went anywhere.

"Keep in touch, Ron." Michael walked back into his office.

He could ring Jessie's mother, just check she got to Sydney all right. And that was a perfectly reasonable request—after they'd brought her back on Saturday night. Or Fred. He hadn't spoken to Fred for years. No, he'd ring her mother.

*

"Well, that was Michael D'Larghi, wanting to know if Jessie got back to Sydney safely," Clare Cranfield said to her husband as she cleared the breakfast table.

"Thank God she did and that was a bloody miracle in itself. I had to go out before I decided to throttle her. Will she ever listen to anyone?"

Clare laughed. "The best, the *only* way, is to stand firm. Make the point a few times. Where were you when our daughter was growing up?" she teased him.

"And what's more, I thank God for boarding school." Lex Cranfield drained his tea and stood up. "You did a good job to stop her from driving back, I must say. How did you do it?"

"I booked her a seat on the plane and, oh, I took her keys from her as well."

Lex had to laugh. "I guess that would have done it." He grabbed his hat and started to go outside. "He's a bit keen, isn't he?"

"I don't think so. It's perfectly natural to ask if she'd got back safely. I think he was worried that she might drive, too."

"You didn't give him her number, did you?"

"No. I thought about it, but if Jessie wants to give out her number she can do it herself. Anyway, he didn't ask."

Lex looked out at the distant craggy mountain range and leaned over to pull on his boots. "Lucky she's taken. We don't need a D'Larghi on the scene." Then he shrugged on his sheepskin coat and walked out the door. "I'll be back in a few hours. Going to check the heifers have enough water. I put them in the dam paddock but it's a bit low. Fred should start the ploughing this week."

"When are we ever going to address a problem head on?" she said under her breath to the swinging door. "It was all a very long time ago."

The D'Larghis were never a pleasant topic of conversation between them.

Chapter 11

"I don't know whether I'm missing the car or not," Alan said to Jessie a few days later when they were lying on the sofa together after dinner.

"It's all very well for you—you catch one bus into town. And you can use a work vehicle for your jaunts into the country to visit your farmers." Jessie broke two bits of chocolate off the bar and handed one to Alan. "I'm missing it like mad. I have to take a bus and then a train. I would like to go and get my car this weekend but we're expected at the Boffins' christening, this Sunday."

Alan made a face. "Would they miss us all that much? Everyone's usually off their face by two. All the kids running 'round causing mayhem, and me feeling there's a huge slap building up inside me."

"Oh, don't." Jessie started to laugh. "They're old school friends of yours—I would have thought you could at least make an effort."

"An effort to do what? You want to go to Cooma for the weekend. How about I go and get the car and you stay?" he suggested. Jessie whacked him with a cushion. "And then you won't, by accident, run into D'Larghi." Grabbing the cushion from her, he held it to his chest.

"I wouldn't. That's not why I'm going. I don't want to ever see him again."

"Right." Alan pulled her to him. "Good answer. You'd better bloody not."

*

It was pouring. *Heavy rain, wouldn't Dad be loving this?* Jessie thought glumly as she set out for work two days later.

Rain in Cooma, why don't you?

No crutches today, but she still hobbled a bit. How she'd have managed an umbrella and the crutches she didn't know. She really needed her car, no matter what Alan said. She leant up against the bus shelter, remembering the set of Michael D'Larghi's shoulders and his long, easy stride, as he walked calmly round the ring with Savior trudging tamely after him. She moved on to that night on stage with Michael, singing his heart out. His eyes holding hers. He had such—Damn. Yuck, yuck, yuck.

The bus she was waiting for zipped past, full again, whipping up a wave of muddy water that she was too slow to dodge. She really did need her car. Surely no one would have a problem with her driving now, it was nearly a week. Maybe her mother could drive it up and have a couple of days in Sydney. Now that was a good idea.

The next bus stopped and she pulled herself up the stairs. She would only be a few minutes late. She flicked on her phone with one hand while hanging grimly on to the pole with the other.

"Mom, how are you? How would two days in Sydney grab you? If you bring the car I can fly you home. My ticket this time … Great."

*

"I can't believe how I've missed you." Jessie bent and kissed her mother through the open window of her compact i30.

"It hasn't been a week, Jessie, and do you mean me or the car? Be honest."

"Mm, maybe the car ... No, you, of course. Alan will be back tomorrow. He's been at a conference for a couple of days, staying in the city. Not a huge distance but he's been very busy, so it's worked out well. How's Dad and Fred?"

"Good. Well. Overworked. I must say, I'm impressed with the car—it drives like a dream. I set the cruise control and it basically drove itself here. I'm looking forward to a drink, though."

"Well, give me your bag and we'll go upstairs and have one."

"I'll carry the bag. Why aren't you on crutches?"

"Not needed any more." Jessie led her mother into the apartment, trying to disguise the limp. "Here, this is where you're sleeping." She showed her mother into her bedroom before leading the way back to the lounge room. Clare sat down while Jessie brought food and two glasses of wine and set them down on the table. "This is a nice place. It was unnecessary for you to give up your bed for me. I can sleep on the sofa," Clare chastised Jessie, eyeing off the antipasto arranged on a plate.

"Try one of these olives, they are so good." Jessie smiled. "We are spoilt, you know. Cooma has this stuff coming out its ears. I've got to really work to find these fat green olives in Sydney, and now I think I've finally found a place that sells them about three blocks from here."

"Honestly, I can sleep on the sofa. It looks very comfortable." Clare helped herself to the pink taramasalata. "Mm."

"Mom, just do what you're told. Have I said just how wonderful it is to have you here?" And wasn't that the truth. It was as though some sort of calming potion had been drizzled over the apartment. Jessie felt as though everything would be sorted out now her mother was here. She hadn't expected this. The mother–child relationship, this reliance on each other—the ties were very real. She didn't need to tell her mother about the problem she was having exorcising Michael D'Larghi from her brain. She didn't have to talk about how she was walking around on eggshells with Alan at the moment.

She felt better already.

"It's too long since we've had time together. You know your father hates coming to Sydney. I have lots of plans for tomorrow, starting with the art gallery. No, starting with a latte and a newspaper at that nice café I saw just round the corner from here. Or is there a better one?" Clare's eyes twinkled.

Jessie laughed. "I've got just the place—now I've got my lovely car back and I can drive to work. It saves me half an hour traveling."

"Are you sure you're right to drive? How is your ankle?"

"I'm fine, Mom, really. Just a bit stiff and it sometimes swells up when I stand on it for too long."

"Well. There's the answer for you. I'll say no more. So this is the sofa." Clare stroked the white leather.

"What do you think?"

"Beautiful. It must have cost a fortune."

"Our first big purchase. Alan thinks we can start with the furniture while we're looking for a house and then we'll be set up for when we move in."

"And how do you feel?"

Jessie shrugged. "A little bit premature. We borrowed money to buy this." She waved at the chairs. "Now we're looking for a dining table. I don't know how anyone can afford it all—even on our wages. Everyone's doing it, though." She shrugged. "What do you think of our artwork?"

"Did you do this?"

Jessie giggled. "Yep, got some canvases and threw some paint around and hey presto—art."

"Very ... colorful."

"You really are abominable. Say it's lovely, or at least interesting."

They turned when they heard the front door opening.

"Alan! You gave me such a fright. I wasn't expecting you till tomorrow night."

"Hi, babe. Oh, Clare. I didn't know you were coming, er, would be here. Did you bring the car up? Jessie said she was missing it."

The three stood awkwardly for a moment. Jessie laughed. "Goodness, I've asked Mom to stay—you must have sensed I'd given away our bed for the night."

"No, Jessie, I won't stay. I can get a room close by," Clare interrupted.

"Clare, you *must* stay. I'll be going back to the conference. I just wanted to see you, Jessie. I have some news."

"Well." Jessie looked at Alan again; he did seem as though he was brimming with excitement.

"I've been offered the job in China! Marketing manager, the one I wanted before. Isn't it fantastic? But they want me to leave in a couple of weeks. So how soon can you get things tied up here, Jessie, and get yourself over?"

"I, um, we've got this place on a six-month lease." Jessie didn't know what to say. "I didn't know you were in line for that job."

"I put my name into the hat last week. I didn't have a clue they would say yes. Don't you think it's what we need to do, babe?" Alan came over and gave Jessie a hug. "I want to get things back to where they were. Before—" He paused. "We'll talk about it tomorrow, okay?" He kissed her on the lips. "Goodbye, Clare, thanks for bringing the car up. Will I see you tomorrow night?"

"No, I'm flying back tomorrow afternoon. Nice to see you, even if it is fleeting. Congratulations. On the job."

"Thanks. See you tomorrow, Jessie. Start packing. This is what we need, babe." And he was gone.

Jessie poured them both another wine. Taking one to her mother, she prowled around the room, looking at her make-shift paintings. The silence stretched out. She turned on her iPod, and music and lyrics tumbled into the room. She sat down. "Oh, brother."

"Isn't this what you were hoping for? You were saying the other day that you weren't ready to come home yet."

"You're right. I did feel like that. I just don't—" She stopped, biting her lip. "Well, talk about a surprise."

"Whereabouts in China?"

"Shanghai, if it's the job Alan talked about before."

"Sounds interesting. You kids all live such global lives these days."

"What are we supposed to do about all this?" Jessie gestured vaguely. "There are three months left on the lease, and how do I leave work? I'm on a contract too, only for a few more months admittedly but—"

"Work out your contract and then follow him up there."

"I'm not sure I can afford this place on just my wage."

"Alan wouldn't leave you to pay for it all."

"No, he wouldn't. Of course he wouldn't."

*

Later that night, Jessie punched the pillow again in an effort to subdue it into submission, and wondered why she couldn't go to sleep. She should be over the moon about going to China. It was a fantastic opportunity—travel, living in Asia, which, she had to admit, she'd been hoping to do.

But it was just not right.

And he hadn't asked, just assumed that she'd be okay with it. As usual. Were all men this autocratic? Certainly her father was—it was nothing new in her life, it was just getting harder to take. She wanted more out of this relationship. So what was she going to do about it?

It hadn't helped that Clare had told her, just before she went to bed, that Michael had rung on Monday. He'd wanted to know she'd got to Sydney okay. She really didn't need to hear that.

Chapter 12

It was dark by the time Jessie returned from dropping her mother off at the airport. They'd had such a good day but now Clare had gone, everything had crept up on her again. She was worried about how she was going to manage the finances. It was all right for her mother to say Alan would help her out but she didn't know that Jessie had paid the bond: three thousand dollars. She let herself in quietly. Alan was home, sitting and reading some papers at the table.

"Hey, babe, come and look at the specifications of the job. There's quite a lot of traveling—I'm covering Thailand and Indonesia as well. They pay for the first month's accommodation until we find something. They have a company, I think, that helps you relocate … Yes, here they are. What do you think?" He looked up. "It's what we need, don't you reckon? To get away."

"I'm not sure when I can get there."

"What do you mean? Oh, your job? They'll let you out of that contract, won't they?"

"I'm not sure."

"What's with all this 'not sure' business? You'll sort it all out and follow me over."

"What do we do with the sofa?"

Alan laughed. "Bring it with us, of course. It's family."

Jessie just looked at him. "Sure. Yes. Let's hit the internet and start looking for apartments in Shanghai."

*

A few hours later, Jessie lay next to Alan in bed. Her eyes were refusing to close, following the shadowy shapes of the furniture and the cracks in the venetians, letting the striped street light in. It had been one week since she'd fallen over in the snow. She tried to think of that as being the event that had changed things so much.

It was also over a week now since Alan and she had made love. At first it had been out of consideration for her ankle and, then there was the conference—but tonight, what was stopping them? All this China business. She hadn't been able to generate quite the enthusiasm she'd hoped while looking for an apartment. Had Alan noticed? There was this cold kernel of dread inside her. What was wrong with her?

She didn't want to go.

Her job, she liked her job. Honestly, earthshattering it was not. A hospital was a hospital anywhere. But it took a lot of energy and hard work to start a new job, getting to know new people, and it was awful leaving them so abruptly.

Who was she kidding? Excuses, excuses.

She had liked being home, seeing the farm and catching up with Patti and David. She really hadn't realized how much she'd missed it, and them. Fred and Sonya and the babies she'd hardly seen. Family was important to her.

She'd left them before.

And when she was home she'd told her mother she wanted to be back in London. Wanted to travel.

She was a nutcase. Did she even know what she did want?

She didn't want to go to China.

Or was it just that she didn't want to go with Alan?

*

On Wednesday night, Alan was later than usual. Jessie was cooking chops on their mini barbecue out on their mini balcony when he charged in, waving a paper at her.

"Look at this, it's all organized—my airline ticket to Shanghai. A stopover in Singapore to catch up with the people there and then Shanghai, here I come."

"Alan, I'm not coming." Jessie didn't even know where it came from.

"What?" Alan stopped on his way to the fridge and turned back. "Why not?"

Now that was a good question. She turned the chops over again.

"Why didn't you say something before? It's going to be very hard to get out of this now, after I've said I'd go."

"No, I didn't mean that you shouldn't go, it's just that I can't."

"Can't? Hold on. Do you mean won't? And where does that leave us? You and me?"

"Something about it feels wrong to me. Maybe we should take a step back and—"

"Is it your job, are they making things difficult for you?"

"No, well, yes, they don't want me to go." And that was the truth.

"And what about Michael D'Larghi, how much does he have to do with this?" Alan was shouting now.

"Absolutely nothing." It had nothing to do with him, she was sure. Something was burning. She took the chops off the grill.

"So, this is it. You're breaking off our engagement."

"I don't want to go to China." She was steadfast. "I'm sorry, we should have talked about it some more. Talked it through."

"You don't want to go to China or you don't want to stay with me?"

"Both," she whispered. This was the hardest thing she'd ever done in her life.

Alan's face was a mixture of incredulity and fury. For the first time she felt a little afraid; this was the second time Alan had lost his temper with her. Sure she'd seen him put his foot down and tailgate cars when he was mad, but now she'd seen him out of control, throwing things around the room, she wondered how far he would go. He didn't look broken or hurt. Just angry. He took a step forward but Jessie had nowhere to go on the little balcony and she stood her ground.

"You know something? Girls who can't commit must have a bit of a problem. I don't know if I could trust you again, anyway." He started to turn away, then changed his mind. "This is just the thing I should have expected from you and your stuck-up family. Graziers," he sneered. "You just haven't picked up on the fact the world has changed. You're all has-beens, now. You still have the land but no money. Your power has evaporated but you're all living in the dark ages and you still think you can dictate the rules to everyone else. Good luck. And particularly with D'Larghi, because he has no respect for your lot either."

Where had that all come from? Is that what he really thought about her family? About her? Jessie was totally shaken. "If that's what you feel, I think maybe this is a good time to part ways. Here." Trembling, she pulled at her ring. To her surprise, it slipped off easily and she handed it back. Alan took it. He was so angry she thought he might throw it over the balcony, but he pocketed it instead.

"I'll be leaving next Wednesday. I'll have my things picked up and put in storage. I'll leave you with the flat but I won't be paying any more rent after I leave. You'll have to find someone else. Shouldn't be too hard."

"Thanks a lot." Why had she suspected this was going to happen? She couldn't afford to stay, so she'd lose the bond money. Well, she wasn't going to ask him for it. She had to take the blame for this. It was her doing. But she felt it was right, down deep inside, she *knew* it was right. It was a funny thing, but sometimes you thought you knew someone through and through and then you realized you didn't know them at all.

*

The next Wednesday evening, when she got home, Alan's packed bags were missing from the hallway and the sofa had gone. She picked up his keys from near the sink. Jessie sank to the carpet and took a deep breath. Now he'd gone, the sense of relief was overwhelming.

Chapter 13

These late autumn days on the Monaro were nothing short of spectacular. The air was so clear and there was a special light warming the countryside, softening it and intensifying the purples and blues of the mountain ranges. Michael stood in the ploughed paddock with its straight, straight lines, the deep rich basalt soil sucking at his boots, and took a deep breath.

"They told me I'd find you here." Renee, in work clothes and pink and yellow gumboots, joined him. "What on earth are you looking at?"

"I feel connected to this view. All that." He spread out his arms. "I can't work out if I belong to it or it belongs to me."

"Bit of both, I'd say. I need to ask you about the fertilizer. Ron's expected back in a few hours and he wants to know where you want it."

Michael threw back his head and laughed. "Thank you, Renee. I'll come on back with you now. You've been speaking to Ron since I talked to him at lunchtime?"

"Oh yes, just a minute ago, he's running ahead of schedule."

"That's good—he'll get a decent sleep tonight."

"I saw Patti Sinclair in town today. You know, the Cranfield's neighbor?"

"Yes, I know Patti."

"Well, she heard today that Jessie and her fiancé are going to China. And I just wondered, had you heard?" she asked Michael innocently, turning for his reaction.

Michael kept on walking. "No, I hadn't heard. Are you sure?"

"Patti said Clare Cranfield had told her, so I reckon it's pretty much on the spot."

"It's probably right then." Michael kept his voice even. But he couldn't help the little jolt of fear that shot through him.

Alan wasn't the right bloke for Jessie Cranfield.

*

In a corner of the large machinery shed were Michael's bikes. His old bike, a Ducati, gleaming and polished, stood in the corner. In pride of place was his new bike, the BMW 1200 GS. Now that was a grand bike. Fast, big and comfortable; you could travel for hours on it. It would go wherever his mood dictated. Today, it was long distance that he needed—a long way there and a long way back. Michael checked the gas and buckled on his helmet. He'd already put on his leather pants, calf-length boots and jacket up at the house. He'd told his grandmother he'd be back sometime, not to keep tea. He turned the key, heard the roar as it started up, the engine perfectly tuned, and was off. Just off. No plans. Just a burning need to ride the demons out.

He'd discovered in his late teens that when things got on top of him, when he felt like hitting out at the world or when he got excited about something, that to go off by himself, on his motorbike, was the answer. He'd bought this BMW five years ago. It was a classic. Take him anywhere, it could go on dirt, power through the roughest country and burn anyone off on the tar. Best of all worlds.

He'd gone through quite a bad patch in his teens. He'd been so angry at the world, his mother—well, it was hardly her fault but he blamed her. An accident. Even now, after all these years, he was furious. It had had such a profound effect on his dad. And, like a ripples on a lake, it affected Sal's relationship with Michael. He just didn't understand. Where was she going that night? Why wouldn't his father talk about it? Why wouldn't he just say she was going to Canberra for the day? Something. Anything.

He believed everything happens for a reason.

It had taken a few years for him to realize his license was his ticket to freedom. To jeopardize that was insane. So he took to riding bikes in his time off. Curving down the Brown Mountain to the coast was a beauty. Then there were the dirt roads around here, roads that crisscrossed the high, flat country, cutting through the open grassy paddocks. They were some of the best rides in the state. Not the best roads exactly but on the other hand, not a lot of law policing it either. With a quick smile, he closed the gate behind him.

He went fast. Hunched over the handlebars, he loved the weight of it, the perfect balance and the speed. It was a fabulous design.

He rode till he felt the angst draining out of him and he noticed the fuel gauge dipping. Not a good idea to run out of gas around here.

His head was clear, finally, and it was so obvious. He didn't want Jessie to go to China, and if he didn't want her to go so much, he'd better tell her. Or forget her, which didn't seem feasible right now, as her face was a permanent fixture in his mind. He sure had enough on his plate without adding another complication to his life.

He pulled the bike around and headed for home.

*

The bike purred up to the machinery shed and he parked it alongside the Ducati. He turned off the ignition, unbuckled his helmet and kicked out the leg. He sat there for a moment until he registered the cold night air starting to penetrate through his haze. The adrenaline was gone. He felt tired and ready to hit the sack. So he'd made his decision, he had to tell Jessie.

Which left him with Sienna to deal with. She'd been quiet since their weekend in Thredbo. Understandably. One thing for certain, out of all this he'd proved to himself Sienna wasn't the right girl for him. Maybe she knew or suspected that he was attracted to Jessie Cranfield. Suppose nothing eventuated with Jessie and she left for China having told him no?

His problem was he wanted Sienna's family to go into the fruit market venture with him. They were in fishing down at Eden, had a couple of trawlers, smoked their own trout and eels. He was to talk to Johnno, Sienna's brother, later in the week. He should have this conversation with Sienna first. Rocky it may be, but he owed it to her. He suspected his nonna would be the worst affected.

He removed his helmet and slipped off the bike and walked back to the house. He shook his head. What will be will be.

No. He'd have to find a way to talk to Sienna.

Sienna first then Jessie.

Chapter 14

Michael stood on the street corner with two of the five men who'd attended his meeting, the Sydney peak-hour traffic snarling beside them. He shook hands with Johnno Fellini, Sienna's brother. This hadn't been the happiest of meetings. Johnno was clearly upset and Michael was pretty sure he knew why.

"Thanks very much. I think it has been productive on all fronts. Thanks for making the journey."

"I will put it to the family. This kind of commitment cannot be undertaken lightly."

"Of course, I understand. It would mean a lot to us to have the Fellinis on board." Michael watched him walk away. There was a bit of bridge mending to be done there. He turned to the other man. "Thank you for coming too, it meant a lot to have a few investors in the room."

"Yes. I think they were quite impressed." The man, older, with a middle-aged paunch and a gray mustache, shook hands with Michael.

"Well it's not often you get five investors in the room, hot to trot." Michael shrugged.

"It's a good plan, Michael, you've thought it out. I'll be interested to see how you get on with the development applications. How long will it take, do you think?"

"We get Fyshwick up and running first. The ACT does most things different to here but the proper DAs are into the council so they know we mean business. Maybe six months? Depends on the council. We're working on Eden and Cooma now. You never know, they're all screaming for development projects at the moment. As long as we can impress on them how big this could be, that we're not just starting another fruit and veg shop down the road. Anyway, I'll be in touch." Michael smiled and raised his arm in farewell until the man was out of sight, then looked at his watch. There was still time. His plane didn't leave for two hours.

He rang the hospital. It was the only contact point he had for her. He was not going to ask anyone he knew for her number.

"Miss Jessie Cranfield," he said to the receptionist.

And he waited. And waited. He leaned against the wall of the building and watched the traffic. Stop, start, crawl, stop, start, crawl. The set, bored expressions on the drivers' faces; such a waste, one per car. Buses swinging in and out of their red lanes, so impatiently.

"Hello?"

He got a shock to hear her voice. "Jessie, it's Michael, how are you?" This was painful. Was that as good as he could do? "Have you got a spare half-hour or so?"

Jessie didn't say anything, so he continued, "To meet up, have a coffee? I have to be on the plane at eight."

Thank God, she said yes.

"Do you know Morelli's, up in Edelstone Street? I'll meet you there as soon as you can get there."

*

Michael walked quickly down George Street, thinking he'd never get there before Jessie, so he looked around for a taxi. Useless—he'd be faster walking. Jessie was driving so she wouldn't be making good time either. How did Sydneysiders stand this endless line of traffic going nowhere? It was getting dark. He threaded his way through the wall of commuters with one thought in their heads: getting home. It reminded him of his days as a second rower in the rugby team.

He pushed open the door into Morelli's and strode past the boxes of fresh vegetables—some, he noted, with the D'Larghi logo on them—to a table in the corner. A quick look around told him she wasn't here yet. His breathing settled. He needed a plan for what he was going to say. Maybe he'd play it by ear.

Watching her walk in, he was aware of a catch in his breath and a sudden lift of spirit. A yearning to take her in his arms. She looked fresh and rosy. Edible. He really had to stop associating her with food.

*

Morelli's. A great place for food, wine and coffee, someone had been talking about it just the other day. Jessie saw Michael near the back as soon as she was inside the restaurant. Why was she so glad to see him? She was not responsible for the smile that wrapped itself around her face, it did just fine all by itself. It was quite dark outside and the light inside was muted. There were lots of people, groups, couples, as she made her way, swiftly, toward the tall figure now standing at the back of the room.

They just stood there looking at each other.

"Hello."

"How's your ankle?"

"Fine. What are you doing in Sydney?"

"I had a meeting. Like a coffee, or a wine?"

"Just a coffee, thanks. I got such a surprise when you rang."

"I wanted to make certain you were okay. I generally follow up all my rescues, make sure they're fully recovered."

"I haven't even thanked you properly. I'm not sure what I'd have done."

"You probably wouldn't have fallen if I hadn't been there." Michael's lifted eyebrows, coupled with a slight smile, made her stomach flip.

"Oh, I can usually manage to get into trouble all by myself, no problem."

"I'm glad I was there."

"Sandy said my skis were found. She's kept them for me. Have you been back up?"

"No, things are getting pretty hectic, really."

"What's happening in your life, Michael?"

The waiter came and they placed their orders. Skinny latte times two.

"There's a bit of a project I'm trying to get off the ground."

"What sort of thing, if you don't mind me asking?"

"I'm trying to start a fresh food and vegetable chain, big stores, to take on the big two. Or at least, to stop them getting away with so much."

Michael smiled at her and her stomach flipped again. Why was it doing that? "I remember, someone did mention it. But that sounds dangerous. They are pretty big people to take on. No wonder you weren't in the mood to look at Alan's contract. Should you be telling me?" To Michael, she'd be part of the enemy camp.

Michael shrugged. "It should be in the press tomorrow. The development approvals are in and the finance, as of two hours ago, is sorted. I'm ready. They probably won't even take any notice. Yet. But I think they might, one day." David talking about taking on Goliath maybe looked like this. Before he saw Goliath.

"Good luck."

"How do you like the hospital?"

"It's okay. Great people, I love what I do."

"How's Alan?"

She stirred her coffee even though she didn't take sugar. "He's fine." So help her, she couldn't say anything more, it was sticking in her throat. Michael didn't need to hear it. "How's Sienna? Please thank her for driving my car back that night. It was very kind."

"Sienna is well, she was a bit upset over our singing the other night."

"Oh, I'm sorry."

"Nothing to be sorry for. It was pretty amazing" He paused. "And a great song. Perhaps we should give it some thought, though, before we decide to do it again." He was smiling and his eyes crinkled.

No doubt about it, they'd proved it that night at Thredbo. Not that Alan was a worry any more. She hadn't told anyone about breaking off the engagement—she didn't feel like telling anyone just yet. What a mistake she'd made. She'd even worn another ring on her finger, so she didn't have to tell anyone at work. Coward. She just needed a little more time.

She finished her coffee. "That was lovely. I should go, thank you again, for everything."

She tried to pay at the counter but the young man in the black T-shirt wouldn't hear of it. "No, no, a friend of Michael's, no. Have a good evening."

*

Full marks for botching that up.

Michael sat down, resisting the urge to follow Jessie outside. He carefully rehashed their conversation and wondered when he should have got down to the nitty-gritty. All it would have taken was, 'Are you going to China?' And then he could have told her, 'I don't want you to go.' And he should have told her his relationship with Sienna was over.

Instead, they'd been perfectly polite. He shouldn't have mentioned the singing. Alan had been furious, he knew. Jessie had pulled away like a scalded cat.

It had started off so well.

Chapter 15

"No." Patti was adamant. "How about we Skype? Have you got time?"

"I'm so tired," said Jessie. "It's been a hell of a day."

"I know. Turn on Skype, I want to see you. Just because you're in the great land of Oz now, doesn't mean we can't see each other."

Jessie knew exactly why Patti wanted to look at her face. She'd be able to pick her unhappiness despair, *whatever*, right off. She got a tea towel and hung it over her face before she turned her laptop on.

Patti chuckled as soon as she saw it. "I knew it. Take it off. Sometimes I think I know you better than I know David, and he's pretty readable. What's the matter?"

"In a word, finances." Jessie downed the dregs in her glass. "I can't scratch up enough for the rent."

"Start from the beginning again. I thought you were going to China?"

"Um, not exactly."

"That glass of yours needs a refill, and I'm going to get one too, be back in a jiffy."

Patti had returned with some knitting and a glass of wine.

"What are you making?" Jessie asked, keen to change the subject.

"I'm not sure exactly, just doing a bit of experimenting with this wool I got from a girl down the road who's breeding black sheep."

"Pretty."

"Yes. Now continue."

*

One hour later, Jessie rang Raven, a girl at the hospital, who had been talking about apartment hunting the other day. "Do you need somewhere to live for three months?" And Raven said yes. Then she rang Belinda. "I know this is short notice, but Patti said you were looking for someone to help with the Growcare project and if I can get out of this position in, say, a month, can you give me a job?" Then she rang her mother. "Can I come home?" And then, "Can I talk about it later?"

Yes. Yes. Yes. Jessie cracked her tea towel like a whip and danced around the apartment. Now who'd have thought it could all be as simple as that? She picked up her phone.

"You're a legend."

Patti laughed at her. "See what happens when you think things through? It will be so good to have you back, Jessie."

*

By Friday, Jessie had returned to ground with a thump. Unfortunately, things hadn't panned out for her exactly as she'd thought.

Raven couldn't talk her boyfriend into paying so much for the apartment. If Jessie'd had any sense, she'd have talked Alan out of it as well. Work said they couldn't possibly replace her in under two months. And Belinda was champing at the bit for her to come on down. "There's so much to do! Hurry up." It still would be all right if it weren't for the damn lease. She could sell the car but she owed more money on it than she'd get.

*

By Sunday night, Jessie thought she was going mad. This turn around in her head was nothing short of bizarre. The thought of going home was so exciting. She couldn't get there quick enough. Working out how she was going to manage the move and when was the problem. If she broke the lease, she'd lose the bond. Still, that wasn't the end of the world.

Walking was helping to relieve the anxiety a little. She'd ended up at Darling Harbour, the crowds thick with tourists. Even though the wind was chilly, it was nothing compared to the Monaro at this time of year.

Her phone buzzed, and she glanced at the number. Not one she recognized.

"Hello? ... Michael?" Jessie stared out at the flat, oily surface of the water before her as she listened. The boats were hardly rocking. The city was turning on the lights—it was very pretty. It was cold too, though, and she shivered, pulling her jacket tightly around her. It must be the wind-chill factor, she thought, as the goosebumps raced up her arms, it certainly wasn't hearing his voice. "Tonight? After midnight? Where? You're not serious ... Okay, I'll be there. No, I'll drive." What the heck, she probably wouldn't be sleeping then, anyway.

This had to be one of the maddest decisions she'd ever made in her life.

*

The big green signs had helped. Jessie looked with amazement at the area ablaze with lights and bustle. She drove up to the entrance gate. Sure enough, the red-haired man inside the kiosk looked up from his screen and gave her an interested glance before waving her through and pointing to a little space further up. She parked and walked back. Michael had said to talk to the man at the gate.

"Jessie? Sure come on in."

It was warm in his office. He handed her a fluoro vest to put on and a visitor ID to hang around her neck. "Michael said he'd be busy for a while longer, but you can go ahead to the café." He grinned. "I'll show you where to go. Just wait a minute." Two big semis roared up beside them. Her friend took the paperwork from the drivers. Then he walked outside with her. "Just stick to the paths, go left and left and right—don't get on the road at any time for heaven's sake. Watch where you're going, it's a madhouse in there." Then he grinned again. "And you can tell Michael he owes me one."

Jessie smiled and pulled her orange fluoro vest round her tightly and set off. Madhouse was right. There were forklifts zooming around, big trucks, huge trucks and little trucks; men waiting with their folders to check off the pallets coming out of the trucks and into the vast sheds. She stopped for a moment, fascinated as a little forklift carefully picked up a pallet piled high with bags of potatoes and deposited it precisely where it was wanted. They made it look so easy. There was a huge amount happening but, funnily enough, no panic. Ordered chaos.

This had to be the café—tables and chairs, everyone wearing their fluoros. Not a lot of women; as a matter of fact, she was attracting quite a bit of attention. She sidled up to the only other woman there: gray-haired, dressed in a yellow apron and deep in conversation with two men.

"Hey Zara," one of them said, nudging his friend.

"Ah, Jessie." She turned around. "I'm Zara, Michael, he tells me you come. I get you a good strong coffee."

"Sounds good, I hardly think I need caffeine—this place is really humming."

The woman eyed her curiously. "Michael won't be long."

Jessie wondered whether Michael brought dates here often. To quell her nervousness, she decided to talk.

"You work all night?"

"Yes, I work nights three times a week."

"Michael, does he come here often?" She was trying not to be nosy but she couldn't help being a little intrigued.

"It's Sundays he comes. "

"Oh."

Suddenly he was there, appearing out of the darkness, huge and solid in the yellow lights, a big grin on his face. She'd not seen him in jeans before, and there was a brown kelpie, a graying muzzle showing its age, at his heels.

"I wasn't sure you'd come." He leaned over and scratched the dog. "This is Frank, my traveling companion."

Jessie laughed. "Hello, Frank." The dog gave her the strangest look. She glanced around. "What an amazing place. This is a first. I've never been asked to go for coffee at one in the morning before."

"Could be a first for me, too," he said quietly, looking down at her.

Well that answered one question, if she believed him.

"Your coffees are ready," Zara sang out from behind the coffee machine, as she pushed the two cups toward them.

"Good trip?" Jessie stirred sugar into her coffee once they were seated at a table. She never had sugar, at least, not for a long time.

"Yeah, particularly after you, um, said you'd come." If she didn't know him better, she'd think he looked a little nervous.

"Where's the truck?" She peered outside.

"It's still being unloaded." Michael looked at her. "Jessie, I wanted to tell you the other night. I lost my nerve, but I think it's important to say things. Tell people what you think, don't you agree?"

"Yes. Sometimes. On the other hand, you know what they say about letting sleeping dogs lie." He didn't return her smile, just looked tense.

"Jessie. I think you should reconsider going to China."

And her answer should be, "But I'm not." But she couldn't resist.

"Why not?"

"There's something going on between us, I don't care what you say. It needs to be resolved. I think you're being unfair to Alan."

"That's all very well for you to say, what about Sienna?" she asked steadily.

His reply was swift. "Sienna and I are no longer involved. Except in a business sense." He was watching her intently. So was the dog.

So Sienna was history. "And exactly how do you propose we resolve this situation, or is it a dilemma?"

Michael reached across the table and took her hand. Oh, there it went again. An electric shock. "We'll find a way." He gave her hand back and then got up. "I don't know why this is, but every time I'm with you I get hungry. I'm just going to order a couple of toasted sandwiches. Do you want any?"

She shook her head and tried to avoid Frank's unwavering gaze.

Jessie watched him, leaning on the counter, chatting to Zara as if everything was normal. She looked round at people talking, some drivers reading newspapers, some watching the television up on the wall. What was Michael suggesting? A physical relationship to release these lust enzymes or whatever they were? A one-night stand? Something serious?

Ridiculous. It had been a long week. It was the middle of the night and she was on this weird high. She couldn't trust her senses or think straight right now. Nor resolve anything. Luckily, Michael didn't know she'd already decided not to go to China and she wasn't going to tell him. It would sound so weak, wouldn't it: "Oh if that's what you think then I won't go." Wonderful.

Michael returned to the table carrying his sandwiches wrapped in greaseproof paper in a bag. He was leaving?

"I've got to get going, Jessie. Think about it, won't you? Please. Where's your car?"

"Down near the gate." She stood up. The dog stood too, waiting patiently.

They walked back along past the stalls that were being set up for the buyers that would descend at first light. Michael pulled her to him suddenly as a forklift came around the corner. Her heart started to thump and she didn't think it was from the forklift.

"Hey, Michael!"

Michael laughed and, with great reflexes, turned to catch the orange that flew through the air toward him.

"There's two, one for your lady." Another orange sailed past and he caught that, too.

"Thanks, Tommy."

"Why don't you bring her over here and introduce us?"

"No way, Tommy, thanks for the oranges."

"Save us a dance at the ball, sweetheart."

"In your dreams, Tommy."

"Drive safely, Michael." The laughter floated behind them.

He handed Jessie an orange. "There you are. From Tommy. But you can forget about dancing with him at the ball."

She laughed. "What ball?"

"They have a huge gala ball in November. Very classy. If you come with me, I will be vetting your dancing partners very seriously—no one under sixty."

"I might go for older men."

"Then you won't be dancing with anyone—other than me."

Jessie laughed again. "I can't believe this place. The sheer energy blows you away. Thank you for asking me."

"Yes, I love it. I always have. It's a different world."

They'd arrived at her car. Jessie didn't want to go, didn't want leave him. He kissed her lightly, just a light brush over her lips. It was like being sprinkled over with fairy dust. If he asked her to stay she probably would say yes.

"Ring me when you get home," he said.

She wound down the window and waited until he was saying goodbye before she said, "I'm not going to China, Michael."

Then she started the engine and drove off.

*

Jessie sat on her bed and looked at her phone. Michael had been the last number to ring. If she didn't ring him, he'd ring her. She texted: *I'm home, thank you. Drive safely.*

I'm glad you're not going to China, was the reply.

Chapter 16

By the next Sunday, her life was a little more organized. She tried hard to put Michael out of her mind but she spent a fair amount of time thinking about him, all the same.

Michael rang once and texted a couple of times. He seemed to be all over the place: Brisbane, Melbourne, Albury, Eden and back home.

She'd decided to break the lease and say goodbye to the bond if she had to. The real estate agent, Roy, had been very negative. "I can't imagine we'll find anyone else at such short notice," he'd told her on the phone and sighed. "But we'll try for you." And she'd handed her resignation in to work and given them one month's notice. She could play hardball with them; it was Belinda who needed her more—every day she called.

More requirements were needed for the development applications Growcare was putting into council and for the grant they were applying for. It was getting harder and harder to get the money, Belinda said. There were seventeen kids in the district, right now, who may be interested—and there'd be more, she was sure, once they got started.

Michael said he'd call on Sunday night again but she hadn't heard a time. Eight o'çlock, eight thirty, eight forty-five. Jessie felt restless. Felt like getting in her car and going to the markets. Would they let her in? Probably not. At eight forty-seven, the phone rang.

It was her mother.

At five past nine, Michael rang.

She made herself let it ring four times. "Hello?"

He wanted her to meet him at Circular Quay. She was to take a taxi.

Wow. She went for her bag and grabbed her coat and with her hand on the door knob, she stopped and laughed at herself. *You idiot.* Four hours she had to wait.

*

Circular Quay was where all the ferries came and went. She hadn't been back since all those free Sundays at school when they went looking for something to do. She'd loved catching the ferry to Manly. There was the shadowy Opera House on the right and the backdrop of the Harbour Bridge on the left. But there were no ferries at this time of night.

Michael must have been watching for her. The tall figure came striding toward her. He'd been waiting beside the wharf at the end of the quay, where the private boats came in.

The big smile was back. "Good timing, our boat's just coming." He gave her a swift, one-armed hug while steering her in the direction of the wharf.

"Our boat?" She'd been rushing and felt a little breathless. She hadn't been expecting a boat.

A large fishing trawler was edging its way toward the wharf. It looked distinctly out of place. She wasn't the only one noticing. People had turned to look. It bumped gently as it made contact and Michael was thrown a rope, which he wound around a thick pole. "Quick. Jump on board."

"Where are we going?"

"Not far.". Michael looked so excited, like a small boy with a big box of chocolates. "Jump."

A large hand reached up and she jumped. The hand steadied her while Michael landed beside her and let the rope out slowly as the boat pulled away.

Jessie couldn't help laughing. "Where are we going?"

"Let me introduce you to Marco and Ronnie." A young sturdy man, in a polo-necked jumper and a yellow slicker, smiled and held out his hand. His offsider just nodded and kept going.

Jessie looked at Michael. His infectious smile was still there. The men—there were three of them as far as she could see—were working frantically to clear up the boat. Nets were being bundled into lockers and piles of silvery, slippery fish were being sorted into foam crates. Weighed. Marked. There was a lot of fish.

"I had to wait till I got Marco's ETA established before I could ring you. I thought you might like a visit to the fish markets tonight."

"Sure, I've never been to the fish markets before. Where have you come from, Marco?"

"Eden, we left yesterday afternoon to get here this morning."

"And you got a good catch, it looks like."

"Medium. There are not a lot of fish around at the moment. But things will improve with the moon."

"The moon?"

Marco smiled at her as he swung the wheel and they went under the Sydney Harbour Bridge. It was dark for a moment.

"Fish don't like a full moon. We get on better when the moon is small or if there is no moon at all."

Once out from under the bridge, Jessie leaned on the rails. It *was* a full moon. The moonlight shone all around them, gilding the black water with gold. The city lights, reaching up into the sky, turned it all into a fairyland.

"This is absolutely beautiful."

Michael came to stand beside her. She felt the fresh salt air on her face and was suddenly overwhelmed by the beauty of the scene around her. They turned into Blackwattle Bay. She scrunched her nose—now there was the smell of fish and diesel and blinding flood lights and men shouting as they steered into the loading docks at the fish market. Michael jumped onto the wharf and pulled the boat up tight with a thick length of rope.

*

Michael and Jessie put on fluoro vests and walked past the negotiating fishermen and the buyers, into the shops.

"Public aren't allowed in until after seven," Marco told her. "And if anyone asks you, you have done the site OH&S course, okay?"

The men at the vegetable shop were arranging and filling their stands with colorful fruit and vegetables but Jessie noticed the bakery shelves were empty as yet. Then there was the sushi shop, still with its covers on, and the restaurants were dark and empty. Everything else was lit up like Christmas.

"Hello, Michael." A trolley of fish crates rolled past.

"You must know everyone, or you're very popular."

"They're all wondering who in the hell you are. Marco will get heaps tonight."

"I won't get anyone into trouble, will I?" Jessie asked, worried.

"Nothing he can't handle, I assure you. Come and we'll find a coffee, I haven't got long."

"Why am I here?"

"Just a welcome to my world, I guess."

Jessie laughed. "A pretty spectacular welcome." She noticed a young man watching her. Actually, as opposed to everyone else, he didn't look so friendly.

"Who's that?"

"Oh, that's Johnno Fellini, Sienna's brother."

"He doesn't look very friendly, I mean, compared to everyone else we've met. Is she okay?".

"She's fine. It's a bit complicated, because it was assumed by our families that we were going to join forces. It's taking everyone else more time to adjust than us. What about Alan?"

"Alan went to China—with my ring."

Michael put his hand out to turn her towards him. "When did this happen?"

"Two weeks ago." Jessie scrunched up her eyes and then opened them to gauge his reaction. Michael looked impassive. He really could be hard to read.

"Both the times I've seen you?" They started walking again through the crates of fish, the talking and the laughing. It was so busy.

She nodded. "The first time at Morelli's, we'd just broken up and I couldn't talk about it, and the second time—I got ornery I guess. I didn't know how to say it."

Marco rejoined them. "I'm off, nice to meet you, Jessie. Will you be staying for the auction, Michael?"

"No, I've got to get going as well. Roberts will be bidding for me this morning."

"There's an auction?"

"Yep, a reverse auction," Marco explained. "They start three dollars higher than the recommended price and go down from there. Registered buyers all have a button and when it gets to where they want, they press the button. Bingo! It works well."

"It sounds totally different to the stock auctions at home, where they start high, then go down, down, down, till they get a starting bid. And then work their way back up again."

"Yep, it's different. The idea came from Holland, selling the tulips. I've seen it—it's incredibly fast. They sell fifty tonnes of fresh seafood here every day. See you." Marco was off, whistling down the hallway.

"So, what are your plans?" Michael turned to her again.

"I've given notice. I am breaking my lease, which is unfortunate, as I will probably lose my bond. And I'm moving back home with my parents. The upside of all that is I'm joining Belinda in the Growcare project, which I am absolutely delirious about."

"Well, I think, all in all, that is a good plan," Michael said slowly. "We might be able to see each other at a time other than two in the morning."

"How do you look so energetic? I have to wonder what you would look like at two in the afternoon. I will probably be asleep." She yawned. "Pity. I've loved this, and the other night, too. And Morelli's." She blushed. She was realizing she quite enjoyed all the times she'd been with him in the last month. It had been crazy. Ordinary meetings at home would be a bit tame. "It's been fun."

Michael called a taxi. They stood together silently until it pulled up beside them. He asked her address, then relayed it to the driver and paid him. He gave her a swift kiss and deposited her into the taxi, and closed the door.

"I'll ring you," he said.

Chapter 17

Michael rang every day.

He was away, traveling all over the country. The next Sunday, he suggested a 24-hour McDonald's close to the markets where he could park the truck. Michael hugged her briefly when she walked in, then reached for her hand. Their fingers interlocked and he wasn't letting go. They ordered and sat side by side at the table. She searched his face. He was quiet tonight. Something was worrying him.

"I told my grandmother this week."

She knew it had been difficult for him, because of Sienna. He'd said his grandmother had loved Sienna.

"What did she say?"

Michael made a face. "Nothing. That is, she hasn't been speaking to me. On Monday, I'll start to get to get long-suffering sighs and by Tuesday it will be full swing to change my mind."

"Will she?"

"No." Michael laughed.

"My mother has a completely different modus operandi when it comes to my brother. She uses a lot of reverse psychology, you know: 'Go ahead, what do you care?' Or, 'Oh, you wouldn't understand what it means to be a mother.' Now I think about it, it could be termed emotional blackmail."

"I get that too, and my grandmother has a double whammy to throw in: 'Your poor mother would hate to see this.'"

"What happened to your mother?"

"She died in a car accident when I was five."

"How awful."

"It was for my father, but as for me, I've been spoiled rotten by my grandmother and Renee, Ron's wife. When one of them said no, the other would always say yes, on principle." He smiled. He was so beautiful when he smiled.

Jessie, careful.

"That explains everything." Jessie shook her head. "Spoilt rotten? I'm not taking you on. If we have a disagreement, you'll just run to your granny or Renee." She nodded sagely.

"How about I promise faithfully never to disagree?" he said intently.

Jessie burst into laughter. "Lucky I've had a brother. I know perfectly well that you can't trust those kinds of promises."

"That's a pity. Although I've never been a brother, so you can't lump me in with that lot." He looked crestfallen, another act, she was sure. "I have to go, unfortunately."

"I'll see you in town, then." She yawned again.

"You'll be there next weekend? Come and have dinner with me, I would love you to meet my family. Mm, maybe if I rope Renee in, I'll get my grandmother to come as well. She hates to play second fiddle to Renee. On the other hand, it will be difficult, I may need a little more time. Maybe I could get Renee to pretend she doesn't like you." He frowned.

Jessie hit him on the arm. "If it's going to be that complicated, I'm not coming. Where's your father?"

"He's been away, but should be home in a couple of weeks. No one knows my father's plans except him." Michael rose and pulled her to her feet. "Come, I'll walk to your car."

They walked out into the dark June night. There was virtually no one around, and Michael pushed her up hard against the car door, reached for her other hand, locking their fingers together, and lowered his head. She lifted hers and closed her eyes.

Nothing happened. She opened her eyes. He was watching her intently. His mouth was so close she could feel his warm breath fanning her face.

"I think a kiss may be in order, don't you?" she whispered.

He smiled. "I'm not sure it's a good idea."

She almost screamed. If he hadn't been holding her hands she might have hit him. Her body was tensed like a bow and she had never wanted a kiss, ever, as much.

"It *is* a good idea. Because, believe me, I might do something brutal if you don't."

Michael laughed, "What exactly?" And with a swift movement, he forced one of his legs between hers. He kissed—no, ran his tongue along her jawbone.

She was a mess of want and need and fury and frustration. "Let me go."

"Uh uh, can't do that either." He kissed her nose. "If you multiply by one hundred what you're feeling right now you will be close to understanding what I'm experiencing." Finally, he kissed her mouth.

They were both breathing heavily when he pulled away. Her legs were definitely not holding her up.

"Go home, Jessie, I'll ring you in an hour."

Heaven only knows how she got back to the apartment that night.

*

She couldn't wait to get home. Five Oaks began to symbolize all that was safe in her world.

There'd been a couple of phone calls from Michael during the week but he'd been away traveling most of the time; on his project he'd said. He'd tried to talk her into letting him organize her move. She'd said no. No, thank you. He was a hard man to stop once he'd made a decision. There was joyous news from Roy: he had someone to take out a lease on the flat and she'd be getting her bond back. Fred was coming down in the ute to pick up her meager belongings and they'd drive back home together. She needed to stop daydreaming and get on with the packing.

A date.

Michael wanted to take her out to dinner when she got home. But she realized the significance. It was a little like a public announcement. Would they go to his home to meet his family? Or maybe they'd all have dinner in town? No matter, everyone would know they were out together. Word would spread like wildfire. A public confirmation for anyone who hadn't heard: she was back in town and having dinner with Michael D'Larghi.

And it was exciting. She laughed at the thought of it all. Surrounded by old newspapers and cardboard boxes she'd scrounged from the local shop, she continued wrapping the plates one by one and packing them in the cartons. The question was—what was she going to wear? Tomorrow was Thursday, it was her last chance to go shopping and get something in Sydney. Paddington was her shopping mecca, there were a whole lot of interesting designers that you didn't have to pay a fortune for. Ugh, there was so much to do. And not enough time.

Chapter 18

Jessie yanked the vacuum cleaner behind her as she made her way through the drawing room at Five Oaks. There must be acres of carpet in this room, though it was beautiful with the afternoon sun streaming in. You couldn't beat high ceilings and natural light. Pausing for a moment, she looked around. The chairs had been re-upholstered in a bright check sometime during the last year, but the furniture was all the same stuff she'd lived with all her life, the round cedar tables and mahogany bookcases and the Tom Roberts bush landscape on the wall that her great-grandfather had picked up, according to the family history, in a gallery in Melbourne for a song—it had to be at least a hundred years ago. For too long she'd been living in cramped rooms on campus and smallish apartments. Taken all this for granted, hadn't she? She pushed on, into the family room and finally into the kitchen, bundling the vacuum into the pantry.

"Finished. Where's Dad?" she asked her mom, who was at the sink, washing a few dishes, wearing her glam purple washing-up gloves.

"I don't know. Fred and he were arguing about doing some chemical shearing. If he doesn't give Fred some leeway, he'll lose him. Thanks for doing that."

Jessie looked again at her mother. She looked tired. Ever since she'd got home things had been a little ... off, was a good word. Moving back in had been sort of strange for them all. There'd been a lot of tiptoeing around and rearranging parameters. Not a word had been said about her broken engagement or Alan. But then, that was her family all over, push it all under the carpet. Let's not make a fuss. "Least said, soonest mended" was their mantra. She joined her mother at the sink.

"I'll do that."

"No, I can do it."

"Patti was saying that Olly is finally moving into a retirement home."

"Very much about time, I believe. Her memory is going."

"She'd be missing Stan badly. They didn't have all that long in town before he died. How will she get on in the home?"

"You know Olly, it'll take her forty minutes before she's organizing everyone, left, right and center."

Jessie laughed. "I must go and see her."

"She'd love that." Clare stopped washing up and looked out the window. It was a great view, down to the bottom of the garden with the willows. You could see glimpses of the creek now it was winter and all the leaves were off the trees. "It's fun having someone else to cook for." She took an onion from the pantry and started chopping it.

"It's not so bad being cooked for." Jessie grinned and picked out an apple from the fruit bowl.

"And for how long will that be, I wonder? Why aren't you heading off to China? I thought you still needed to satisfy that wanderlust."

"Mom, I've got the perfect job. Besides which, I've met someone."

Her mother stopped chopping the onion and wiped her eyes. "Oh, tell me more?"

Jessie handed her a tea towel for her eyes. "After I met him, suddenly Alan and I felt all wrong. I wouldn't be feeling like this about someone else if I truly loved Alan, would I?"

"Feeling like what?" The onions went into the pan and Clare started on the carrots.

"Lust. I'm so curious, and I want to know why I'm feeling like this. Frustration like you'd never believe—lust."

"Sounds like fun." The carrots joined the onions sizzling in the pan.

"Sometimes yes, sometimes no. Haven't you felt like this? Not knowing where you're going?"

"If I have, I've forgotten. Who is it?"

"Michael D'Larghi."

In went the stock and a cloud of steam rose from the pan. "Oh damn! Jessie, stir this for me. I think I've burnt myself. I'll be back in a minute."

"Mom, can I help?"

"No, no, I'll be all right."

Jessie stirred briskly. She wondered why her parents hadn't been asking much about Alan. Maybe they were disappointed about the breakup, not jumping for joy, which was what she'd expected. Fred had made a good comment in the long telephone conversation they'd had as they'd traveled back in convoy, from Sydney. "Good work, Jessie, he was a prig."

And then she'd told him about Michael. He couldn't stop laughing.

"Stop it, Fred, you'll run off the road."

But she couldn't help grinning herself. To think, all those years she'd entertained that huge, silent crush on the brown-haired, dark-eyed Italian friend of her brother. Little Jessie Cranfield, mad about the bad boy who was constantly getting into trouble. Who had millions of girls fawning over him. Jessie frowned, remembering Michael's conversation. What had happened to his mother, she'd never heard about it. She looked up as her mother came back into the kitchen.

"Do you know Michael's mother died?"

"Yes, I heard about it. It was a long time ago, Jessie."

"Do you know the story, what happened?" she asked.

"No, not really. Very sad." Her mother picked up the car keys. "I'm off to town."

Jessie looked up, surprised. It was five o'clock. Her mother was always going to town these days. She did pilates and yoga and Thai cooking classes and golf.

"It's five o'clock. Where are you going?"

"Marge is having a few of the quilters around for drinks this evening to have a look at some new materials she's got in. Turn the soup off in an hour, can you? I'll be back at about seven."

And quilting. She'd forgotten quilting.

*

"Where's your mother?"

"Hi, Dad. Gone to Marge's, she'll be back soon. You're late in."

"The steers I drafted off yesterday decided to go back to their old paddock and I had to get them back before they all got mixed up again. As it was, I had to draft off about three."

"You selling them soon?"

"I'll wait until I hear the market report from Wagga this week. What are we eating?"

"Soup, steak and boiled potatoes and spinach—or broc-coli—which do you want?"

"I'd prefer not to eat spinach."

"Okay, broccoli it is. There are some mushrooms, too."

"Good, I'll just go shower and change." He disappeared down the hallway.

Clare entered the kitchen, dropping her bag. "Oh you've got dinner ready! You are an angel," she said, going straight to the sideboard to pour herself a whiskey. "Where's your father?"

Did they have no idea where the other was? What did they do when she wasn't there to ask? "He's just changing." Funny, it wasn't how she'd imagined coming home. She knew how the ball boys felt at Wimbledon. Fetch this, fetch that and then duck out of the way. Her mother was taking nervous little sips as she leaned against the sideboard.

"Come on, come and sit down, and tell me about the quilting materials." The table was set, three plates and water for everyone.

"They are stunning—from Switzerland and Italy. The colors are simply beautiful. On Saturday night, Marge is having an exhibition of some quilts she has on loan and wants us to come 'round." Her mother sat down with her whiskey.

"Ah, you're back." Lex walked in and sat. "You've got a drink. Jessie, do want one?"

"No thanks, Dad."

"I was just saying, Marge wants us to come for dinner on Saturday."

"Not my thing. You go if you want." Her father didn't sound very excited.

"Jessie, feel like coming to have a look?"

"No, Mom, I'm going on a date. With Michael D'Larghi." She smiled happily at them both and began to serve out the food.

Honestly, she couldn't have got a better response than when she was sixteen and told them she was going to a country party. Both her parents dropped knives, forks and chins.

"Over my dead body." Her father snorted, got up from the table and left the room. Her mother paled, but she'd already been looking pale. So maybe it was her father's reaction that had upset her. Maybe they thought she was too old for dates.

"What's the matter with Dad?" She leaned forward, feeling suddenly nervous as well. "Mom, I'm so excited. Nervous and excited."

"When have you been seeing Michael?"

"When we sang together, when he rescued me at Thredbo and we had the best times to meet in Sydney– at midnight, when he brought the truck down." Jessie laughed.

"Isn't it a little soon after Alan, and breaking your engagement? You couldn't be ready for someone new, surely."

Should she be grieving for Alan? For her engagement? Well, she wasn't. "No, I mean, yes, I think meeting Michael could have been the main catalyst. Suddenly everything between Alan and me didn't seem right any more. The thought of going to China simply crystalized everything." She looked at her mother.

"Mom, are you all right? Is it the mushrooms? You look terrible."

Chapter 19

She'd wanted new everything. Nothing that Alan had touched. So she'd done late-night shopping in Paddington on Thursday. A silky burnt-orange dress that came to mid-thigh and black leggings. And her beloved Stella McCartney pumps; she couldn't part with those.

Not bad, she thought, peering at herself in the mirror in her bedroom—it only did half of her at a time.

She went into the family room where her mother was watching television. "How do I look?"

"You look lovely. Is that dress a bit short?"

"No. Dad was a bit strange the other night when I told you about my date with Michael. I hope he's going to be friendly. You know I'm not sixteen any more. He really hasn't got the right to make those kinds of comments. I think I can ask for a bit more respect when it comes to who I decide to go out with."

"He probably doesn't want to get too involved in case you ditch this one, too." Clare gave a little laugh. "You don't realize what it's like. As a parent you invest a fair bit of time and energy into your child's partner, you get to liking them, and then bang—away they go—never to be seen again. It's disconcerting."

She didn't feel her parents had invested much time or interest in Alan. Jessie went over to her mother and held her by the shoulders and looked her in the eye. "That may not happen this time. It feels different, very different. How did you feel when you met Dad, at the beginning?"

But there was a knock on the door and she didn't wait for an answer. She ran to open it.

"Hi." Michael was holding a bunch of flowers, a big bunch. She blinked.

He looked down. "They're for your mother."

Jessie stood back as Michael gave Clare the flowers. There were butterflies in her stomach and she felt suddenly shy. What was happening? She felt she'd stumbled into a sixties movie and Sandra Dee was going to walk around the corner. Really, when had she gone on a date from home? Never. One reason was the fifteen miles from town. Boys had come and stayed and she'd gone out with other girls into town, but a date? In England, you went everywhere as a group: "We'll all meet at the pub." But a dinner date?

Never.

Even Alan, now she thought of it, the first time they'd gone out, had said, "Let's go to the Test on Friday night—the Wallabies are playing." And there'd been about twenty of them. Since they'd got engaged—nothing even remotely like a romantic dinner.

Michael looked gorgeous. She couldn't take her eyes off him. The theme was black—jacket, pants and shoes. Mm. Was she allowed to say that or would it embarrass him? It probably wouldn't embarrass him. She didn't have to say anything, he was conversing smoothly with her mother. All she really wanted was to have him to herself. It had been a long, long week.

"Should we be going?" She couldn't help interrupting the riveting discussion on town politics between her mother and Michael, which she knew absolutely nothing about.

Michael's car was familiar from their trip home from the snow.

"Nice dress." Michael glanced over admiringly.

"Nice shirt." Feeling it, she was sure it was silk.

"Hang on, you're not allowed to do that."

"What."

"Touch on the first date."

"What?"

He chuckled. "Just thought I'd try a bit of reverse psychology."

Jessie reached over and stroked his arm.

"Mm, no touching and definitely no kissing."

Jessie leaned back in the seat and sat with her eyes resolutely closed.

"What are you doing?"

"If I'm not allowed to kiss I'll just sit here and imagine what it will be like when you kiss me. It's called emotional blackmail."

"Jessie." He swerved over to the side of the road, jerked the car into park and reached for her. He pulled her onto him and they fought to get closer to each other, Jessie pulling at the jacket to feel the silk of his shirt underneath. Their mouths clung as he tried to do the same.

"Oh, shoot. Your legs are so long." She was sprawled over him. "Maybe this is not such a good idea. My dress doesn't come apart. It has to come off all in one go."

"Right." Michael took a deep breath. "I'm on."

Jessie giggled. "No, you don't."

"What a ridiculous dress to buy. Don't you think these things through? Does any planning go through that head of yours?"

"You plan enough for the two of us. It's my job to throw up some challenges. I can't make it too easy for you. She climbed reluctantly off him and went back to her own seat, pulling down her dress from where it had ended up, somewhere around her waist.

"Food, maestro."

Michael leaned over, pulled her dress down another inch, patted her leg, and then slid in a CD. Andrea Bocelli filled the car. She wasn't at all sure that was going to be effective in cooling her down.

"We can't go into town with all the windows fogged up." He wound his window down. Jessie laughed, followed suit and stuck her head out the window.

"I need cooling off, too. I can't meet your family looking all hot and bothered."

"We aren't meeting my family tonight."

"Why ever not? I thought that was—" She stopped, disconcerted.

"Tonight is just us." He smiled at her but, somehow, she felt the subject had been closed.

*

Jessie wasn't surprised to find they were eating at Leo's. It had the best reputation, opening at six in the morning with the bakery and for three nights a week as a restaurant. Michael knew everyone in the place, of course.

After he'd kissed nearly everybody and waved at all the others, they sat down at a table near the back.

"A quiet dinner," Jessie said as she picked up the menu.

"Not on your life." Michael grinned. "This is going to be a night this town remembers. Our first date." And he leaned over and kissed her fingers.

"Stop it." Jessie pulled her hand away. Then she ran her bare foot up his leg.

"If you do that again I will take your foot and kiss it out in the open where everyone will see."

Jessie looked at him. Weighing up her options, discretion was probably wiser. On the other hand...

"Hey Michael, good to see you here." Leo himself came up and slapped Michael on the back. "And Jessie, great singing the other night."

"Thanks, Leo." She smiled. "How's Katrina? I haven't seen her for ages."

"Katrina is pregnant with her third baby and is a very busy girl."

"Oh, say hello for me." Three kids. Good Lord. Jessie had gone to primary school with Katrina. Leo had a tribe of kids, and Kat was the fourth, if she remembered rightly.

Leo and Michael started to talk about wine and she tuned out. This restaurant was always busy; Leo served wonderful food. Tonight, it was full already.

"What would you like to eat?" Michael asked.

"The scallopini, always. Thanks. What about you?"

"Lasagne for me, but we have to have starters."

"Oh, well I'd better have a look then. The arancini are always wonderful." Michael passed her the menu and their knuckles grazed. She went from feeling confident and really good and happy to feeling shy and bashful and uncertain all of a sudden. What was wrong with her?

Jessie looked blankly at the menu. Then at Michael's hand fingering his water glass. That hand had been strong on the steering wheel; it had held her against the car that night in Sydney when she'd wanted him to kiss her. Damn, she wanted him to do it again—kiss her senseless.

"Water?"

"Oh, yes please."

"The wine is from Victoria, I think you'll like it. Leo recommended it."

"One thing you can't grow on the Monaro is grapes."

Michael smiled and leaned forward. "That all may change shortly."

"Why?"

"Climate change may make higher altitudes more suitable for growing grapes. So you never know, in ten years we might be making wine around here." He poured them both a glass of wine and lifted his to toast. "One thing for sure—if we do, it will be good."

"Why do you say that?"

"Limestone country is very good for grape vines. Do you know the meaning of the word 'Monaro'?"

"I've always thought it meant a high plain, or is it Aboriginal for fast car?"

"No. Monaro is the local Aboriginal word for a woman's breast." Michael took another mouthful.

That was it. She was blushing. That's exactly what they looked like, the low folded hills on the Monaro. Her nipples were hardening and all he'd had to say was the word "breast."

Michael laughed softly. Damn it, he was doing it deliberately. "And they called the car the Monaro because one of its designers was on a holiday at the snow, drove through the town and saw the name on the county council building, the Monaro Shire. It was a true light-bulb moment. He raced home and copyrighted the name."

The food had arrived. "This looks so good," she said, then changed the subject. "Belinda has gone away for a week, studying the other Growcare centers around the state, but I'm looking forward to getting into it all with her."

"There's a shed on one of our places you might be interested in."

"Thanks, I'm only number two, but I'll run it past Belinda on Monday."

"So when did you and Belinda get to be friends?"

"Through the plays at the theater. We were always competing for the same role. I got Peter Pan but I was devastated when she got Annie." She looked down at her food. "Then I was away more than I was here, first boarding school, then uni, then the UK."

"Where you met Alan." Michael looked at her, considering, as though he wanted to ask more.

"Your turn." It seemed a good idea to change the subject.

"My grandparents brought me up, oh, and Ron and Renee, bless them. Dad was MIA, working, working, working. My grandfather encouraged me to play basketball, insisted I went to uni and made me apply for the basketball scholarship to Scottsford."

*

When they'd finished eating they walked down the main street, hand in hand. Holding hands felt strange—tingly and comforting at the same time. Natural and weird. Embarrassing and yet so much what she wanted to do it outweighed the embarrassment.

"The place hasn't changed much from when we were kids, has it? " Jessie observed. "On the other hand, it's completely different to what it would have been like forty years ago. Building the dam certainly changed things around here. Ten thousand migrant workers plonked down in a country town."

"It's certainly kept its mojo better than a lot of other country towns in the drought." They walked past the newly painted D'Larghi Motors sign.

"Wow, that looks good. Someone must be flourishing." Jessie grinned.

"You could say that." Michael looked proud, and Jessie felt like kissing him.

Maybe she should. Get it over with and maybe then she could stop thinking about it all the time. This was his office wasn't it? Why didn't he ask her in?

"Mom was saying the other day that this part of town used to be filled with nightclubs, you would walk down the street and hear seven different languages. She said it was like living in Rome, only better."

"Why better?"

"'Cause in thirty-seven minutes you could be home." Jessie laughed.

"I guess it has become more of a ski transit lounge now with everyone passing through on their way to the snowfields. Different kind of money, but we've adapted."

They walked on down the street.

"I think I'd better get you home." Michael stopped and put her hand to his lips. "Thank you for a lovely night."

"Yep. Thank you," she said reluctantly.

It couldn't be going to end now. It had all gone so fast.

*

They pulled up outside the house at Five Oaks. The light was on at the front door, but thankfully, there was no irate father standing there.

Jessie looked at Michael's profile. He really looked beautiful and very serious.

"I've told my nonna about you, but as yet I'm still getting the heavy sighs response."

"It might take a little time."

He pulled her to him and the kiss that she'd been waiting for all night happened. Kisses were funny things. She'd been unable to think of anything else for five hours, but now she was left feeling frustrated and wanting more. He sat back. She knew this wasn't the time, it was just …

"See you soon." Jessie walked her fingers up his chest until he caught them and stopped their journey.

"You'd better believe it, Jessie." He touched her briefly on the lips and tucked a lock of hair behind her ear. "Go now. Goodnight."

Chapter 20

Michael bounced the ball, then threw it through the hoop again. The hoop his grandfather had put up for him at the back of the house when he was twelve. Despite the cold, foggy morning, sweat was running off him. How long had he been at it? Half an hour probably—normally it was a sure-fire way of working off steam—but he wasn't sure he felt much better. The fog swirled around him, blanketing his thoughts and the repetitive bounce, jump and shoot.

Bounce, shoot, bounce it again. Damn the real estate guy, Roy, whatever his name was, he needn't have told Jessie that Michael had taken over the lease on her flat. Not taken it over, just taken out another six-month lease. He was going to need a pad anyway, somewhere in Sydney, over the next six months. Bloody hell.

Bounce, bounce, bounce, shoot.

He'd been going to ask her over for lunch to meet his grandmother before she'd rung him, furious, this morning. So, let it ride or pursue?

Bounce the ball, shoot.

He hadn't done this for ages. But he was getting his rhythm back.

Bounce, jump, shoot.

Hell, you'd think he'd detonated an atomic bomb when he'd told his grandmother his relationship with Sienna was finished. Sienna had taken it pretty well, considering. She said it had been pretty obvious from the night of the concert. At least she'd understood that he'd fallen heavily for Jessie. The family had more of a problem with it. And the grandmothers. His nonna had to realize that arranged marriages were a thing of the past. It was his mistake to have gone along with it in the first place.

Jump, shoot, bounce the ball.

He didn't really understand what the problem was with Jessie's parents. The Cranfields were part of the old world. There was a new one now. The power had shifted. His star was ascending. It wasn't due to luck, though; his grandfather and his father had worked really hard to build what they had now. It was up to him to build it up further, he knew that.

Bounce, missed. *Damn.* He bent over to retrieve the ball.

"Michael."

Panting slightly, more than he liked, he stopped and turned. His nonna's thick brows were drawn together and she was wiping her hands on her apron. Her hair was the gray of steel wool and caught in a bun. Although not happy, she was obviously over the sighing.

"Nonna. How are you this morning?"

"I think you should come in and have some breakfast."

Michael grinned and walked over to give her a hug. "Nonna, I'm starving."

"Ugh. You shower first." She pushed him away. He tucked the ball under his arm and accompanied her back to the house.

"You went to Leo's last night with Jessie Cranfield."

"You've been talking to Leo."

"Mm." She folded her arms. "And Lorna."

Leo's wife. Well, it was out, but he'd expected nothing less.

*

Facing a huge plate of eggs and bacon and his favorite spicy sausage, normal breakfast fare for him, Michael tucked in.

"When's Dad expected back?"

His grandmother poured coffee, passed it over and leaned back. "One month he is away. He should be back next week."

"Have you heard from him?"

"No, he never rings when he's back in the old country. He's staying with the Lorinze cousins this trip, and going back to Portofino."

"Do you remember Portofino?" Michael buttered more toast.

"Of course I remember. It was such a beautiful place, on the water, with the harbor full of boats and people who come for holiday. A very happy place, Portofino. But the war was over and there were no jobs. We were lucky." Maria shrugged and took Michael's empty plate over to the sink. "When Gino got told, we had three days before he had to leave. We got married and it was two years before I could come to join him." She started to chuckle. "Australians didn't know what spaghetti was, real spaghetti. Only that tinned stuff, so there was much upset until they sent some *real* spaghetti up from Melbourne. Then Italians insisted on their own mess. That was all before I came. Gino wrote to me about it."

Michael had heard it all before but he loved his nonna telling him about the old country and beginning their new life in Australia. It was amazing. His grandfather slept in a tent, with no heater and no blankets. He apparently got under the mattress, fully clothed, on top of the wire base, to keep warm. It was an extraordinary story.

Michael put more wood into the glass-fronted heater that warmed the house. "Can I ask Jessie to come for lunch today?

I would like you to meet her." He went up to his nonna at the sink and put his arm round her. "It's important to me."

"I don't think it is a good idea." Maria frowned. "Sienna rang yesterday. She is a good, loyal girl. She said you needed time and she had to give it to you. You shouldn't have hurt her, Michael."

He hadn't said anything about needing time. He thought he'd been quite explicit. Sienna had been calm and understanding.

"If I hurt her, I am sorry. Sometimes there's nothing you can do about that. No, Nonna, this is important, I want you to meet Jessie."

Another sigh. "Okay. We just have the regular."

"Whatever you do will be good, thank you."

But in the end there wasn't a problem. When he tried Jessie, she didn't answer her phone. He rang the Cranfields, only to hear she'd gone off somewhere and she'd ring back. She didn't.

Chapter 21

"More coffee, Jessie?"

"No, thanks, Patti. Why do they do it to me? Am I so pathetic I can't even sort out my own leasing arrangements or take the rap for my own decisions? No—I've got to be rescued. It's the same with Dad and Fred. They never include me in the farm. They pat me on the head and fob me off. Boy's business!"

Jessie was so angry. She'd been angry since the phone call from Roy at eight thirty this morning.

"Men's business," Patti prompted.

"Men. It was like I was never tall enough or old enough or big enough or anything enough ..." Jessie trailed off.

"Which is why you got the hell out of it. Remember?"

"I suppose."

"We've had this conversation before, Jessie. It's their problem, not yours. Don't get it muddled up with Michael's gallantry. It sounds very chivalrous to me. Quite thoughtful. I mean, if he needed a pad—"

"He would have got one before now, though, wouldn't he? It's just so infuriating. I don't want him to be like that."

"Thoughtful and chivalrous?"

"Nope, exclusionist, high-handed and chauvinist."

"Michael rescued you before, on the mountain, didn't he?"

Jessie gave a weak smile. "Yes, but that was because I sprained my ankle, and it was his fault anyway—he challenged me to the race."

Patti didn't answer, just looked at her skeptically, but she let it go. "Belinda will be back tomorrow and you can get stuck into the Growcare project."

"I've been thinking that we could set up a social club for the kids, one night a week, listening to music, watching movies. Grown-up stuff. What do you think?"

"I think it sounds wonderful. You've got no idea what a difference it's going to make to our lives. David will love it. He's growing up so fast. You think they are going to stay small forever and all of a sudden, *whoosh*. But please continue, the first date you've ever been on and ..."

"It was beautiful," Jessie said wistfully, chin on her hands, and then, with a complete change of mood, said, "Why did he have to spoil everything? We've got a lot of shared history, you know. He was Fred's friend and he remembers me when I was little. We grew up in the same town. We know the same people." Jessie got up and began to pace restlessly. "That might be a slight exaggeration. Did you know about his mother?"

"No. She died, didn't she? I don't know anything about it. So there was no problem with the night itself, going to dinner?"

"That was fine, but I don't know why he felt he had to intervene and take up the lease."

"Have you told him how you feel, discussed this problem you have with overbearing men?"

"No." Jessie looked skywards and sighed. "Not really."

"Well then." Patti picked up the coffee cups.

"Sometimes you are too practical for your own good." Jessie had to laugh. "All right, I will, I will."

There was no doubt her head was in a mess. Driving the short road home from Patti's, Jessie mulled it over.

She was overreacting, yes, but why?

A lifetime of being treated as someone who doesn't make decisions. Patted on the head, encouraged. Her family loved her to bits, but did not respect her as an adult. Nine years between Fred and herself probably hadn't helped.

So how much of it was her fault? Did she play the baby sister role? She nodded. To perfection … Ugh. It was too difficult and here she was home already. She turned the car off and just sat there.

So, why was what Michael did wrong?

He should have talked to her. On the other hand, to give him his due, he probably wasn't used to consulting anyone about his decision-making either.

The other worry was her father. He'd basically disappeared over the weekend. She'd asked her mother if there was something wrong but Clare hadn't known of anything worrying him, apart from the usual: too much rain or no rain, cattle prices, and the wool market plummeting. She slipped in a CD and jumped when she realized it was Andrea Bocelli, the same one Michael had played last night. Turning it off, she switched to the radio and also checked her phone.

There were two text messages, one from Michael—no—two from Michael.

I would love you to come to lunch, here. That was so brief, she laughed. It was way past lunchtime. Then the second message. *Sorry I missed you. Have left for Sydney.*

Well, Michael, have a good one.

Jessie pulled off her coat and paused as she walked into the kitchen. Her father was reading Saturday's newspaper in his chair by the fire. Her mother was making tea. It was only just four but it was getting darker by the minute. A peaceful, familiar scene.

"I have had enough." Her father thumped the paper on the table. "Fred is caught by every single new fad that passes by. While I'm still here we'll do things my way. Damn it, Clare, what does he think I've been doing the last forty years?"

Oh dear. Maybe not so peaceful.

"I think it's called youth," her mother said calmly.

"I think it's called bloody stupidity. They've been trying chemicals for at least twenty years, with people realizing the idea is crazy and doesn't work—not remotely. I've read about it and talked about it and now, hey presto! He's going to solve the wool industry's problems, just like that."

"Um, hi."

Her father rattled the pages of his newspaper and retreated behind them again.

Her mother looked up and smiled. "Hello, love, would you like a cup of tea?"

"That sounds good. What's the problem, Dad?"

"Don't ask. I'm sick of the subject."

"Well, actually, I am asking." Jessie took her mug from her mother, who frowned at her.

"A new form of shearing, chemical shearing—they give the sheep a needle, put a net 'round it and in a couple of weeks the wool has fallen off." Her father took the chocolate biscuit handed to him and grunted. "Happy?"

"No. What's wrong with it? I thought we were running out of shearers these days, that they are a dying race?"

"I've already argued this out with Fred this afternoon—I'm not going to put up with having to argue with another ill-informed person. I've got too much to do." He folded the paper, put it under his arm and marched out of the room.

"Well, that was successful." Her mother sighed. "There are days when I wish he hadn't given up smoking."

"I didn't know Dad smoked."

"He gave up the day you were born."

"Why is it such an effort to have a discussion about the farm or politics with my father?"

"I don't know. I do know it's not worth it."

"You know something, Mom? I've only just realized it, but you are part of my problem. With Dad there is only one point of view, isn't there? His. You give in to this chauvinism all the time. You don't stick up for yourself and so I don't. *Didn't*. I do now," she said with a new resolve. "Why do you do it?"

"Years of compromise. Working out the best way to handle your father. Oh, by the way, Michael D'Larghi rang."

"Thanks, I got his message." Jessie left her mother standing at the sink.

*

Work at last. Growcare had an office in the main street almost opposite Leo's café. The office had been a clothing shop that closed down the previous year and Belinda had been given the use of it until it was leased again. Jessie used her new key, walked in and looked around. There were two desks, two chairs, a filing cabinet and a computer. Her confusion over her father's behaviour and anger at Michael's unnecessary actions hadn't passed. Or was it anger with her dad and confusion over Michael? She sighed. Maybe she should write a song about it.

Before she could even work out which desk was hers, the door opened behind her.

"Jessie, I was going to be here first. Hello and, boy, is it good to see you." Belinda enveloped her in a big hug and led her to the desk by the window. "There you are, sit down." Triumphantly, she produced two coffees from her bag and stared at the lids for a moment before placing one in front of Jessie. "Now, don't panic, but these are the main things you need to get acquainted with first." She pulled out a bundle of files tied with different colored ribbons from the deep filing cabinet drawer.

"Green, council regulations; red, Health Department requirements; blue, EPA, which include building quotes and architects drawings; orange are the ones I want to kill; and black, they're dead already. "

Jessie started to laugh.

"You may well laugh, my friend—I'd like to see if you're still laughing an hour from now," Belinda said with mock severity.

Jessie looked at the mound of papers in front of her. There were so many of them. Belinda's phone rang. Belinda winked at Jessie and sat down with her coffee.

"Yes, Michael, that is a wonderful idea and we can … yes, Jessie's here too this morning. We'll see you in ten." Belinda ended the call and spun around, laughing.

"That, my darling Jessie, was Michael D'Larghi. He wants us to go and look at an old shed that he can give us—if we want. He thinks he can move it on some flat top trailers to our land. That would be incredible. It sounds enormous. He'll be here in ten minutes to pick us up."

Her stomach dropped. Who needed a dose of Mr D'Larghi this morning? There was no reason not to hope for a reprieve. "I can stay here if you like—and try to get my head around this stuff."

"No way. I need your ideas on this, too. Oh, it's so good to have you here, Jessie. Two heads are infinitely better than one."

"This head may be better off if you left it in the office."

"Uh uh. Michael asked if you were here. He's our landlord, you know, owns half the block actually. Anyway, Patti told me you guys had dinner on Saturday night. What's he like, Jessie? Tell me. On a score from one to ten?"

She grinned. "Nine and a half." It was true. What was she making all the fuss about? It was up to her to set boundaries if she wanted them. Tell them, no, *show* them that she wanted more, needed more—what? She looked blankly at the papers. *Consultation*. That was the right word. Happier, she rummaged in her bag for a lipstick.

Michael walked in looking amazing, fresh, good enough to eat, and carrying a box of fruit. His hair curled slightly over the neck of a black sweatshirt and his eyelashes were thick. No one would guess he'd been driving all night. He put the box down on her desk. She smiled politely.

"Thought you two might like some apples from Tumut and oranges from the Riverina." He noticed the pile of papers on her desk. "This looks a little like my office at the moment." He laughed. "I don't suppose there's much difference between trying to get an NFP project up and running and going through the DAs for our fresh food markets. We'll have to trade notes on some of this stuff, Belinda. Hello, Jessie." His smile was easy.

That smile knocked her heart into her ribs so hard it hurt.

They hopped into his car, Belinda in the front, and drove about two miles out of town to a small farm. Jessie got out to open the gate. It was old and the hinges had nearly rusted through, but she began to pull it across. Michael got out of the car and joined her.

"Hey, let me do that, I hadn't realized it had got so stiff." He took the gate from her and heaved it open enough for the car to get through.

"Do you want me to close it?"

"No, we'll leave it open, we won't be long." They stood there a moment just looking at each other. Somehow she couldn't think of anything to say. She wanted to apologize for missing his call yesterday but she had no words. If she stuck to her guns, he would be doing the apologizing.

Belinda stuck her head out of the car. "What are you two doing?" Jessie couldn't get back to the car quick enough.

They drove along a dirt track close to the fence until they came to some scrubby snow gums with their wiry, white trunks. The track wound through the trees and came up to two old nissen huts, standing in an open space in the middle of the scrub.

"Are these the sheds?" Belinda asked.

"Yes. They are pretty basic. They were used to house some of the European immigrants who came up here to work on the Snowy. My grandfather bought them at some stage and had them put here. I don't have a use for them." He shrugged. "So if you think they might be useful we could move them for you."

Belinda clutched Jessie as they stood and looked at the two long, semicircular, corrugated-iron huts. They were a little rust stained but appeared sturdy. They walked over, climbed the couple of steps and pushed in the door. Cobwebs garlanded the walls and grass was growing up through the rotted floorboards.

"How old are they?"

"I think they were left over from the Second World War."

"Do they leak?"

Michael laughed. "No idea! We'd have to test them. Doesn't look like it."

Belinda's phone rang and she excused herself and walked outside, talking and gesticulating to whoever was on the other end.

"You still mad with me?" Michael asked Jessie, leaning against the doorway.

"No. Yes. I think it's my fault. I'm not giving out the right signals—that I am a capable twenty-six year old who can look after herself."

"I see."

"It was very kind and thoughtful of you but a little over the top."

"Over the top?" Michael frowned at her. "I like looking after you. And I need somewhere to stay in Sydney for the next six months while I'm setting up my project. It will double as an office in Sydney."

"Next time could you talk about it. With me." She sounded a little breathless. Michael had come closer, very close. It was distracting her from the point she was trying to make.

"I like the sound of 'next time.'" His voice was low and so sexy.

"Hey, you two." Belinda took the stairs two at a time and joined them. "Let's get measured up. How can we test them for leaks, Michael? Would we take the floorboards or leave them behind? There's not enough light for a potting shed but we could use them for tools or machines. Or an office? Thank you so much, Michael. Do we want both, Jessie? What do you think?"

*

Michael got out of the car when he dropped them off and leaned against the driver's door, his hands in his pockets.

"Oh, Jessie, could I have a minute?"

Jessie didn't miss the wink from Belinda as she walked back into their office.

"Did you get my messages yesterday?"

"I did, but not until about four and you'd left for Sydney. The reception around home is abominable. I was at Patti's. Sorry."

"My grandmother wants to meet you—she was hoping you could come yesterday."

Jessie felt herself turning red. She hadn't realized. "Oh, I'm so sorry! I didn't think, I thought it was just you.'"

Michael just looked at her. "If that's an apology, be careful, you could be digging yourself into a hole." Then he laughed.

"I am going to be away for the rest of the week. Would you like to do something on Friday night?"

To her surprise, Jessie heard herself say yes.

Chapter 22

Now why had she said yes? She asked herself that question one thousand times until she finally admitted it was simply because she wanted to see him again. Considering she couldn't get him out of her head, it was a reasonable assumption.

That breakthrough was on Wednesday. Time was moving excruciatingly slowly. She was going into town each day and working with Belinda, who wasn't exactly helping, as her favorite topic of conversation was Michael D'Larghi.

"What did he say?" she asked again, her eyes huge behind her glasses. "What are you going to do on Friday?"

"I don't know. 'Do something' was all he said."

"I think you should think of somewhere to take him."

"You've got to be kidding! You don't tell Michael D'Larghi where you're taking him."

"Why not?"

"It wouldn't go down well."

"You might be surprised. Cook him dinner."

"Where exactly? He's already got hold of my flat in Sydney," Jessie grumbled. "I'm not the best cook in the world either."

"Don't be so negative. We'll think of something. Ask him to dinner with your parents."

155

"I haven't even been game to tell my parents we're going to see one another again. I'm still ducking from the flack I got last weekend."

"Come on, it couldn't be that bad."

"Suppose he's organized his grandmother again?"

"Suppose he hasn't. Come on, Jessie."

But at the last moment, on Thursday night, Jessie discovered her parents were going to a friend's place at Jindabyne for dinner on Friday and were thinking of going skiing for the weekend.

Friday morning she burst into the office grinning from ear to ear.

"Well, what's happened to you?" Belinda looked up.

"I have a plan."

At ten past ten, she texted: *Michael, are you happy to leave tonight to me?*

He answered swiftly: *Yes, pick me up at the airport. What are we doing?*

Wait and see.

Now, wasn't *that* going to drive him crackers?

*

The snazzy little plane from Sydney bounced a couple of times before it pulled up in front of the small Cooma terminal. Jessie watched impatiently as the stairs were rolled out toward it and the red cones marking the passengers' path were placed on the tarmac. Michael D'Larghi was third down the stairs. He was carrying a briefcase and wearing suit pants, an open-necked shirt and a red woolen jumper. It was windy and cold.

"Where's your coat?"

He grinned. "I'm straight off the plane from Brisbane, didn't need one there."

She just stood there drinking him in. They were surrounded by the chaos that was Friday six pm at the airport. They knew most of the people and too many of them were staring.

"Do you have to get a bag?"

"No, no bag. Where's your car?"

He stood quietly at the passenger side while she tried to unlock the car. For some reason she kept hitting the wrong button.

"Unlock damn you, wait a minute, here we go." Jessie laughed at her nervousness.

Then they were in and Michael slung his briefcase over on to the back seat, and then fiddled with his own seat to give his legs more room. Then he reached for her, pulling her toward him.

"How about a hello, how are you?" Jessie couldn't help it, her voice shook.

Michael just shook his head, burying it in her neck and breathing in her scent.

She wound her arms around his neck. Despite his lack of a coat he was warm and smelt of coffee.

"I've been thinking of doing this for the last five hours. I'm way past hello, how are you. I want to know where we are going and does it have a bed?"

Jessie started to laugh. Her thoughts had been running along those lines as well, but they were hardly—that is, now it looked like a certainty, she felt a little nervous.

"Are you extremely tired or are you suggesting something else?"

"What do you think?"

"So you think I'm a pushover on the second date, do you?"

"It's not our second date. I've known you forever and I can't wait any longer. And your car's too small." He leaned back and closed his eyes. "Come on, Jessie, let's go."

She looked over at him, almost asleep already. Was he always this autocratic? He had been traveling for the last five hours, so she supposed she could cut him a little slack.

He hadn't even asked where they were going. And she couldn't help it, she smothered a laugh. It did have a bed.

*

They drove into Five Oaks. Michael hadn't said anything, just opened one eye as they'd rumbled over the ramp. She turned to him.

"Wake up. Welcome to Five Oaks, home to Cranfields for one hundred and fifty years."

Michael stretched. "I haven't been asleep. Just conserving my energy. I guessed where you were going when you turned left out of the airport."

Jessie giggled. "Damn, I am so transparent."

They walked into the big empty kitchen and Michael backed her against the counter, his arms either side of her. He was so tall. She had to arch back to look into his eyes.

"Coffee, tea or me?" she offered.

"Did I hear you say that? Did my ears deceive me?"

Michael had her wrapped in his arms, a place she was enjoying, she must say. He straightened, lifting her off the floor and depositing her on the bench in front of him. Her legs twined around him.

"My prisoner. Or am I yours?" he whispered in her ear. He was crushing her. His hands slid up her arms. Warm lips on her neck and she could hardly breathe. His hands sliding on her bare skin. Exploring. "My God, Jessie, where are your parents?"

"Out. For the night. For the weekend, actually."

He stopped abruptly. She opened her eyes. Michael looked surprised.

"For the whole night?"

"Mm hm." She put her arms around him and hugged him. The kitchen door banged.

"Mom," a voice called out.

"Who's that?"

"Oh no," Jessie whispered. "Fred."

Michael let her slip to the floor but he didn't step away.

Fred looked stunned as he came round the corner and saw Michael D'Larghi standing with Jessie in his parents' kitchen.

"Where's Mom?"

"Gone away for the weekend."

Fred looked lost for words. He couldn't take his eyes off Michael. Recovering slightly, he came forward to shake hands. "Hi Michael. Didn't expect to see you here, how are you? Um, Jessie, we're in a bit of trouble, Sonya's cut her finger, or rather, she's cut the tip off, it won't stop bleeding and I want to take her to the hospital to have someone look at it. I thought Mom was here, the lights were on. I don't suppose you could look after the babies for us? We could be a few hours. You know what emergency is like.

"Everything's here. It's all set up for them in the old blue bedroom down the hall ... What do you think?" He stopped, uncertain. "It's just a matter of giving them their bottles and then putting them into bed."

*

Jessie, one arm grasping a squirming twin, and a nappy bag in the other, turned to Michael, who was holding the other baby, as the taillights disappeared down the drive.

"Didn't Sonya look awful? Poor thing, she was as white as a ghost."

"Can you remember all the things she told us?"

"Not a thing."

"What's your one's name?"

"I've no idea, one's Bill and one's Bob, but I've never been able to tell which one's which. Do you know anything about toddlers?"

"No, foreign territory for me."

"Pity. I haven't had anything to do with a baby since I looked after David. I've barely met these two. Come on, let's go inside."

Jessie dumped the bag on the countertop and her child on the floor. "One thing I've learned—you don't put the bag and the child anywhere near one other. Wait a minute." She ran down the hall and returned, struggling with a wooden box. "Here are the toys Mom keeps for them." She knelt on the floor between them and burrowed into the box, coming up with two trucks. "Here you are, red one for you and blue one for you." The baby who got the red truck immediately put his down and reached for the other truck. The blue truck baby hung on grimly and started to cry.

Jessie looked with horror at Michael, who grinned and got down on the floor, too. "Here," he said with quiet authority, and both babies stopped and looked at him with interest.

"I'm not sure whether it's the deep voice or whether they're just sizing you up for their next kill," Jessie whispered.

Michael ignored her. "Come on, you two. Let's load these up and get them to Sydney." By the time she got back with the bottles, there was a road to Sydney, a service station, a market and a park set up from the chair to the sofa and back again. Both babies were totally immersed in the game although she wasn't convinced it was the same game Michael was playing with them. Whatever, all three looked extremely happy.

"I'm sorry it took me so long, I wasn't sure how hot to make them, then Fred rang and said they had them cold, so I had to start again."

"How are they getting on?" Michael barely looked up.

"Okay, it's a bit of a wait still, they've seen the triage nurse but the doctor will still be a while. She can't have stitches, apparently." Jessie plopped down on the floor and handed him a bottle. "Which one do you want?"

"Blue truck, come on, fella, drink time." He settled his back against the wall, the baby in his arms, looking so comfortable Jessie started to laugh. How come a man could hold a baby and look so darned sexy?

"Okay red truck, come to momma." To her surprise, the other one toddled straight into her lap and settled himself before grabbing the bottle from her.

"I can't believe this, what have you done to them?"

Michael grinned at her. "Trucks will do it, every time, no problem."

By the time the bottles were finished the children were almost comatose.

"How do we get up and put them into bed without waking them?" Jessie whispered.

Michael shrugged and looked at her. He put his charge down carefully on the floor and rose to his feet, then bent to take Jessie's child from her.

"Okay, thank you." Jessie got up. "Here goes." She took back her nephew and led the way into the bedroom already set up with two cots, a change table and pile of nappies. "Oh no. We have to change their nappies?"

Michael looked horrified. "I played trucks, you change nappies," he whispered.

Jessie put down her baby on the change table and picked up the nappy. "They're different, how do these work? David's used to have tabs."

"I think they're pullups. They don't open." Michael leaned over her shoulder. His nearness made her clumsy.

"How do you know?"

"Because I watch television."

"Very funny," she whispered back. But by the time she had the nappies on and the babies in their cots, both boys were sitting up and not looking the least sleepy.

"What do we do now?" She straightened from her last futile effort to make red truck lie down and looked at Michael, who was leaning against the wall watching her.

He reached for her and drew her against him, holding her as they looked at the babies. It felt so good to be nestled in his arms.

"We sing."

"Of course, what will we sing?"

"Oh, when the Saints …"

Jessie elbowed him. "No, 'Rockabye baby.'"

"I don't know it, you sing it."

So, with Michael's arms around her, she began to sing the old lullaby that her mother had sung to her so many times. After a while, he chimed in. They were making music again. The babies obediently closed their eyes and settled down and were asleep in minutes. Jessie pulled the quilts over them.

"We're very good at that," Michael said as they tiptoed out of the room, leaving the door slightly ajar. "We could rent ourselves out as baby whisperers."

*

Michael was watching the television. Jessie was banging pans around in the kitchen, fixing something to eat. She didn't sound very happy. Fred had rung twice, probably to have something to do, more than worrying about his kids. Maybe he was checking on his baby sister.

It was getting a little bizarre. Michael was stuck. No car, no transport out of here, forty minutes from town. He could hardly take Jessie's car—if she had an emergency with the twins, she'd be needing it. The most absurd thing was—he didn't want to go. Normally he'd be running a mile, tonight he just wanted to be with Jessie. Whatever, however. What was happening to him? He'd had fun playing with those two little tykes. Putting them to bed—what was the matter with him? Getting soft in the head.

"Dinner's ready." Jessie handed him a beer. "It's the only one Dad's got, I hope you like it," she said.

"Hey." He pulled her to him, down onto the sofa. "It's fine, don't worry. It's okay. It's just one of those things, you know?" And he started to sing: "Just one of those things …" Jessie collapsed into laughter against him. "There's nothing we can do about it. So chill."

"Thank you." She kissed him softly.

And didn't that make him feel a hundred feet tall.

*

At half-past eleven, Fred appeared at the door, looking tired. They carried the twins out to the car and handed them to Sonya, whose finger was pristinely bandaged.

"Are you guys all right?" Jessie asked.

"Thank you so much, I can't believe we ruined your night, I'm so sorry."

"Don't be silly, I'm glad you're okay."

Michael and Jessie stood together and watched the car disappear.

"It's exhausting. How do they do it?" Jessie said as they returned to the house. "We've only been at it four hours—and three of those, they were asleep. How do you do twenty more?"

"Let me show you, it's called resuscitation, or survivor reviver." He stopped in the dark hall and turned her to face him. "Stand quietly, put your arms on my waist, open your mouth and I breathe gently into it, then I touch your lips with my tongue and, no," he admonished, "leave your hands on my hips, you are not revived yet. Close your eyes, then I run my fingers lightly down your cheek and along your jawline."

Jessie started to tremble. Extraordinary things were happening to her nervous system. "I think you should stop."

"I think you're right." He put his arms around her and gave her a hug. "I can't do this anymore either and be held accountable. You see, if we were their parents, for a proper survivor reviver, we'd just tumble into bed. I seem to remember you mentioning a bed?"

"Michael, we can't. Not, not with the babies and Fred and Sonya …" She looked helplessly at Michael. "I just can't."

This was unbelievably embarrassing. She ended up offering Michael the spare room, which he accepted gracefully. Not gratefully, but he really looked exhausted. Jessie had given him a towel and showed him where the bathroom was and gone into her bedroom and closed the door. This was just like getting on a train and not knowing where you were going. But it wasn't stopping and there was no getting off, that she did know.

This nervous intensity had been missing from her relationship with Alan. It had been easy going compared to this. Good mates they'd been, really. This was so much more—explosive. Like traversing ravines and abseiling down cliffs. Maybe they just needed to get it over and done with, and then everything would be back to normal. Make love, fuck, whatever. But for now, it was all on hold.

She wasn't all that tired. How did that song go, "Wired for Sound"? She was wired for something. It took her a long time to get to sleep.

Chapter 23

"Would you like some more toast?" Jessie refilled his cup with tea. There was a distinct feel of frost inside the house this morning. Michael wasn't sure if it was because Jessie was regretting turning him down last night. Maybe she'd expected him to beat her door down.

"No, thanks. I probably should be thinking of getting back. There's a fair bit to do before I go to Sydney tomorrow night. Dad's away still, so I'm looking after his things as well."

The phone rang. Jessie got up to answer it. She covered the mouthpiece.

"Fred and Sonya are wondering if we would like to go over for morning tea?" she asked him.

"Sorry, I think I'd better get back to town. Some other time."

He didn't particularly feel like explaining himself this morning, or listening to Jessie try to excuse his presence in the house last night. It had been a long time since he'd felt so uncomfortable in a situation. It was obvious no one knew he was there, not Fred and obviously not her parents. And it just didn't sit right.

*

Jessie drove him back into town after breakfast. His car was at the car yard. A big wind had got up and was blowing unimpeded across the treeless landscape. They didn't even discuss going back to Five Oaks.

Jessie broke the silence. "Rain coming, or snow."

"Looks like it." The phone reception had finally come back and Michael was going through his messages. There were plenty. "Well, that's it. Should keep me going till this time next week."

"Are you going away this week?"

"No, only Sunday night as usual. I'll get on to Belinda about those huts. You'll have to put in a DA, but it's no good until you know where you want them."

"No, that's right. I'll talk to the architects on Monday—I don't know yet what restrictions are on our lease." Jessie had pulled up. The car yard was open and there were a few people wandering about already.

Michael could see Ron approaching across the yard, firm intention written on his face. A truck problem, at a guess. "Jessie, maybe we can catch up later in the week. Ring me when you're in town and available."

*

Available. Jessie felt like spluttering. Just who did he think he was? Available for him? Never.

She started to settle down as she drove home. It really wasn't his fault. She'd been the one to pull back. She was going to have to tell her parents that she'd invited Michael to stay the night. Or get Fred to not say anything. It was too complicated. It wasn't her house, but on the other hand, she was twenty-six; she was beyond answering to anyone who she was—or wasn't—going to spend the night with. Or lying about it.

She had to be honest. It was the best way to avoid trouble.

*

The beef stew was simmering on the stove with mashed potatoes in the oven and freshly picked broccoli ready for the boiling water. Jessie surveyed her tidy kitchen critically and thought she was as prepared as she could be. Headlights swept around the drive and she heard her parents getting out of the car. She poured them all a glass of wine and took a deep breath.

"Hi. How did it go?" she asked her mother.

Jessie listened to her talk while she finished making dinner. They were sitting at the table when the conversation got around to her.

"Now tell us about yours, darling, did you have a good weekend?"

"There was a bit of drama. Sonya cut her finger and Fred asked us to look after the twins while he whisked her off to hospital."

"Oh no. Who's us?"

"Michael D'Larghi was here for dinner. Mom, Dad, I wanted to tell you that I invited him back here on Friday night. I should have told you before you left. Well, asked," she amended.

Their reactions were extraordinary: her mother went white and her father, red. Neither said anything.

Then her father turned to her mother and said, "I told you so." And he walked out.

So much for being up front and honest. It was a slight over-reaction, especially since nothing had happened between her and Michael. But neither of them stayed to hear that bit. She was very sick of being treated like she was eighteen, that was for sure.

*

It was after breakfast on Monday, before she left for work, that Jessie heard the conversation between her father and Fred—she supposed—on the phone. She walked in behind Lex as he was talking.

"We do not do business with D'Larghis. Full stop. No, I will not listen to any more. I don't trust them. And I have good reason. No, Fred. Don't ask me again."

He clicked the phone off and turned abruptly to see Jessie standing there.

"What's all this with D'Larghi? Couldn't you find someone better than that? I don't want him muscling in here, trying to do business with the family. Don't think it's you he's interested in. He's just trying to get to Fred or me. Don't be a fool, Jessie." He was shaking with anger. And he turned and walked out.

Jessie just stood there, transfixed.

She'd thought she was immune to her father's ranting judgments of the people in her life. There was always one reason or another, but she was not going to take this lying down. This was a mistake. He just didn't know the Michael she knew. They could be two completely different people, from the way he was talking.

She burst into the kitchen. "Mom, what do you and Dad have against the D'Larghis? You are both behaving abominably."

"Don't talk to me like that! We have a right to know who you are inviting into our house."

"Yes, I understand that. I did things the wrong way round. I should have told you first. I mistakenly assumed I lived here, too. And I hadn't realized you both think I'm still sixteen. But is there anything else that's the problem?"

"There's always been rumours, you know, about the Mafia, drugs, protection rackets. I've never heard anything concrete, but the D'Larghis have done pretty well for themselves, haven't they, in a short amount of time."

"That sounds more like sour grapes to me. You should see how hard they work. It's not true. Can't be true," she stated hotly. "What do you think of Michael?"

Clare looked out the window, sipping at her coffee. "More to the point, what do you think of him?"

"Michael D'Larghi is—" She stopped and considered. "The best thing that's happened to me. But after the debacle with Alan, I feel my judgment could be severely flawed. How do I trust my feelings this time?"

"I don't know, darling, feelings are important but there's more to it than that. I'd take a little more time, perhaps. Are you, um, seeing him again?" Her mother's voice was cool but she clutched her mug tightly.

"I don't know." Jessie gave her a big hug. "This could all be an unnecessary conversation. He may not want to see me again after Friday night." She sounded miserable. "Could you find out what Dad's going off about? Talk some sense into him. I really don't understand it. Tell him I'm a big girl now and capable of making a decision or two. Even if they might be wrong. You've got to let me run with it."

For the life of her, she couldn't imagine why her parents were so against the D'Larghis. Maybe moving home hadn't been such a hot idea.

Chapter 24

Belinda walked in with two skim lattes and two warm apple and cinnamon muffins from the corner café.

"What happened? Sit and relax and tell me everything." She plonked one coffee down in front of Jessie and sat nursing hers while she passed over one of the muffins. "Mm, they are so good." She fixed Jessie with her direct stare. "Now."

"Nothing. I stuffed up. I'm not sure, but it is all very embarrassing."

"Great. What did you do?"

"You try moving back home when you're twenty-six *and* have been living with someone, and then try and work out what the rules are. You can't go back eight years and going forward appears to be a no-go situation. I know it's not my house but *really*." Miserably, she crumbled off a piece of muffin. "Fred had to take Sonya to hospital 'cause she'd cut her finger, so he burst in and asked us to look after the babies. And so it kind of put a dampener on everything and so—nothing happened."

"Oh." Belinda sat back and put her muffin down, somewhat deflated. "That's not good. But what did Michael say?"

"He was pretty fantastic about it all but he probably never wants to see me again. I wouldn't blame him." The more she thought about it—and she was certainly thinking about the over-the-top reaction of her parents the other night, when she'd told them she'd invited Michael home—she had no idea what they were on about. No one behaved like that any more. It was pathetic.

"I'm moving out." The decision was made. Just like that. Staying was intolerable.

"What?"

"You heard me. I'm going to find somewhere to live in town. I do not understand where my parents are coming from. I refuse to comply with the stupid ideas of a century ago—they were terrible then and even worse now. I'm really disappointed in my parents, you know."

"Hi, Joan." Belinda welcomed a middle-aged, rotund woman with a wave. "Joan, this is Jessie Cranfield. Jessie, Joan's the admin manager at the hospital."

"Ah. Just the person I was looking for. Hello, Jessie. I was wondering if you could do a couple of days for me up at the hospital? My OT has gone away for a month and I'm snowed under. Heard about you coming back home from Olive, you remember Olive? She used to work for your folks. She mentioned you were here and I thought you'd be just the one to help us out." She smiled at Belinda. "You'd be able to spare the girl for a couple of days a week, wouldn't you?"

Belinda groaned. "I may as well tell you, Jessie, you haven't a hope of getting out of it. Joan Roberts here is our militant commander. You don't say no to Joan." She turned to Joan. "Now, this girl is very precious, no more than a couple of days for a couple of weeks, hear?"

"Of course I can help." Jessie laughed. "Actually I'd welcome the opportunity to see how it all works up here. But tell me, how can I get in touch with Olly? I've been meaning to go and say hello."

"She's just moved into the retirement village attached to the hospital. I'll give you the number."

*

All in all, it worked out beautifully. A couple of days' extra pay from the hospital to help ends meet and when she went to visit Olly—their beautiful Olly, who, with Stan, had lived and worked on the property for years, and was more family than some of her relations—Jessie discovered she had an empty house she could rent.

Jessie was back after lunch. "It's perfect." She waved the key at Belinda. "It's even furnished, because Olly can't take all her furniture with her. Only her bed and a chest of drawers and a chair. So I'm set."

"Didn't Olly drive the school bus?"

"She used to work in the house when Fred was young, but when I was in primary school she did. She used to look after me a lot."

"What luck. That's perfect."

All that was left to do was to tell her parents.

And wipe Michael D'Larghi out of her mind and thoughts. Which was not going to be particularly hard, as she was going to be frantically busy over the next few weeks. Wasn't she?

"Mom? Dad?" There was no one home when she got there. She'd forgotten what her mother did on Mondays She was probably still in town. Jessie walked into her bedroom, pulled down her suitcase and started to pack.

One hour later, there was still no one around. It was almost six o'clock and totally dark. Jessie went into the kitchen to begin getting dinner. She may as well; she couldn't leave until she'd told them. No more secrets. She'd learned her lesson.

She was peeling potatoes when she saw the lights of the ute park in the garage.

It was going to be her father first. The back door opened and the boots thumped on the floor and the tap went on as he went straight to the laundry to wash. He stuck his head around the kitchen door and saw her.

"Oh Jessie, how long will dinner be? I've got a few calls to make. And then I'll go take a shower."

"What time will Mom be home?" she called after him, but she was asking an empty space. No reference to the arguments of the morning. All pushed out of the way, as usual; ignored, as though nothing had happened.

Jessie impatiently turned on the television. And waited. At seven thirty her mother came rushing in.

"Thank you so much, darling, I was held up and couldn't get here earlier. That looks and smells delicious. You are a good girl. I'll get out of these clothes and be back in a jiffy."

She was back quicker than that. She walked in to the family room with a startled expression on her face. "What are all those suitcases doing in your room, Jessie?"

"I'm getting a place in town—Olly's house. I visited her at the retirement wing at the hospital and she offered to rent me her place for a while. I've just got a job at the hospital as well, so it will be handy not driving in and out every day." She was such a coward. Why wasn't she telling them what she really thought?

"Oh. What has your father said?"

"Nothing, that is, I haven't told him, he just stuck his 'round the door and he's gone to have a shower."

"Right," said Clare and she went to tell Lex, obviously. But they both said nothing when he came in.

They sat down to dinner. It was a quiet one apart from the scrape of knives and forks on the plates. They passed the salt and pepper and Lex poured water for the three of them. *Typical, let's not rock the boat. Or spoil dinner with an argument, or didn't they care?* The sooner she got out of there the better.

"How's Olly?" her mother asked.

"She's wonderful, as usual. Making the most of the situation. She likes the home because she doesn't have to cook dinner any more, she said. Or wash up. Just as good as a holiday, she said. Hasn't seen you for ages, said to tell you any time you'd like to drop 'round, she'd love to show you her room."

"Very good. I must do that." Clare stood up. "I suppose you'll be leaving in the morning. You don't need anything?"

"No. Thank you."

"Good then, goodnight."

That left her at the table with her father. And she really didn't have anything to say to him. Her parents were incredible. They'd become two automated, oh-so-polite ghosts. Say nothing, don't make a fuss, was the way they coped with crises. She looked at her father down the other end of the table. As far as he was concerned, she'd gone already.

She shouldn't feel disappointed, it was what she expected.

*

Tuesday morning it was her turn to buy the coffees. She ran into Michael in the café. Literally ran into him, and nearly spilled two boiling hot coffees all over him.

"Hey Jessie." He steadied the coffees. "How are you?" And she promptly burst into tears.

He guided her to one of the outside tables, concerned, and sat her down.

"What's wrong?" he asked her gently as he put sugar into one of the cups. "I presume this is for Belinda? I'll get her another."

Grown up and in control she was not.

She took a breath and a sip of the coffee. The burning liquid helped ground her. "Hi Michael," she said brightly. "How are you this morning?"

"No, I asked you first. Anything wrong?" he asked.

"No, it's all good. I'm moving into town—actually I've moved already, this morning, into Olly and Stan's house."

"That's a bit sudden, isn't it?"

"Joan Roberts from the hospital asked me yesterday to work for a couple of days a week, just for a little while, and it seemed a good thing. Well, everything fell into place."

'Your parents are okay with it?"

"Yes, fine."

Michael sat back in his chair, watching her shrewdly. She was glad it was only a little white lie. She wouldn't like to be in the witness box with him as interrogator.

"Feel like going to the movies tonight?"

"Thank you, yes, I would." And didn't the coffee taste a bit better.

1983

His wife knew. She followed her with her eyes when they were picking up the children. Their boys. Who were now mates. Had he said something? It mustn't get out, that much she did know—her husband would not tolerate it.

She'd been mad, crazy. So foolish. If only she hadn't done it that first time.

Her car had started wandering and then she felt the whoop, whoop, thump. She'd pulled over and looked with horror at her front tire. Flat as a pancake. They'd only had the car a few weeks. What was she to do now? She didn't know how to change a tire. Looking up and down the lonely road there didn't appear to be anyone else around to do it either. She opened the boot. Great, now she was going to be late home, another black mark against her.

If only she'd known how to change the damn tire. Then it would never have happened. If only. Her life ruined because no one had ever told her how to change a tire. Surely it should have been one of the first things she was taught. All these lonely, country roads.

He'd stopped, and of course it hadn't been a problem. He'd changed the tire. And they'd laughed a lot. He'd been so easy to get along with and she'd needed a laugh at the time. It had been another disappointing month. And this time the cramping had been really bad and the bleeding so heavy. If only they could have another baby.

But she shouldn't have taken him the bottle of wine to thank him. She didn't have to do that and it was fate that there was no one else there when she'd arrived at his house. They'd drunk it. No, she couldn't blame him. Not entirely. It was just circumstance. Opportunity. And it was naughty and wicked. She'd hurt her husband badly, if he ever found out. He mustn't ever find out.

She'd come to her senses a month ago. No more, she'd told him.

And never again, never again. She'd promised herself she'd never do it again.

Chapter 25

It was dark in the movie theater but she could see Michael's profile in the glow from the screen. The column of his throat when he threw his head back and laughed. The smell of the popcorn. The strangeness and the familiarity of the bulk of him sitting beside her. She was so aware of his arm sliding across the back of her seat.

"I think we should go away next weekend," he whispered.

"Why?" That was a fair question, she thought.

"I don't know about you, but these steps we're taking, one step forward and then one step back, are driving me crazy. I want you, Jessie."

This was a strange place for this conversation.

"Do you want me?" he asked.

"Shh, yes, I do." But he didn't hear her.

"What did you say? Please, Jessie. Come on, think about it."

The person behind shushed them both.

"Michael," she warned.

"No parents, no town, no one but us—how about it?"

"Sounds incredible." He was tickling her ear. She laughed. The person beside her gave her a frowning glance.

"Just say yes."

"Yes."

Michael straightened up. His arm was suddenly not along the back of her chair any more. He'd grabbed her hand, intertwining their fingers. "Good."

God, she was a pushover.

*

Wednesday night, Michael rang from Sydney.

"It's very strange being in your flat. I feel you around me."

"I hope it's not Alan's presence you feel."

"No, definitely not."

"That's good. How did you get on with the builders?"

"There's a delay in the start date."

"That sounds familiar. Wouldn't it be wonderful if you could have a good idea and then get everyone on board and get it up and running in a couple of months?"

"Where's the challenge in that?"

"Okay. How're you going with your plans for the weekend?"

"Don't you worry, it's under control."

The suspense was killing her.

*

Thursday, he rang from a country town that had an abattoir.

"Today was a good day. I caught up with a great guy who's going to buy the meat for us, and it will be killed here and packaged how I want."

"We had a good one too. I met some of the kids and we had a preliminary look at what they want and what we can expect. They are so enthusiastic, I can't believe it, it makes everything worthwhile."

"So I'll see you tomorrow in Sydney? You know where to come."

"Yes. What do I bring?"

"Not much."

Jessie laughed. "You're not very forthcoming."

"I can't wait, Jessie."

"Neither can I. Oh boy, neither can I."

"Seven, you can get there by seven?"

"Oh, yes."

*

Jessie was five minutes early and saw Michael as soon as he reached the top of the escalator—he was taller by a head than most of the people milling around the departure lounge at the airport. This time it was all Michael's plan. Payback, he'd said. You will know nothing, just get to the airport by seven o'clock.

Jessie hoped all these people knew more about their destinations than she did. It didn't seem like it: they all looked totally clueless.

"Hi."

"Jessie." He took her hand and led her straight out again, down the long escalator. She looked at him, simply not believing just how wonderful it was to see him again.

She became aware that they were not going toward the check-in counter. Not again. "You've changed your mind." She pulled him to a stop.

"No. Have you?"

She shook her head. They were off again.

"Where are we going?"

He grinned at her. "Mystery tour, remember?"

It didn't take her too long to work out they were heading toward the light aircraft section.

"Have you got your driver's license?" he asked. "We'll need it to show the man at the gate." And that was about all that was said until they were loaded onto a small, twin-engine airplane with the blond, too-young-looking pilot helping Jessie in and showing her how to buckle up.

Five minutes later they were in the air. Sydney stretched out below them, ribbons of headlights snaking home in the peak-hour traffic, the city twinkling—the sheer scale of it was breathtaking. She could see the brightly lit tankers out on the black sea, then they were banking, turning back toward the city and heading west.

Michael produced a bottle of sparkling pinot and two glasses. "Here's to our weekend."

Speechless, she raised her glass. Didn't Michael know this was driving her crazy? Surprises were all well and good but this was taking it to the extreme. She wasn't good at waiting for surprises.

"How's your day been?" he asked.

When they landed forty-five minutes later, she realized she hadn't stopped talking and she still didn't have a clue where they were. Moonlight showed up a small private airstrip with white markers. It seemed to be on top of a hill, smooth and flat like a billiard table.

"We could be the only people left in the world," Jessie whispered as the plane disappeared and became indistinguishable from all the stars in the night sky. "Where are we?"

"This is the Kranjee Valley, on top of the Dividing Range, and it has to be one of the most beautiful places in the world. Not quite as good as home, but almost." Michael chuckled. He stood behind her with his arms around her. She felt so—safe. Considering the nervousness she'd felt over the last week, it was quite strange.

"Come, we'll see it better in the morning."

Michael picked up their two cases and they walked almost to the edge of the cliff before Jessie saw a low-slung house clinging to the cliff edge, its long glass windows overlooking the valley.

"Wow. Who lives here?" she said, awestruck.

"A friend of mine owns it, and it's ours for the weekend. There's a resort a couple of kilometres away and they manage it for him, keep it warm and stocked with food." They walked down a short path to the carved, front door that had been lifted straight from India or Indonesia. Inside was warm, the fire was lit, and a magnificent garlicky smell wafted out of the kitchen. Michael flicked on the lights and Jessie noted more signs that someone had been there recently: bread rolls wrapped in a napkin, wine glasses and a bottle of red on the table, which was set for two. It was too perfect.

She'd had enough of games. She'd had enough of mysteries and being polite. She wanted him hot and out of control. A bit like her. There simply had to be a resolution to this massive attraction or she might explode.

Remember Alan, she cautioned herself. He'd been a mighty mistake. But the caution didn't work; she could barely remember what Alan looked like.

All she could see was Michael. The shape of his jaw, the dark stubble lining it, the column of his throat, the hair on his chest disappearing down behind the third button on his shirt. The shape of his mouth.

He poured the red and handed her a glass. Was it her imagination or was the glass trembling? The dark liquid quivered ever so slightly. She put her hand around his on the glass. She brought the glass and his hand to her mouth, took a sip and then kissed his fingers, running her lips over them gently. She felt them tighten around the glass. The red wine was an aphrodisiac—and that was the last thing she needed.

The wine mixed with the scent of Michael and she put her hand to his chest. There was heat, the silky feel of his shirt, the roughness of his pants, and suddenly she needed to touch his skin. He was moving away, back to get his own glass.

"Would you like a massage? We can get someone up here from the resort, if you like."

Massage? He had to be kidding. "You've been here before. When have you been here before?" What a stupid question. Did she really want to know that he'd brought someone else here?

"My friend organized a dinner here, flew us all in—he was one of the sponsors of our basketball team. But we all took up the offer of the massage. I can recommend it. Then there's a spa out the back and a pool and they can bring horses round in the morning if you feel like a ride."

What kind of a dinner: all men, men and wives, or men and girlfriends?

"Why don't you have a massage? I'll read a magazine or go outside for a while."

She sounded annoyed. *Relax, smile.* He was probably nervous too. She walked over to the floor-to-ceiling plate-glass windows and pulled the curtains across.

*

Michael watched Jessie standing over by the curtains. Her beauty was so—what was the opposite of ethereal? Earthy, real, tangible. He wanted to hold her and taste her, feel her body under his and—What was the matter with him? Ever since he'd dispelled the fear that she wouldn't be there, when he first saw her standing in the throngs at Mascot he'd been increasingly nervous. He'd been on some rollercoaster ride. To be honest, this wasn't the kind of thing he did. Girls, week-ends sure, but this was Jessie. It was so important he got it right. And he was messing everything up. The last few times they'd tried being together hadn't worked. This should. Now he was afraid it might be overkill. It was so incredibly special, he'd thought Jessie would love it as he did.

"There's a great music selection, or an iPod if you don't feel like choosing." Maybe he'd understand a little better how she was feeling if she chose the music. He walked into the kitchen and checked the casserole in the oven. The vegetables were in a plastic container, ready to go into the microwave for one minute thirty, according to the Post-it. Easy. Nothing to do here. He felt a soft pair of arms hug him from behind.

"Just so you know who's kissing who exactly. It's me. Kissing you."

And he turned, pulling her into his arms and leaning back against the bench and lifting her up and it felt good. Her legs wrapped around him and she tasted like hot chili. Her mouth fit his and her body was—not close enough. Jessie was fighting with his belt and he was touching bare skin and she was so hot, making little moans into his mouth.

"Stop," he panted. Condoms were in his bag.

His phone rang. They both looked at it, buzzing on the countertop where it had fallen out of his pocket. He leaned over and switched it off. He saw her feel in the pocket of her jacket for her phone. She carefully took it out and turned it off and set it beside Michael's.

"Good thinking."

They looked at each other. Was that a shadow of uncertainty he saw in Jessie's eyes?

"Perhaps we'd better have something to eat. It smells cooked."

Chapter 26

"What was your favorite thing at school?" Michael pushed his empty plate away.

She followed suit. "Running, I was quite a good runner."

Behind him, the fire was dying down. He was backlit and she noticed the shape of his ears. They were neat and set close to his head. She liked them. His hair was crisp and curly and recently cut. She liked it, too.

"What distance?"

Michael offered her more wine. Jessie covered her glass and shook her head. That was the last thing she needed. "Eight hundred. I trained for skiing and the eight hundred was in my comfort zone. What about you?"

"Basketball, and it took me a long way. Why did you choose occupational therapy?"

"Patti and Paul had David and it threw them so badly. There just wasn't much support for parents of Down's kids. People shied away from them, as though it was catching. Patti said one day it was like going traveling: you'd organized for Paris, booking rooms and learning the language, but then they put you down in Moscow instead. Can you imagine?" She looked at him. "You can't. It would be such a shock. So

I wanted ..." She shrugged, embarrassed, and sat back and straightened her fork on the empty plate. "Okay, you."

"D'Larghi's. What can I say? Trucks and vegetables. Vegetables and trucks. We've been carting vegetables in and out of the district for sixty years. Ron was taking me to the markets with him when I was six years old. I've always been able to do anything I've ever wanted to do since. Lucky really."

He got up and reached for her plate. She stood as well. "I can do that."

"What's wrong?" Michael, at last, asked her.

"I want to know why your grandmother has a problem with me."

What I really want to know is why you are standing there collecting plates. And I want to know when you are going to take me to bed.

"She's old school, from a different time where families had a big say in who you married. My father's marriage was arranged. My mother was brought over from Italy and they'd never met."

"Michael." She took the plates from his hands and set them down on the table. "I think we should take pressure off ourselves and stop thinking this is so important. I haven't felt this explosive lust before. It might all vanish into dust. How would I know? How do *you* know?"

Michael started to laugh. "You're right. One step at a time." He put his plate down and took her hand.

"No pressure," she said softly.

"Okay. I'll just stoke up the fire."

Now *she* was all nervous. During the eight or nine months she'd been with Alan things had quietened down on the love-making front. He was often quite late to bed, or he was away, and they didn't make love all that often toward the end. She went to her suitcase, which lay on a wooden blanket box at the end of the bed next to Michael's. They looked funny sitting there side by side. Much more companionable than she and Michael. Maybe she should take everything out of each case and mix it up all together. Anything, to get back to where they were good, kissing in the kitchen. That was good.

She pulled out the shirt and undies, the entire contents. There wasn't much more than that in it—ah, yes, a packet of condoms. Michael had said not to bring much. She'd thought it was funny at the time. But now, oh hell. What had he brought? She opened his case. One shirt and a pair of undies, the same as her. She started to laugh, Oh, and a packet of condoms. Thank heavens. Great minds think alike. Her shoulders shook.

"What's the matter?" Michael came up behind her, worried. He put his arms around her.

She couldn't help it, "Look." She pointed to the empty cases. "You said not to bring much."

"Good girl. I like a woman who does as she's told," he growled in her ear. And he pushed her down onto the bed. At last.

*

Every garment came off slowly. That is, he tried to make it slow and Jessie fought and struggled to whip everything off. "Patience, wait." But she wouldn't. He took both her hands in one of his and stretched them out above her head. Kissing her, he lost it as well. He had to keep stopping and running his lips down her throat to the pulse point just above her collarbone and licking her, breathing in her scent. Every time he touched her she bucked or wriggled. Her breasts were magnificent and when he touched her between her legs, she almost screamed.

Finally, she struggled free and half sat up with her hair falling in her eyes.

"If you don't do it now, I'll kill you." She reached for a condom packet and tore it with her teeth. "Put it on."

Then he was inside her and the two of them melted together. Like it had been when they sang. One voice. Each one drawing more out of the other until he felt her climax just seconds before he shuddered and came.

Chapter 27

Jessie flicked the down feather, escapee from one of the pillows, under Michael's nose. He was fast asleep. She shouldn't wake him, he must be exhausted. Talk about stamina.

She should be exhausted too, but she felt she could climb mountains, swim rivers and—"Climb Every Mountain" popped into her head and she started to hum. An arm came around her, tucking her into his body.

"Sleep."

"I can't." She wriggled. "Can't we get up?"

"If you really insist and I say, 'I think I can,' a few times, something might happen but I can't promise anything." He bit the back of her neck gently. "I have this incredible desire to eat you. In another life, could I have been a vampire, do you think?"

"Oh." Jessie turned underneath him, her eyes wide. "Edward or Wolfman?"

"I have no idea who you're talking about. What do you think?"

"It depends on which book. I think the Wolfman." She closed her eyes. "Eat me."

Michael started to laugh. "You are insatiable. What have I got myself into?"

"Me, just me." And she couldn't help it. Even to herself, she sounded as if she was purring.

*

When they woke next, Jessie jumped out of bed and raced to the curtains. The bedroom lie adjacent to the large sitting room and shared the same view. It was incredible. Down below, the valley snaked its way off into the distance as far as she could see: mountains, bush, weird rocky outcrops and those fabulous red sandstone cliffs.

Michael came to stand beside her and handed her a white toweling gown. She put it on and followed him into the kitchen.

The fridge held a big bowl of fruit salad and tubs of yogurt and packets of cereal stood neatly on the bench.

"You do breakfast and I'll clean up our mess from last night," said Michael.

He passed her on the way to the sink and they kissed. The connection was incredible. His lips were soft and the smell of her on him and the taste of him was to die for.

When they parted, she blinked. "I can't see any mess. This is fairyland and the fairies have been."

"As long as it isn't vampire land and the vampires have been."

"I don't think they have yogurt for brekkie. Look, there's frost still on the western side of the house. It must be cold out."

Michael smiled down at her. "Maybe we should stay inside."

Jessie went to put the coffee machine on. "Where's the toaster?"

"Over here." They collided again and started to laugh.

"You know." Michael pushed her gently back against the counter as he reached around her to put the bread in the toaster. "You could marry me and we could do this every morning. " He bent down and kissed her on the nose.

Jessie pulled back, suddenly serious. "No." There was that M-word again. She'd ignore it.

"That's it—just no?"

"You don't understand. I made a terrible mistake with Alan." She shook her head. "It's not that I think you're anything like Alan, it's just that my life is starting to take off, I love my job, really love it, and I just want to go with it for a while." Michael looked so hurt. "And I'm just not ready."

"You sure that's all? I can wait."

Jessie looked at him steadily. "Being engaged doesn't have a whole lot to recommend it. I've just been engaged and I don't want to do that again. Married but not, you get all the downsides—the commitment, the sacrifices, the compromises—all without being married. I want—I want this fizz."

Laughing, she threw herself at him and wrapped her arms around his neck. He caught her and lifted her easily onto the counter so she could look him straight in the eye.

Resting her arms loosely round his shoulders, she told him, "I'm not ready. I can't believe how selfish I'm sounding. I want to go with this for a bit, I'm enjoying my freedom—it's pretty special, too. Please don't hate me."

She felt for the bowl of fruit salad that looked as if it might be pushed on to the floor and cradled it in her arms. Why did she feel like crying? Damn it. She'd know if and when she wanted to marry Michael, be his wife. Right now, she didn't. She looked at him hoping for—what? A glimmer of understanding, not the cold of the other night. She was deadly serious. Did he understand how important this was?

*

Jessie was stubborn. He knew that. What had he said to himself before—he was going to enjoy these skirmishes? Maybe not so much, not if he wasn't winning. She had to be feeling hesitant about walking right back into a relationship so soon after breaking up with Alan, and he had pushed her to the limit for that. *Back off, D'Larghi, what man in his right mind would be knocking back a relationship with no commitments?* Yes, he wanted to tie her up, heave her over his shoulder and take her back to his cave. He'd been the sensitive, talkative, "exploring his feelings" sort of man, many times before, because it's what he thought women wanted—and he could take it or leave it. But no woman had ever made him feel so possessive.

So, decision time, D'Larghi. Time to back off.

He picked a piece of apple from the bowl of fruit salad, ate it, then fished for a piece for Jessie and fed it to her. "Okay."

He pushed a lock of that dark red hair back behind her ear and kissed her. The tang of apple mixed with Jessie. He caught the bowl as it fell out of her hands and put it down safely on the bench before getting back to the task at hand.

*

Maybe Michael had withdrawn from her a little, but that was when they were up and walking around. Not in bed. No, it was hot and sexy, and transported her to heights she had never been to before. They got up to eat. And shower. That was usually a disaster and they would end up back in bed.

"This is it, Jessie. Last one."

She giggled. "No, it isn't." She jumped out of bed and raced to find her case, which had fallen to the floor. "Look!" She held up her packet triumphantly. "There's more. Ta da!"

"What foresight! You are remarkable. Have I told you that?"

"So what would we have done if we had run out?"

"I don't take those kinds of chances."

"And if I'd said I was safe would you believe me?"

"I don't play with the odds, Jessie."

"Yet you're a risk taker."

"I like to know the odds are in my favor."

"Aren't I a risk?"

"Mm," he grunted. "And I'll take you any time you like."
He rolled over on top of her.

She had a lot to learn about Michael D'Larghi. He was
such a control freak—he pretended he wasn't, but she knew
how he liked to make the decisions. She liked pushing him out
of his comfort zone.

Michael looked at her lazily. "What's going on in that
beautiful head of yours?"

"I don't think I know you very well. How well do I know
you, Michael?"

"There's no rush. We've got plenty of time."

"How serious was it between you and Sienna?"

"It was comfortable. I told you it was. For me—I can't
speak for her, but I don't think it was a serious thing for her.
It was more ... suitable, courtesy of our grandmothers. Sienna
has always been a good mate," Michael said. "Alan, now, he
was a serious contender, he had me worried for a while."

"I'm so fickle. I thought I loved him, and suddenly there
you were and I realized." She broke off and buried her head in
her pillow. Michael pulled her over again and gently pushed
her hair off her face.

"It's okay, trust your feelings."

"Right now, I trust no one, particularly myself or my
feelings or my analytical powers."

"Let me take you through the things we did last night, very
slowly, and see if I can recreate a situation for you. That will
help you resolve things."

"I simply can't think of a better idea." She gave a little sigh and lifted her arms up around his neck.

Michael undid the knot of the bathrobe and as it fell open, he bent to kiss each nipple. "Jessie. You are incredibly beautiful. This is like opening a present on my birthday. Only we won't have to take so much time undressing this time. We can get to work on the playing part earlier."

Thank heavens she was lying down, she felt her legs relax, open, then he went exploring …

They laughed and they both reached for the new packet of condoms at the same time.

*

Jessie gathered up the bathrobe, which had fallen on the floor, and wandered into the kitchen. On the bench lay two neatly folded tracksuits and two pairs of sturdy trainers. She picked up the pair of shoes in her size and raced back into the bedroom.

"Where did these come from?"

Michael's eyes were closed. "I rang the resort and asked them to send some up. Hope I got the right size?"

"You mean they came in while—while we …" She trailed off, horrified.

Michael grinned. "No, I rang them just before we dropped off to sleep. They said they were bringing dinner as well. Did you find anything to eat?"

"I didn't look. What are the tracksuits for?"

"Well," Michael said, "I thought you might like to go for a walk and as neither of us had anything suitable for hiking in—"

Michael had the breath knocked out of him as Jessie landed on top of him.

"That is such a good idea. Let's go now." She scrambled off and pulled down the doona, revealing Michael's naked figure.

"Oh, you are gorgeous, did you know that? Your legs are so long and everything—" She stopped.

"Everything?" Michael asked, but he couldn't quite keep the grin off his face.

"Yeah, Everything is … quite perfect. Why are you so golden? Your skin is different to what I—" She screamed as he suddenly pulled her down on top of him.

"My mother was from the north of Italy. They are different to the people of the south. That's where I got my height and my coloring."

"I'm sad I won't get to meet her. She must have been beautiful."

"Yes, she was very beautiful. However, you're right, we should go outside." He patted her bottom and pushed her off. She pulled the doona back up again and raced to get into her tracksuit.

*

"What time is it?"

Michael pulled his phone out of his pocket and switched it on. "Around two thirty."

"Have we had lunch?"

"I did." Michael looked at her. "You may have missed out."

Jessie let that comment pass right on by. "Have we got a compass? I wouldn't want to get lost here." Michael lifted his phone in answer. "The trails look quite well marked. What an extraordinary place. What are those rock statues, standing in the middle of the valley?"

"I think they're called pagodas."

The afternoon sun was hitting the red sandstone cliffs on the eastern side of the valley.

"Just imagine being one of the early settlers and seeing all that land waiting for you and no one but you to claim it."

"I think there may have been a few native inhabitants looking down not so happily. But you can't deny that Australia was a gift to all those land-starved Englishmen and, I might add, all the job-starved Italians, too." He laughed.

They were scrambling down a rocky trail toward the bottom of the valley.

"My grandfather got the news he was accepted, married my grandmother the next day and then sailed for Australia two days after that."

"What did he do?"

"He was a carpenter by trade, but when he got here they really wanted mechanics so he ended up doing that. Eventually, he bought a truck and started carting out of the markets to the Monaro."

"What did your grandmother think of Australia?"

"She was very worried there was no food here because every time he wrote to her, he complained about the food."

"They were so brave, weren't they? Migrants from Russia, Germany, Yugoslavia, Poland and Italy; people who'd been shooting each other three years before, leaving everything they knew to come across the world and end up in Australia. Which must really have seemed to be the end of the earth. But the magic worked, didn't it? They built the dam, so there was electricity for Sydney, water for the M.I.A. *and* Cooma became multicultural, way before the name was coined. Was your father born here?"

"Dad was born in Italy nine months after my grandfather left. Luckily for him." Michael sat on a fallen tree. "Here, sit for a minute. Okay, tell me about your family."

"Cranfields were crofters and came from the west of Scotland. My great-great-grandfather was a tough old man. But it's hard to differentiate the tough men of the Monaro from their roots—I mean, where they came from probably had an affect but so does the country here, must be something in the soil or the air." She gave a little laugh.

"I love that poem by Banjo Patterson. I'm rambling. Michael, I want to ask you something." She couldn't leave it alone. It had been building inside her since her mother mentioned it.

Jessie screwed up her eyes, took a breath and rushed in: "Did your family ever have a connection to the Mafia?"

Michael didn't reply and the silence dragged on and she finally looked at him. She was shocked by the fury in his eyes.

"What do you think?" His voice was controlled, belying the anger she could feel radiating from him.

"I don't think anythng, it's just that Mom mentioned it when we were talking about the D'Larghis."

"So, it's not just me, it's my whole family who are the drug runners, is it?"

"I didn't say drugs. Just a yes or a no is all I need." It wasn't possible for her to feel any more miserable. Why had she started this?

"And what if it's yes?" Michael's voice was getting lower and more angry.

"I—hell, I don't know. I want you to say no, I guess, so I can tell Mom to pull her head in ..."

"Well, she's not the first person who's thought it. I've lived with the rumours and speculation all my life. I just didn't think you would be asking me this."

His phone started to rumble. She could almost feel the vibration from where she was standing.

Michael took it out of his pocket and looked at the number. He frowned. "It's Belinda ... Hello? Sure, I'll put her on."

"Jessie, I'm sorry but your dad is frantic. Your mom's just had a stroke and she's in intensive care and he asked me if I knew where you were. Your phone isn't answering, so I had to try Michael. Can you get back from wherever you are?"

Chapter 28

Michael didn't have to answer her question. She knew he wasn't involved with the Mafia. But now was not a good time to bring it up, she thought as she looked out of the window at the mountainous terrain and olive-green bush below. The forests filled with trees going forever and ever, winding rivers, snaking through the valleys. The plane ride was taking too long.

Michael had done everything. It had taken them half an hour to walk back to the house. She'd felt stiff and awkward and had stumbled more than a few times, but Michael had been there with a steadying hand. The plane had arrived in under two hours. He hadn't said much, only asking where her mother was and telling her to be strong.

They'd barely talked since. Had she ruined everything? How important was the yes or no to the question she'd asked? She couldn't answer that. Right now, it wasn't important at all. It was so hard to take in this was really happening.

Michael dropped her off at the hospital. He gave her a quick hug and wished her luck. It was so awkward. She didn't know what to say to him. She'd hurt him, she knew. But she couldn't cope with all that now.

She thought she'd heard him call but she was already running up the stairs. And she didn't want him to see the tears.

*

The person in the bed was a stranger. That wasn't her mother. It was totally different looking at someone you love, lying in a hospital bed attached to all those tubes and masks and beeping machines. The shock had her flying into her father's arms, speechless. Her father was the calm one. Jessie found it so easy to be calm and objective when it was someone she didn't know. Where was her professionalism, her experience, when she needed it? Disappeared, completely.

"It's okay, Jessie. Hush." Her father patted her awkwardly. "I couldn't find you. Don't you ever go away again without telling me where you are, promise?"

"Yes, I'm so sorry. How is she?" Holding on to her father's hand tightly, she was finally able to look again at her mother. The left side of her face drooped and her eyes were closed.

"We don't know much, just waiting for the results of some tests. But it's a big one. They have her in an induced coma at the moment. They're talking about airlifting her to Canberra. It's a nightmare. I really want her to stay here where we know everyone. But if she has to go …"

"Dad, if she has to go, there'll be a good reason. Don't worry."

She made herself go to the notes at the end of the bed. Cold hard facts were what she wanted. Her father and her family needed her to be professional.

Fred came in, embraced his father, then hugged her. "Jessie, love, they found you. Thank God." He was so like their father—a big softie. The tears welled up again.

"Sorry." She swiped at them. "Tears won't help anything at this stage. I'm sorry, but this is a waiting game now. We just have to wait and see how much damage has been done and then wait and see how—or if it—mends. From what I can see in the notes, no one can tell anything much at the moment."

＊

And it just got worse, so much worse, Clare regained consciousness two days later but she couldn't speak or move. Neither side. Then there was jubilation when she got some movement in her right hand. Then a little more in her toes.

They were soon totally into the hospital routine. Jessie ran in and out between clients. Clare was alive, but only just. Lex hardly left her bedside. He had more or less moved in with Jessie at Olive's house. She'd insisted one night that he stay—she really didn't think he would manage the drive home by himself. And he'd stayed. He was so gray and exhausted she thought he might topple over. Essentially, standing up for herself and moving out had ended up being a help for them all.

But they never mentioned Michael D'Larghi. It was as though Jessie's weekend with Michael had never happened.

It was so hard to believe there'd been a time when her parents had been happy and well and life was normal. Her world had shrunk to the route between the hospital, the Growcare office, home and back to the hospital again.

She'd never been on great terms with her father and now, despite living under the same roof, the gap between them just got wider and wider. How she missed having her mother to talk to. They'd always had each other and it was so easy to tell her anything.

＊

Jessie walked along the wide corridor, forty-one, forty-two, forty-three: here it was. She knocked.

"Hello, come on in, it's open."

"Olly. It's me, Jessie. Oh, Olly." Shocked, she looked at her leg, encased in a white stocking, stuck out on a stool.

Olly was watching the television. The same tightly permed hair, soft and white, with glasses perched on the end of her nose, knitting needles resting in her lap, and a brightly colored ball of red wool lay where it had fallen on the floor.

"Jessie, I do believe."

She dropped to her knees in front of Olly and wrapped her in a big hug. "What have you done to your leg?"

"It's just one of those stupid ulcers. We've got it under control. How's your mother? I'm sorry I couldn't get there when we're practically in the same building but I thought it might be better to wait."

"Don't worry, I don't really think she recognizes anyone. I've bought you some chocolates, and a photo I found in one of your drawers. Look, you and Stanley."

"Thank you." Olly fingered the photo softly and smiled down at it. "I'd wondered where that had gone. It's a bit difficult when you're not doing your own packing up. How're you getting on, love? I'm so glad you're in my house."

"The whole family seems to have moved in at the moment. Dad is staying to save driving in and out of town, and Fred stayed the other night. It's so wonderful to be able to have it, but we have to get down to business. Where or who should I pay the rent to?"

"We won't worry about all that at the moment. Until the house is sold, I'd much rather have someone in it. How about a cuppa?"

"I'd love one, but aren't you supposed to be having dinner? Everyone else is downstairs in the dining room."

"Mrs Roberts said I could stay up here for dinner whenever I liked, and I felt like it tonight. It's a lovely place and all the staff are truly wonderful, but it's a bit daunting, all those people. I'm used to having dinner by myself."

Jessie got up off her knees and went to the little bench that served as the kitchen, just a sink, two cupboards and a microwave. She put the kettle on.

"We're going to get back to the rent, Olly. If you just give me a bank account, I can put it straight in."

"I don't rightly know, love. You'll have to ask Mrs Roberts. I've been getting a little confused lately, that's one of the reasons I agreed to move in here."

Jessie brought over two cups of tea and put one down on the table beside Olly.

"It's not much fun growing old, is it, Olly?"

"Not much, Jessie, no. At least Stan was spared all this, He'd have hated it."

"He would," Jessie agreed. Stan had worked for the Cranfields for about fifty years, for Lex's father and probably his father before that. He and Olly had lived in the manager's cottage that Fred and Sonya now lived in. They'd come in the fifties, in the golden age, when wool was 'a pound for a pound.' When Five Oaks was employing gardeners and a dairyman and housemaids. And they'd stayed until they'd had to force Stan to retire and he and Olly had bought a house in town. They'd had no kids. So who *was* looking after Olly's affairs now? She would ask Joan Roberts. Jessie put the framed photo she'd found on the bureau next to another photo of Olly driving the school bus.

"I remember you driving the school bus; without you, I'd have been dead meat. It was a terrifying place. Particularly as I was such a cheeky little brat. A few years on a country school bus really toughens you up. But Fred says you used to work for Mom, cooking and stuff—you used to make the best chocolate cakes, he said. What happened, why weren't you working for us when I was growing up?"

"I started in the house with your grandmother, then I worked for your mother until, well until we had a little falling out. Then I got the job driving the school bus."

"Oh." Jessie wondered what had happened between her mother and Olly. She hadn't heard anything about that before.

"So tell me all your news, Jessie."

Jessie looked at her a bit oddly. She'd asked the same question a couple of days ago when she'd visited. Olly must be having a bit of a memory problem.

"I spent the weekend with Michael, remember, I told you I was going away before Mom got sick?"

"Oh, of course, your poor mother. So this Michael, is he a nice boy?"

Jessie laughed. "Well, I probably wouldn't call him a nice boy—he's pretty terrific, though. Do you know the D'Larghis, Olly?"

"The D'Larghis?" Olly looked suddenly stricken. "No, I don't know them."

"Michael was in Fred's year, they were friends once. I'm sure you'd have met him, if he'd come home on the bus with Fred."

"Michael D'Larghi. No, I don't remember him. I didn't drive the bus then." One of the knitting needles rolled off her lap and Jessie reached to pick it up for her.

Chapter 29

"How can we involve the council more?"

"I've been bombarding one of the councillors daily. We've got all our insurances covered and certificates, but we need their support before we can get state funding and we need state funding before we can get council support. I feel like I'm banging my head against a brick wall." Belinda got up and pasted another letter on the noticeboard at the end of the room they used as an office.

"It's been two years since they agreed to lease us the land. It's a peppercorn rent but it gives us some certainty, some standing in the community." Jessie sorted through the documents on her desk. "How do we get it out into the community more, you know, awareness ... What about an afternoon tea or barbecue at the local supermarket on a Saturday, or the pub? With flyers showing in pictures what we are trying to do?"

"That's a good idea, but we need the go-ahead first. All we want to do is to give these kids a choice. We've got Endeavour Industries, and House with No Steps, but this is different. Now they will have the opportunity to be trained in a variety of jobs, to see how far they can go."

Jessie laughed. "You sound as though you have learned that off by heart."

"I've said it so often over the last few years that I do know it off by heart. If only I could get someone to listen to me."

"And don't forget the practical side, growing Australian natives for a wholesale market—LandCare need them, everyone needs them. It is such a worthwhile project, why is it so hard?"

"In a word: bureaucracy. Jessie, you're exhausted. Take a few hours off, go and smell some roses somewhere. How's your mom doing?"

"Slowly. And I mean *slowly*. And I'm not sure if that's slowly up or slowly down. Dad's counting how many times she blinks. Yesterday it was five. He's sure she's trying to communicate. It's very frustrating." She sighed and pushed at the pile of papers in front of her. "I can't take a day off—look at all this stuff."

"I didn't say a day, I said a few hours," Belinda said. "Come back after lunch."

Jessie looked out the window to the main street. The sun was shining at last; the past few days had been overcast and windy, not that she'd seen too much of them. Sun. People were smiling out there. And walking. Living.

"Okay."

Jessie felt bad for a while but once in the car and driving out toward Five Oaks, she settled down a bit. She hadn't been to see her friends for a week. She drove right through the gates, past the house, where she noticed the lawns needed mowing, and pulled up at their paddock. They were right down the end near the dam. She got out of the car and called and whistled. Savior raised his head first, looking around and starting to walk toward her. Dolly ignored her as usual, then when Savior had got to within fifty yards she lifted her head and started trotting toward her, arriving at almost the same time. They nuzzled her, fighting for attention, pushing each other out of the way. Jessie laughed. "You fools."

What an uncomplicated love theirs was. She had no food with her, so it wasn't about greed or selfishness—then again, it might have something to do with jealousy. "I'm the favorite," they were saying, "no, I'm the favorite." They blew soft air into her face and made her laugh once more.

"Stop it. Yuck. Yes, I'm fine and thank you for asking. My mom is not so good. It's so hard pretending she's getting better. Dad won't accept it, but I don't think she's ever going to talk again. Or walk. It's just awful. Two weeks ago she was fit and strong and alive. Now she's been cut down and is just lying there. And everyone pretends that it's all right and she's getting better when she's not. No one is realistic with a sick person; they prevaricate, and they pretend, and the last thing anyone does is look at the truth."

She put her arms around Dolly's neck and buried her head in the soft brown winter coat. The tears came. She let them fall. God, she was tired.

The sound of an engine getting louder cut through the peace of the countryside. She lifted her head. Fred was approaching quite quickly in his white ute and he braked hard when he got to her.

"How's Mom?" he asked out the open window.

"Okay, the same. I'm just having a couple of hours of R and R."

"I was worried when I saw you over here, thought something might have happened."

"Sorry. I should have realized it would look bad. I just needed some time out. How are you fellas getting on?"

"She's not getting any better, is she?"

"No, I don't think so, but it's early days and we don't know whether there's another stroke in the offing or if she'll slowly make her way back. It just takes so much time." There she went, same old stuff. Couldn't she at least talk straight to Fred? "Fred, it's just awful. No one knows anything and I don't know how Dad keeps going day after day."

Fred was out of the ute in a second and hugging her. "Hey, I don't know how you keep him so strong. It's okay. We think you're doing a great job. Sonya and I appreciate what you're doing so much. Why don't you come over for lunch?"

"Thanks, Fred, that would be great. In a minute, okay?"

*

Jessie sat on the floor in front of the warm, glass-fronted wood fire in Fred and Sonya's big kitchen, a pair of wild nearly two year olds climbing all over her.

"This is just what I needed. Hey, don't pull my hair."

Sonya laughed. "Total chaos, you mean?"

"Yes." Jessie tickled one twin and then the other and was almost bowled over by their rush to get back and be tickled some more. "How do you keep it up?"

"I don't start it," Sonya replied dryly. "Come on, you two, it's time for your naps." She picked up a twin under each arm. They squealed and squirmed like a couple of piglets. "Say bye bye to Aunty Jessie."

Fred was sitting at the table reading the paper. He looked so like their father that Jessie felt a large lump well in her throat.

He put the paper down. "So where were you before it all happened?"

"I went away with Michael D'Larghi, to a place in the Dividing Range." No one had mentioned the weekend since her father's first words to her. He certainly hadn't brought it up again and Jessie had thought everyone had conveniently forgotten. Not that she'd been able to forget any of it. Not the good bits, the bad bits, or the awful, awful bits.

Fred looked puzzled. "So why didn't you tell anyone? Oh, except for obviously Belinda."

"Mom and Dad had been so negative about him. I really don't understand it. They think he's running drugs and involved with the Mafia."

Fred burst out laughing. "Don't be ridiculous."

"I wish I was. They made me so mad, that's why I moved out. It wasn't so much not telling them where I was going, it was more like we hadn't spoken since I moved out." She turned to look at him. "I heard Dad talking to you about it on the Monday morning."

Fred paused. "Oh, that conversation. I never thought too much about it. Dad goes over the top sometimes. You know, Michael would never be involved in all that. He was always honest. Why do you think he got himself in so much trouble? He was too honest for his own good." He grinned. "We were quite good friends in kindergarten."

"What happened?"

"No idea. Just went our own ways, I guess. Then his mom died. So, what's going on between you two?"

"Coffee anyone?" Sonya walked back in and fell into a chair. "Peace and quiet for forty-five minutes."

"Oh no, I've got to run. Thanks for lunch. Bye, Fred." She kissed him on the cheek. "And thanks for, you know. Bye, Sonya."

"Hey, wait a minute you haven't answered my question."

But she let the door bang shut behind her.

*

Frank lay with his head on his paws following Michael with his eyes. The dog always picked up on his moods so quickly. And his mood wasn't good at the moment.

He turned his head when he heard a knock at the door. Frank stretched and got up and went to the door, tail wagging. How did he know?

"Michael, it's Renee, are you there? Can I come in?"

He threw down his pen and got up to open the door. "Sure, come on in."

"Welcoming committee." Renee smiled at the two of them and bent down to scratch Frank behind the ears.

"I don't know how but he always knows when it's you. How are you Renee? Heard from Ron?"

"No, I haven't. I just heard about Clare Cranfield. It's terrible, Michael."

"Yeah, it's terrible." He sat back down at his desk and played with the basketball he held in his hand, twirling it around on one finger.

"Is Jessie okay?"

"No, not really. You can imagine what it would be like."

"Yes, I saw Patti down the street—she said everyone was in shock. How was the weekend?"

"Good. Did Nonna tell you I went away with Jessie? You can't keep anything to yourself 'round here, can you?"

"Not something like that. I heard her talking to Sienna."

"Geez." Michael was disgusted and dropped the ball. "It's none of her business."

Frank got up and pushed the ball back to Michael with his nose. He picked it up again.

"What's wrong, Michael?"

"Nothing." Around went the ball, balanced on his fingertip.

"Really?"

"I am just so bloody sick of it."

Renee didn't say anything, just waited.

"Jessie thinks we are part of the Mafia, or her mother thinks we are."

Renee started to laugh. "Well, she's not the first! You've been dealing with that since you were ten years old. Do remember when you came home with the bleeding nose and you wouldn't tell us what happened? It took us ages to find out who did it. I mean to say, Michael, you are of Italian descent and it comes with the territory."

"Racial prejudice! Why can't people just leave it alone? Judge people on who they are. I don't mind generally, I just didn't want Jessie to be one of them."

"Well, look at it this way, if Jessie really thought you were a member of the Mafia, she probably wouldn't have asked, would she?"

Michael smiled slightly. "I guess not."

"And parents tend to want to protect their children from making bad decisions. Give them a break."

"How do I persuade them that I'm not a bad decision?"

"Be yourself. Don't create problems where there aren't any to begin with. I would have thought Jessie could need a huge amount of support at the moment."

"Thanks." Michael looked up with one of his special smiles. "You could be right. I seriously like her. The problem is, we don't seem to be getting a clear run. If it's not her parents, it's my grandmother, or this project that's taking up so much time. Or her mother getting sick."

"Hang in there, Michael, I'd like to meet her. Give it time. Oh, and by the way, I'd watch Sienna, if I was you. She and Nonna are thick as thieves."

Chapter 30

Her little car followed the familiar road back to town. She was certifiably mad, she realized, thinking over the conversation she'd had with Fred.

Reverse the situation. How would she feel if someone had asked her if she robbed banks in her spare time?

Had she ever in her life had such a wonderful weekend?

Had she ever in her life had such wonderful sex?

Had she ever in her life met a man like him?

Jessie drove back into town wondering how she could have been so influenced by her crazy parents. She picked up two coffees at the corner café and walked determinedly back into the office. Belinda looked up and whistled.

"Well, if that don't beat all, the desired effect in just—" she consulted her watch, "—four hours. I want to know what the magic elixir is."

"You know when you realize you've been incredibly stupid, how do you turn everything around?"

"That doesn't make any sense." Belinda took her coffee, sniffing it gratefully. "What about an apology? You know, as in abject apology, down on your knees, complete with hair shirt, confessions, the lot. I'm a forgiving person." She grinned.

"Very funny. I'm not apologizing to you." Jessie grimaced. "The lot, you're sure? How about, 'Can I cook you dinner?'"

"Who are we talking about here?"

Jessie didn't answer, just took a sip of her coffee.

"Ah, let me guess? Michael, huh? How good a cook are you?"

"Medium."

"How about, 'Can I buy you dinner?'"

"No."

"Then it depends on what you are offering for dessert." Belinda grinned again. It wasn't hard to grasp her meaning.

"I've been such a fool."

"I'm so sorry about interrupting your weekend last Sunday but your father was devastated. It was rotten luck."

"That had nothing to do with it. I'd managed to ruin everything all by myself before that."

"So what's it going to be, dinner or dessert?"

"Ha ha, I think I might need handcuffs and a rope or two."

"Now there's a thought." Belinda blinked appreciatively. "But we'd better put it aside until after five o'clock—there are about twenty-five people I need you to ring." Belinda handed her a sheet of paper, with the numbers scribbled on it. "Start at the top."

*

Michael closed the door behind Renee feeling unsettled. He hadn't experienced this before. Exorcising Jessie should be a breeze. He'd never had a problem getting over a woman. There was that girl in the States he'd fallen madly in love with, but she'd rejected him, and after the initial shock—he didn't think it had ever happened before—he'd fallen out of love with her, quick time. Mostly he'd been the one to move on. So why couldn't he do it this time? He was so worried about her, with her mother in intensive care. It must be a terrible time for the family. If only he could do something to help. Probably the best thing was to keep the hell out of her way. He walked over to the sheds and chained Fred up to a post inside.

"Not this time, fella." He bent over to give him a pat.

He rolled out his old Ducati and went hell for leather out of town, on the road to Bobundara, desperate for some thinking time. The afternoon was overcast but there wasn't much chance of rain. It seldom rained in the country around Cooma. It only snowed a couple of times a year and it didn't even stay on the ground most of the time—extraordinary when the snow fields were only a hop, skip and a jump away.

His project was coming on well. He wasn't sure Jessie's and Belinda's efforts were getting anywhere, though. Was there something he could do, he thought, as long as Jessie didn't get to hear of it? He smiled. He'd be accused of interfering in her life again. *Jessie, if it's a friend you want, a friend you'll have.*

He couldn't help it. He hunched over the bike's body, gripping with his knees and cornering smoothly. He loved this road for its corners. And the fact it was mostly uninhabited by traffic. He loved hearing the satisfying hum of the engine. Mile after mile of smooth dirt, with the fence posts flashing past, the silvery pastures a blur. He had slowed down, pulling over to have a drink from the water bottle he always carried, when he heard his phone.

He was not all that surprised to see Sienna's number. "Hi Sienna, yes, you're coming through in an hour ... Yes, I'll meet you in town. Thanks."

He looked at the phone as he put it back in his pocket. Sienna was ringing quite frequently as she'd become the liason for the Fellinis. They were still an important piece of his project, the fish and seafood section. She had good ideas and a fresh approach. Now she wanted to meet up for a coffee.

He shrugged, there was just time for him to get back. And he'd find out soon enough what this was all about.

*

"Good luck, Jessie." Belinda looked up as Jessie opened the office door.

"Thanks, I'll need it." Jessie looked up and down the street as she closed the door behind her. The dark had settled around the town already even though it was only five thirty. *Bring on the shortest day*, Jessie thought. *We're ready.* It was wonderful to think that the days would be getting longer again soon. A positive attitude was what was needed. She felt more focused than she had in a while—ten days, to be precise.

Now where would she find Michael?

The car yard would be a good place to start. She set off with a confident stride until she noticed a tall man across the street. He was wearing leathers—tight pants with a leather jacket—and a helmet dangling from one hand. How could she mistake that body? There was a woman dangling from his other arm, a woman with long brown hair. She'd seen that hair before. Sienna.

Well, that hadn't taken long.

Chapter 31

"So Sienna, how's things?" Michael and Sienna sat down in the back of the café at a table for two.

"Good, Michael, and you?" Sienna said calmly. He could depend on Sienna to be controlled and calm, there was little worry she'd make a fuss or throw a hissy fit in public. After Jessie, maybe she was a little too measured. He loved Jessie's way of bubbling up, her passion. There wasn't too much control about Jessie. He really should stop this comparing.

"All good. Are you on the way home? What do you want to drink?"

"An iced water, thanks," she said. "Yes, I've been in Fyshwyck for a few days. I've been sorting out the opposition to the fish side of things up there. How many venues there are already in competition, how much and when is interesting. I've been thinking people buy their fish on Friday but if we concentrate on Thursday to hit them with the specials and bring the most fish up then? We make them think fish on Thursday."

"Good thinking."

"When do you think we'll be ready to go?"

"Next week they're supposed to be starting on the building. So I would say six months, tops, you should work

215

on being in." Two iced waters were brought to the table. "The contractors have promised they can get the building up in four months."

"How're things with Jessie?" She fiddled with the cap of the bottle.

"Jessie's mother had a stroke two weeks ago. She's in intensive care. Jessie's very worried about her." He sat up straight. "Which you know already, as you've been talking to Nonna."

"Uh, yes, Nonna told my grandmother—you know how these things get about."

He was certain that things got around between those two with the speed of light. Over Sienna's shoulder, he saw Jessie walk in. The café was reasonably full of after-work regulars but it wasn't crowded. Jessie lifted her head and looked him straight in the eye. Ah yes, he couldn't help a little smile. He had a feeling seeing him was no surprise to her. He stood and waved her over.

"Jessie, come and join us. You remember Sienna, don't you?"

Jessie approached with a challenge in her eyes that he remembered well. Good. It was better than the lost, defeated look she'd had when he'd left her at the hospital. He pulled up a chair. "What would you like?"

"A coffee, please. What brings you to Cooma, Sienna?"

"Just passing through, on my way home to Eden. Michael suggested catching up."

He'd have to let that pass, he'd look stupid repudiating that untruth, but he couldn't resist a glance at Jessie. Her wide-eyed look of surprise had him wondering but not for long.

"He suggested we meet here when I finished, too! We often have a coffee after work—my office is just over the road from here. What a lovely surprise, he didn't tell me you were coming."

Michael was stumped. He thought he might go and leave them to it. On the other hand, it might be more interesting to stay. Sienna was older and more sophisticated, but he'd put his money on the fighting spirit in Jessie at the moment. That look on her face was a classic.

Sienna turned to him. "I'll be seeing you in Fyshwyck then, in a couple of weeks? Will you be staying over?"

"Probably not." Not if his interpretation of the frown that had appeared on Jessie's face was correct. "With a bit of luck, I might not be necessary to the building operation. It's good you're doing this research now."

"I want to have everything ready for you."

"Thanks, I appreciate it. I've got on to the abattoir in Sefton and they are going to package meats under our Take Five label. A fair bit of cryovac meat. I've organized a buyer who will buy exactly what I want."

"That's all sounding good." said Sienna. "If there's anything you want me to do, give me a ring. Well, I suppose I'd better be off. Nice to see you again, Jessie. Bye, Michael."

They accompanied Sienna back to her car and waved her off, Jessie sticking like glue to Michael's side.

Michael couldn't help it, he started to laugh. "Miaow."

"I'm sorry. That is, I'm not sorry. I saw you two walk in and I just wanted to know—" She broke off.

"Wanted to know what?"

"Whether I'd ruined things completely. I didn't want you thinking I didn't care about you. That I don't believe in you," she said quietly. They stood side by side, watching the traffic streaming past. "I am really sorry for that lack of trust. You didn't deserve that, Michael, you must believe me. I was coming to find you when I saw Sienna and you walking along. That wasn't true was it, that you told her you wanted to catch up with her?"

"No."

"I didn't think so." She breathed out again.

"I think it's time you came to meet my family." Michael smiled down at her and took her hand.

"Who's in your family, apart from your grandmother and your father?" Suddenly Jessie felt inexplicably shy.

"There's Ron and Renee Fraser, they've been living with us—well, ever since Mom died. Renee has been my surrogate mom and Ron introduced me to the passion we have shared always—trucks."

"And your father?"

"He's away at the moment. Suppose I can arrange something for Friday night, can you come over?"

"Sure, I'd love to." She was smiling up at him and he couldn't help it, he couldn't stop the smile on his face, either.

*

Jessie opened the front door of Olly's house. There was a light on in the kitchen.

"Dad. Oh, you're back already." Her father sat, hunched, on a stool at the kitchen counter. He'd shrunk in the last couple of weeks.

"What's wrong? How's Mom?"

"Just the same, maybe a little better, Oh, I don't know, it's so hard to tell." He banged the bench in front of him suddenly, giving Jessie a fright. "What if she never gets better?"

"Every day she stays alive cells are repaired in her brain, you've got to believe that. I've seen absolute miracles happen. You have to just wait it out." Jessie put out her hand tentatively and touched her father's arm. He didn't respond and she turned away. "Brrr, it's cold in here. You're sitting in the cold. Let's turn on the heater. Have you eaten?"

"No, I'm not hungry. Have you heard from Fred today?"

"Yes, I went out there, had lunch with Fred and Sonya and the babies. You should get out there, Dad, it would do you some good to get away. Mom will be fine for a couple of hours."

"I just can't, Jessie, what if—"

"No, Dad, sitting and waiting is very debilitating. Honestly, it would do you both good."

"I just want her to get better."

"I know, Dad, I know." And this time she did put her arms around him and gave him a hug.

*

They'd turned the television on and her dad had eaten the regulation three chops, potatoes and peas that Jessie had cooked. She'd perservered, despite being told he was not hungry. Her father now even had a beer in his hand.

"So what's news on your work front?"

"It's terribly frustrating," said Jessie. "Everything hinges on this approval we need from the department. Belinda is lobbying like mad in Canberra, hoping we can get the federal pollies to make a commitment, but so far, no good." Jessie tried not to sound too eager or astonished. She wasn't used to her dad asking her questions.

"Have you thought about getting the service charities involved, Lions and Rotary? They pull quite a bit of weight, state wise."

"I'm sure we've tried but I'll ask Belinda." She got up to take away the plates. "Michael's asked me to meet his family on Friday night."

Her father put his beer down. "I don't think that's a good idea, I don't want you to go."

"Why ever not?" Jessie stood with the plates in her arms.

"I don't like the D'Larghis, never have. I can't believe you could think of doing this, Jessie. I'm the one who needs you right now. And your mother needs you."

Jessie swallowed her reply. She'd work it out. There was no need to make things worse for her father tonight. It was the first time they'd started talking properly and she didn't want to ruin that. But there must be a way around it. Maybe Fred could come in for a couple of hours.

"Promise me, Jessie, just for a week or two, don't leave me, *us*. Please."

"Hey, of course I won't. I'm here for you, Dad. You know that."

Chapter 32

"Fred, can I drive Dad out for lunch today? We can bring some pies, if you like. I think he needs to get away from the hospital." Jessie, the phone tucked under her chin, managed to pour two cups of tea.

"Great idea. We're at the sheep yards this morning. You can meet us there. Oh and pies sound great."

"There you are." Jessie turned to her father, handing him the Vegemite with a smile. "That's what you need. A few hours away. Mom will relax without you hovering and they will look after her beautifully. Belinda's in Canberra and I reckon I've got a couple of hours owing to me." Jessie grinned.

"I don't know, suppose—"

"Suppose nothing, let's go."

Her father got quieter and quieter on the trip out.

"Pull up here, Jessie. I think I'll go in and have a look at the mail and sort a few things out. I'll get the ute and come over when lunch is ready." He was out of the car and stomping up to the house before she could argue. At least she'd got him this far.

Jessie carried on to the Five Oaks sheep yards. The sun was out but there was a chilly wind blowing across the paddocks.

The yards were protected from the worst of the wind by a row of huddled pines. Fred was standing at the drafting gates, Sonya was pushing the sheep up to him and the twins were sitting in their stroller, calmly watching the proceedings.

"What are these beautiful babies doing out here?" Jessie said, getting out of the car, shivering. "They'll freeze to death.'"

Sonya turned around. "They're rugged up, and quite happy, as long as they have their snacks. You can offer them a little drink from their bottles, if you like. Where's Lex?" She turned back, at Fred's grunt of exasperation, to push the sheep along. "Okay! I'm concentrating."

"Jessie, come and help. Two of you might get them through quicker," Fred shouted at her.

Jessie looked blankly at the sheep milling around in the yards. How long had it been since she'd been in the yards with the sheep? She laughed. "I've got no idea what I'm doing, but sure," she said and hopped over the fence.

"Do you do this a lot?" she asked Sonya, as they let the next mob into the drafting yards. "I mean, with the kids and all." The sheep huddled down at the opposite end of the yard. They walked around the back to push them up.

Sonya laughed. "I love it, and the kids love it, and it means I get out of the house and do things with Fred. So if it's possible, yes, I do it."

"I've never done it. There was always Stan or Fred, or one of the jackeroos. Or all of them."

"Well, there are certainly no jackeroos now, Stan's long gone, and Fred needs me." She chased a sheep that dived out of the mob. "No, you don't."

"Mom never did it, either. I can't remember her ever getting into the yards with an animal in them. Hey, Fred, can you remember our mother ever in the yards?"

"No, I can't. It was Gran who was the tartar—she was adamant about no women in the yards. You didn't know her, did you? She died before you were born." He was frowning, concentrating on separating the sheep coming through into three mobs. Then the sheep stopped and he waited as they pushed the sheep up to him again.

"Where did all these sheep come from?" Jessie asked, looking around. "There must be hundreds of them here."

Sonya laughed at her. "Nine hundred and eighty-four to be exact."

"I thought we owned cattle? Apart from a few killers, Dad never had many sheep on the place."

"We used to have sheep many years ago. I don't think Dad liked them all that much."

"Getting back into sheep is Fred's doing." Sonya rushed past her, clapping her hands. "He loves the wretched things, says they do so well on the Monaro it was a pity we didn't have more. He wore your father down. You know: drip, drip, drip. Hey," she shouted and waved her arms. "Up you go."

"Well, I think things are about to change around here. With Dad gone AWOL, I'm going to need some help." Fred grinned. "A female workforce, now, that might get Dad so angry he'll get going again. He never wanted one—but I don't have a problem with it. Not at all."

"So what are you drafting the sheep for?" Jessie clapped her hands. "Shoo."

"If you look closely, you will see there are blue dots and red dots. Blue are the twin lambers, red dots are singles, and no dots will be very late or not lamb at all. They were ultra-sounded three weeks ago and we dotted them then."

Jessie watched Fred as he talked and at the same time, dexterously drafting the sheep three ways. She was quite impressed with her brother.

"Ultrasound sheep?"

"Welcome to the new age, baby sister."

Jessie looked around at the dwindling mob on their end of the race. "We've nearly finished. How about I take these babies back to the house and put the pies in the oven and ring Dad? I'll take your car with the car seats, shall I?"

But by the time Jessie had struggled getting the two babies out of their stroller and into their car seats and buckled them in, Fred and Sonya had finished anyway. As she waved to the other two, she saw they were fighting over who got to drive her car but she thought she saw Sonya slide into the driver's seat first. She grinned. Fred and Sonya had a good time together. She was a great girl. They had married just before she'd gone over to England so Jessie hadn't had much to do with Sonya. Fred was lucky, she was a lot of fun. Those nine years between Fred and Jessie had meant they'd never been close. He'd been part of the Bachelor and Spinster balls generation, she'd been more picnic races and—what? Uni parties, she supposed.

Her parents had lived in a different time again. Workmen all over the place; women weren't encouraged to pitch in, not on the bigger properties around here. It was more a case of tennis parties or go and get a job in town. Her mother hadn't gone to tennis parties or got a job in town. Niether had Clare and Lex had the kind of fun Fred and Sonya had together, not that Jessie had observed.

*

They were driving back into town when Jessie checked the time. They'd only been a couple of hours—she wouldn't be too late.

"How did you enjoy your bonding session with your grandchildren?"

"They are a pair of holy terrors."

Jessie laughed. "There's lots of Cranfield fighting spirit in there."

Her father just humphed and looked out the window. Then he said slowly, "Sonya thought they might come into town Friday and we might all have dinner together. What do you think?"

Not Friday night, no. "What will she do about the twins?"

"She said they could get a sitter. It's been a while—I don't know if I could do it … without your mother." Jessie knew they should do it. Her father needed to know they would continue to be a strong unit, no matter what happened. He was right. He needed them both, no—*all of them*—right now. She had to go.

*

Michael walked into the kitchen, where his grandmother was washing up methodically. He took a tea towel and attacked the pile of plates. They had a perfectly good dishwasher and he didn't know why his grandmother refused to use it.

"Jessie has had to cancel dinner on Friday night."

"Oh. That is too bad, is her mother worse?"

"No, she says her father needs her at the moment. I can understand that."

"I can understand that, too. She must be a good girl. She can come another time. Are you going up to Fyshwick tomorrow?"

"Yes, I'll be away for the night." And he'd pretend he wasn't as hurt as he felt. "Nonna, did you like my mother?"

"Of course I did! That is a terrible question, Michael. Why would you ask me that? She was very beautiful."

"I know she was beautiful, I remember that she was very beautiful—do you know she used to talk to me in Italian when no one was around. But why does no one talk about her?"

"You father, he gets very upset."

"Yes, I understand that, but you don't talk about her either. Or her family. I know all your family backward."

"I didn't know her family. She came from the north. Your grandfather had a friend on the Snowy Scheme, Russo—he was killed in an accident. It was very sad. Gabriella was his daughter. Gino brought her out here after her father died and she and Sal got married." She shrugged. "She had no family."

"Was she happy, Nonna?"

"It was hard for her to settle in. I'm not sure she really wanted to come to Australia. She was a good mother. She loved you very much. She pined for the old country. Maybe too much."

He wanted to ask where his mother had been going that day but he didn't. Maybe he didn't want to know the answer.

Chapter 33

Jessie called Michael the moment she was alone after her family dinner. She'd been phoning him quite a lot. It was filling up her days quite nicely. Not to mention the nights. He always answered, too.

"Hi Jessie."

"You're in the truck."

"How did you know?"

"You sound different. Why are you in the truck when it's a Friday night?"

"I'm taking it to Fyshwick for a service. It'll be there first thing in the morning. How did dinner go?"

"Terrible. The dynamics without Mom are disastrous. Dad was miserable—there was a moment I thought Fred and Dad were going to kill each other."

"What was the problem?"

"Chemical shearing. Don't ask me to tell you what that is either. But then Dad went back into his shell again."

"It's bound to be hard for everyone."

"You're telling me. Mom was the bubbly core of this family and I had no idea how much she kept the peace all the time. I'm not particularly good at it—that much I do know."

"You'll all work things out, and soon your mom will be back."

"Thank you," she said softly. "I need to hear that sometimes."

"Good night, Jessie. Take care."

"You're staying the night? I hope Sienna's not in town."

Michael laughed. "No, she's not. And I wouldn't notice her if she was."

*

On Saturday night, Jessie came home to find a box of fruit on the verandah. She picked up her phone.

"Thank you for the fruit."

"My pleasure, how did you get on today?"

"I took Dad out to Five Oaks again. The hospital staff were so grateful the other day, I knew it was the right thing to do."

"So did your father enjoy it?"

"You know what he did? He mowed the lawns. I helped Fred and Sonya in the yards. Fred despairs of getting Dad back working. At least I got him out of the hospital for a couple of hours."

"He probably wanted time to be by himself."

"Yeah, you're probably right. Goodnight."

*

Sunday night they talked for hours while Michael drove to Sydney.

"I wish you were here and I could see you for an hour or so. All the fun has gone out of coming to Sydney."

"You flatterer. You know you have a great time down in those markets."

"Everyone asks me where you are."

"Yeah, right."

"Honestly. They've got a book going."

Jessie laughed. "Seriously?"

"Yep, You're coming to the ball with me in November, apparently. Odds are two to one."

"Don't let Sienna hear of it."

"Oh, ye of little faith."

*

By Tuesday night, Michael was home.

"Did you see the frost this morning? It was a beauty."

"No, but I heard about it from Fred. There was no water out on the farm, the pipes were frozen, the sliding door on the shed wouldn't open and Fred had to get boiling water to defrost the windscreens. And to top it off, the battery on the old tractor gave up the ghost."

Michael laughed at her. 'Negative, negative, negative. You have to change the way you look at things."

"A century and a half of programming? You've got to be kidding."

*

When her phone rang on Thursday and she saw it was Michael, she nearly knocked it onto the floor but luckily caught it before it hit. So she sounded breathless when she answered.

"Hello?"

And this time when he asked her to come for dinner on Friday, a posse of wild horses were not going to stop her from saying yes.

*

The D'Larghis' property was quite different country to Five Oaks. The brick homestead was surrounded by river flats with rich alluvial soil, the paddocks were ploughed in straight furrows. Some fields grew rows of cabbages, some were being fallowed. Irrigation equipment was set up over the paddocks, lying idle. Everything looked neat and tidy, with big Colorbond sheds housing tractors. There were so many, from the quick look Jessie got as they drove up the drive, after first crossing the Murrumbidgee over a small wooden bridge.

Once a Federation brick cottage, the homestead had obviously been built on to a few times over the years. Inside, there was a lot of wood paneling and the bare brick walls that had been popular thirty years ago. There were heavy red curtains, a bit fussy, with loads of ornaments on the bookshelves and lots of leather furniture. The table was loaded with heavy silver candlesticks and too much food. Crusty breads and colorful salads and dishes piled high with vegetables and different meats and cheeses and olives.

Jessie could hardly believe she was here. Her father had been difficult in the last twenty-four hours, begging: "Please, Jessie, don't go." And when that didn't work, she'd got the cold treatment, but not before the warning: "Don't turn your phone off. If your mother takes a turn for the worse ..."

"If that happens, Dad, I'll only be three-quarters of an hour away" she'd replied patiently.

And what had she gotten herself into? From her first step into the D'Larghi home, Jessie knew she was on trial. Michael's grandmother, Maria, was watching her carefully, and though Renee Fraser was being really friendly and sweet she was carefully watching her, too. Renee said she knew Clare from the days of the PTA when Michael and Fred had been at primary school together. From what Michael had told her, Renee had been his surrogate mother. One thing Jessie was sure of, the two women in Michael's life were guarding him carefully. Who guarded the emperor in the old days? If she remembered correctly, it was the Praetorian Guard, so she'd better watch her step. Her only ally was Frank, Michael's dog, who'd come up to her wagging his tail, totally delighted to see her again.

"Thank you. This looks wonderful." She took the plate handed to her by Michael's grandmother. Ron hadn't made it back in time so it was just the four of them. To eat all this food.

"How's your father doing?" Renee passed her a tomato and eggplant dish. Jessie thought it was called ratatouille, but she wasn't sure.

"He's, well, he's not doing so brilliantly." Jessie helped herself and passed the dish on to Michael. "He spends most of his time sitting with Mom and driving the hospital staff insane."

On the wall above the mantelpiece was a portrait of a young woman. Golden hair and big brown eyes, her face quite solemn.

"Is that your mother?" she asked Michael. She couldn't help feeling he was even being guarded from above. She passed the bread along.

"Yes. Gabriella."

"She was so beautiful. And look at those photos." She caught sight of a series of about twenty pictures, all simply framed, on the other wall.

"They are old photos of the camps and the times of the Snowy Scheme," said Michael. "Our first truck. There's my grandfather. There's my grandmother, the day she arrived from the old country, laden with food. That's all she'd heard about for the last two years, how hungry my grandfather was—she thought she was coming to a desert."

"They are wonderful, a great way of remembering the past. I must go through our old photos, there are so many, while—oh." She'd almost said "while my parents are still alive." That was stupid.

"And how's Fred?" Renee filled in the gap. "He was in Michael's year. He was a lovely boy."

Jessie laughed. "The twins are keeping him and Sonya very busy."

Michael was quiet.

"So you are working hard on this project, Michael tells us." Thank goodness for Renee.

"Yes, we haven't got quite as far as he has but I hope we get going soon." She looked helplessly at Michael. "Where's Ron tonight?"

"Ron and the truck have been held up at the ports. There's a strike and he can't get unloaded."

"Oh that's a shame."

"He's not happy, that much I can tell you."

There was the sound of the front door opening. Everyone looked at each other, a little startled.

"Who's that?" Renee asked Maria.

"It must be Sal. Sal, you didn't tell us you were back," Maria called and stood up.

A man in an overcoat walked into the room and went over to the fire, rubbing his hands. He turned to face them. "Hello, Mama, Renee, Michael." Then he saw Jessie sitting next to Michael.

"Clare," he whispered. His eyes were shocked, as though he couldn't believe what he was seeing.

"No, Dad, This is Jessie Cranfield. Welcome home."

Sal D'Larghi reluctantly dragged his eyes off Jessie to look at his son. "What is she doing here?"

Michael looked disconcerted, as though he couldn't believe what his father was saying. "Jessie's come for dinner."

"Get her out of here. Now!" He stormed out of the room.

Jessie stood up and Michael joined her and put his arm round her. "No, stay. I don't know what's the matter with him but you will not go anywhere."

"Michael, I can't."

"Yes, you can."

She looked to Maria, who seemed to be in shock, and then to Renee, who looked horrified.

"He's just got home from an overseas trip. He must be exhausted, not know what he's saying," Renee said, trying to excuse him.

"Oh, mio dio, é impazziti. Please excuse my son, Jessie. I think Renee's right. He must be ill." Maria looked so upset. "Michael, you go and talk to him."

Jessie wasn't sure what to say or do. Renee sat down and Jessie followed suit.

Michael came back with a set face and went over to Jessie. "Come." He turned to his grandmother, who was still standing. "Nonna, we'll go."

"What did he say?"

"Nothing."

"I'm so sorry, Jessie. It doesn't make any sense." Renee gave her a quick hug. "Don't worry, we'll sort it out. It must be something that happened on the trip."

Michael put his arm round her and led her to his car, Frank following them. He opened the door and put her in and held the seatbelt out for her to put on. "You go home, Frank, good fella." He got in and looked straight ahead.

"Jesus, Jessie. I have no idea what that was all about."

"Well, whatever it is, it's on both sides. My parents, both of them, have been incomprehensible. I thought they were just out of date. That it was all a throwback to a hundred years ago." She turned to face him in the car, the glow from the dashboard lighting up her face. "Is it me?"

"Or me." Michael started to laugh. "I'm sorry, it's no laughing matter. We're going to have to get to the bottom of it." He put the key in and started the car. "I can tell you now, it won't make a scrap of difference to the way I feel about you."

"Or me you." Jessie bit her lip. She still couldn't believe it.

Chapter 34

Jessie stuck her head into the hospital room. Her mother was out of intensive care now, but she still had a room to herself. Privileges of a country hospital—when it was possible, you got a room to yourself. The room was empty of visitors and nursing staff but full of soft beeps. The sun was streaming in and the flowers she'd bought were a cheerful mix of yellows, reds and pinks. Her mother lay motionless in the bed, just her eyes letting them all know she was alive. And the rise and fall of her chest. Jessie smoothed the blanket over her, then she picked up Clare's lifeless hand. It had never been so still. Her mother was always using her hands, they would shape and flutter and exclaim. They were beautiful hands, so soft.

"I went to dinner with the D'Larghis. Michael's family. Oh, Mom, please talk to me, *please*. It was so horrible. What do the D'Larghis have against us? You need to get better so you can tell me. Did you have a fight? Was it some deal that Dad and Sal got involved in?" But all the answer she got was the soft beeping from the machines, and the noise of a squeaking trolley being wheeled up the corridor outside the room.

"Why did Michael's father call me Clare? Mom, you've got to tell me what's going on," she whispered and put her mother's hand to her cheek. "Wake up, please."

She looked up as her father entered. He had a shopping bag full of newspapers and a magazine or two. And a bottle of soft drink and a packet of chips.

"Hello, Jessie." He sank into the low chair on the other side of the bed and methodically put the papers and contents of the bag on the hospital table. It was as though something essential had been wrung out of him.

"Dad, you look awful."

"Ah well, I suppose I could say the same about you. What's happened to you?"

They hadn't spoken since Jessie's return on the Friday night.

"Dad, I—could you tell me what happened between you and the D'Larghis? I just don't understand it. It's all very strange. I met Mr D'Larghi the other night, when I was at dinner, and he basically told me to get out of the house."

"He what? That fucking bastard."

"You see, there *is* something, isn't there? Please tell me."

"No. And that's an end to it, Jessie. What happened is finished and it would do no one any good to drag everything up again. No good at all. Just stay the hell away from them."

Jessie could tell that she was the one who had to leave the room. There didn't appear to be a way forward at this end. Maybe Michael was doing better.

*

"Nonna and Renee are just as bamboozled as I am," Michael said on the phone from Canberra. "Dad just says it's none of my business."

"That's exactly what I'm getting. Well, I have an idea. Olly had some falling out—as she put it—with Mom, when Fred was about five, I think. She might know something."

"Do you want to wait till I get back? I should be finished here by tomorrow night—no, I'm taking the truck to Sydney. I won't be back till Monday morning."

"I wish you were here."

"So do I, Jessie, so do I. Take care of yourself."

It was so simple. She'd ask Olly. Olly would tell her if she knew anything. It must have been a fight between Michael's father and her father, or did it go back even further? Their grandfathers probably knew each other, too. Hell. Michael's nonna didn't know of any disagreement. It had to be an argument over land, or a deal gone wrong. Things couldn't stay as they were, that's for sure.

1983

It wasn't to have happened again. It was the last thing she wanted but he'd had too many drinks and he was being too obvious. Everyone had too many drinks at the picnic races. Her husband had quite a few as well, but even he'd start catching on if she didn't get the idiot out of there. So she took him to his car. Her heels were sinking into the rough grass; why had she worn such high heels? Then she'd stood looking around wondering what to do. The last race was over. Most people had retreated to their tents and settled down in small groups, a drink in their hands, on their fold-up chairs. Ties loosened and hats askew and maybe more than a few sunburned shoulders. The last of the sandwiches were being handed around. It had been quite hot today.

Where was his wife? She should be doing this, not her. It was getting hotter in the late afternoon, not cooler. She fanned herself with the printed race program. Horse owners were leading their horses out, putting them on trucks and trailers to take them home.

He couldn't drive, that was for certain. Wait, there was Olly, working over in the food tent for the members—she'd do it.

Chapter 35

Jessie walked along the corridor to number forty-three. She knocked, but there was no answer. She pushed the door—it wasn't locked, and she stuck her head inside.

"Olly?" No answer. The room was empty.

Jessie went back down the stairs to the large sitting room. Olly was there with a group of women playing cards. She looked so involved and happy. Oh damn, Jessie couldn't ask what she needed to know unless Olly was alone.

She went back to Olly's room after seven o'clock. Surely she'd be back in her room by now. Knocking gently, she pushed on the door. It wasn't locked this time either.

"Olly?"

Olly was asleep in her chair with her leg in its white stocking raised on a stool in front of her. Jessie tiptoed in, not sure whether to wake her up or not.

"Olly, are you awake?"

"Oh, who is it? Jessie. You gave me a fright! What time is it?" Her voice was all quivery.

"Just after seven. Do you want to go to bed? I can help you if you like."

"No, it's pretty early, isn't it? Seven, good lord, if I go to bed now, I'll be waking up at midnight. Let's have a cuppa. How's the project going?"

"Slowly, slowly. How does anyone get anything done in this country, that's what I want to know? It's not a question of let's get something going, it's more, 'You can't do that. What are you thinking?' And 'It's not our fault you can't do it,' oh no, it's 'Somebody else says you can't do it.'" Jessie put the milk in the cups. "Here you are. I dropped by this afternoon and you were downstairs playing cards."

"Was I? Oh, yes, I remember now. We don't play for money, apparently. If we had, I would have won something."

"I'm not surprised, an old pro like you, you were always playing cards."

"I suppose I did at that. Stan and I played anything going—five hundred, solo, poker—anything but bridge really."

"Why didn't you play bridge?"

"Stan hated it for some reason. How's your mother?"

"No change, really. Olly, I need to ask you something."

"What is it, dear? You know I'll help you if I can."

"I told you about Michael."

"Michael who, dear?"

"Michael D'Larghi. I mentioned him the other day. His father Sal—they're big in transport and vegetables." Jessie trailed off as she realized Olly didn't seem to be listening—she was far more interested in the television.

"Sorry, I'm trying to find out what happened between my family and the D'Larghis. I feel something did, but no one will say anything, not Dad or Sal D'Larghi and they're the only ones who seem to know. Except maybe Mom, and she can't say anything."

"I'm sure I don't know any Michael."

"Yes, you do, he used to come and play when Fred was in kindergarten and you were working for us then." Jessie was

241

starting to get frustrated. This was so hard. "Fred told me that much."

"Let it go, Jessie, please don't ask me. I made a promise to your father a long time ago."

"You promised Dad what?"

"That I wouldn't say anything. And I haven't and I won't. Not after all this time."

"Did it have anything to do with Gabriella? She died in a car accident. Michael says his father doesn't talk about his mother, never has." No response. She was making such a mess of this.

There was a knock on the door, followed by a smiling curly-headed woman sticking her head around the door.

"Olly, you ready for bed yet? Oh, you've got a visitor. Sorry."

"No, Susan, I am ready for bed, thank you, Jessie was just going." Olly had definitely perked up.

Susan bustled in. "Oh, good, I wanted to have a look at that leg. Hello, Jessie."

Jessie farewelled Olly, leaving her with Susan, and walked out to her car, parked in the dark hospital car park. If her father and Sal weren't making such a big deal of this, she could deal with not knowing. But add to that her mother's behavior before she'd had the stroke … Lies and untruths and sidestepping were just making it all worse. Why hadn't they just got over it? She rang Michael.

"Michael, hi. I feel like I'm in some weird remake of *Romeo and Juliet*. If I remember correctly, she took a fake poison and he killed himself. How about we don't do that? Promise?"

She got into the car and plugged in her phone. "I'm going home now. See you in a minute."

*

Michael was waiting for her on the steps of Olly's house. She got out of the car and flew into his strong arms. Why did this feel so good? It was so safe. So right. She clutched him tightly.

"Michael," she breathed his name, taking in his scent—the wool, the leather jacket and jeans. The solid reality of him was so much better than the anticipation. "Come inside." She pulled him to the door.

"Jessie, I won't come in."

Jessie stopped trying to find the key. "Why not?"

"I just wanted to make sure you were home safe. I've got stuff to do." He kissed the top of her head.

"We are not going to let them beat us," she said fiercely and then her expression changed to hopeful. "Well, how about just for a minute?"

"No, we are not." Michael laughed at her. "I think tonight, let's not make a fuss."

"Upset my father, you mean." She looked up at him. "He can go to hell."

"So Olly didn't know anything?"

"Only that she promised my father she would never tell anyone. What on earth could it be?" She stared at Michael. A growing horror began to take shape. "No, surely not. They wouldn't. It's impossible, isn't it? An affair—my father had an affair with your mother and Olly found out and he told Olly never to tell anyone. Oh God, Michael, surely that couldn't be right. And then your mother ... Sweet Jesus." The ramifications were banging around in her chest. No, it couldn't be true.

She looked down at her bag. Her phone was ringing. She fished it out just as it stopped. "It's Dad. I don't know if I can talk to him."

"Jessie, that's all supposition. There's no hard fact in there. Don't jump to conclusions."

Jessie just looked at him, sighed and pressed reply. "Dad, hello ... What? Okay." She closed her eyes as she ended the call. "Mom's just had another stroke."

"Oh, no." His arms were wrapped round her again and she didn't want them removed. She was in a safety net that was just about to drop her back into the cold, dark ocean.

"I was going to go and see her this afternoon and I didn't," she whispered. "I feel bad about this—a second stroke is not good,"

"Come on, I'll take you to the hospital."

*

Michael didn't come in. They ran into Fred and Sonya as they went up the hospital steps and Michael passed Jessie over into Fred's care, kissing her lightly and telling her to ring him. Then he was gone. The three of them rushed into the hospital together. When they got to their mother's room, they stopped.

"You first." Fred had his hand on the door.

"No, you," Jessie whispered. "I'm so scared."

"Come on, you two." Sonya shook her head and pulled them in with her.

Lex was sitting beside the bed holding Clare's hand. He looked up when he heard them but he couldn't see them—his eyes were filled with tears running unrestrained down his face. "I told her I loved her but I'm not sure she heard me." He blew his nose fiercely on a large white handkerchief. "Your mother passed around ten minutes ago."

He sat on the chair looking at the figure in the bed. "It was a massive stroke this time, there was nothing anyone could do ... I just wish I knew she heard me. I loved her so much."

Chapter 36

It rained for three days.

"If you needed any proof that Mom is having a say up there, this is it," Jessie said to Fred. "She knows there's nothing Dad would like more than to have three days of this soft rain."

"He's a mess, isn't he?" Fred sat on the sofa in the family room. Jessie sat on a stool at the counter, elbow deep in notes and letters from friends of her mother's.

"Awful," Jessie agreed. "So am I. It's as though our lives are in suspension. The earth has stopped spinning. The only normal thing in our lives is the twins. And sympathy cards have to be the worst piece of communication humans have devised over the last two thousand years. They are truly frightful." She started to laugh. "Can you imagine what Mom would be saying if she was here reading this nonsense?" She grimaced. "On the other hand, I've never had to write one. So maybe I'd better shut up."

"Do we have to reply to them all?"

"I suppose so, Dad will know. He's up to strength in all this protocol business. Lucky for us. Where are all the photo albums?"

"In that sideboard, I think. Why?"

"I want to put together a picture memory, you know, of Mom, play it at the funeral. We have some great photos but I don't know where they are."

"Have you seen Dad this morning?"

"No, not since breakfast. Yes, here they are. Thanks, Fred."

"I'll love you and leave you with all this high-tech stuff."

"I'd love photos of Mom's stage performances over the years. I guess the theater would have some." She was flicking through the pages. "These are all of us growing up. Oh, Fred, I can't bear it."

She hardly noticed Fred leaving. All she could see were these photos of her dad and her mom, and Fred and her mom, and herself and her mom. Standing with their arms round each other, making faces at the camera. God, she looked so happy.

So in love. There was Fred, he had to be five, in his school uniform and her mom and dad were looking at each other. She felt sick. This had to be at the same time Lex was being unfaithful. She felt like tearing the photo into a million pieces, then shouting and stamping on it. How could he have done it to her?

She didn't really trust herself not to say anything. And she couldn't do that to him, not now.

How she missed her mother. There was this nasty hole inside her that hurt, when she let it. She'd learned to put in the bung. That was called being strong.

It was so hard to accept death was real, not just a word. What was the difference between being dead and saying "dead"? She just couldn't get her head around it. She told herself it was better this way, her mother would hate being reduced to being a body in a bed that couldn't move or talk or laugh. She would have really hated it.

Oh Michael, talk to me. He was ringing her late at night on the home phone and she'd take it into bed with her. The phone didn't stop during the day. Her damn mobile didn't work out here.

And when everything got too bad she'd sidestep a little, think of something else.

It's not fair dammit, she was far too young.

Three more days until the funeral. Three endless days. How were they going to get through them? The funeral couldn't come soon enough. They'd spoken to the minister, the church was organized and her mom was to be cremated, so they wouldn't have to go to the graveside. Everyone was to come back here for the wake.

The phone rang again.

"How are things going?" It was Michael.

She picked up the phone and walked outside in the drizzly rain onto the stone patio to get some privacy. "Hi, it's a mad house. Thank heavens Sonya is helping with the cooking. The café is catering but we need so much food. The trouble is, you can't tell how many people will come, or how many will come back to the house, or how many are intending to stay. We've got the shearer's quarters, so I'm making up all the beds. The florist in town is wearing a track out here. There are so many flowers in the house it's starting to look like we're the shop.

"And I'm okay. I just didn't see it coming. I know she's better off, and even though you tell yourself that, time and time again, it doesn't seem to work. Where are you?"

Her father stood at the open French door out to the patio, a photo album in his arms.

"Jessie, are you mad? Don't stand out in the rain. It's freezing. What are you doing with all these photos?"

"I've got to go. Ring me later." She came inside.

"Who was that?"

"Michael. And it's no good frowning like that Dad, he's coming."

"And if I said he was not welcome, said this is not the place for him?"

"I'd ask you again, Dad—why?"

Her father was silent. He turned and went back into the dining room.

*

"Are you going?" His father sat at the outside table cleaning his gun. It was still raining but he was protected by the glass roof that had been erected a few years ago. He'd had the twelve-gauge shot gun for many years. It had a polished walnut stock and steel double barrels and all the moving parts were laid out neatly on the table with his little bottle of oil and the small, soft rag that he always used.

"Jessie wants me to go."

His father didn't look at him, picking up the barrels and squinting down them. "And if I asked you not to go?"

"Dad, this is ridiculous. Whatever happened between you and Lex Cranfield is over. Done, finished."

"I'm not sure it is over." He rubbed the already gleaming stock lovingly.

"Of course it's over," Michael insisted. "I don't know why you're protecting him—I suppose it's my mother you're trying to protect. Jessie and I have already worked it out. They had an affair. My mother was leaving you, I suppose, when the car crashed and killed her. It's not all that hard to put together." He stood before his father, furious and angry. Sick of the deception. Sick of the lies.

"Except you've got it all wrong. I was the one, son—Clare and I were the ones who had the affair. And then my mistake was to fall in love with her." He shrugged.

Michael looked at his father, stupefied. "I think you can answer one question for me. When did this affair end?"

Sal looked squarely up at him. "You can rest assured, son, you were five years old and it lasted barely a couple of months. The scales fell off Clare's eyes just as I realized I was falling in love with her. She loved Lex. Unfortunately, you can't choose who you love. And I have loved her all this time. You can't go to Clare's funeral. Neither can I. If I was Lex Cranfield, I might kill you."

1983

Gabriella was dead. The five trees flashed past. She was home, she put the brakes on and the car skidded and skewed around at an angle. Her heart was thumping and her mouth was dry. Getting out of the car, she dropped the keys on the ground. On the news, she'd heard it on the news on the radio, coming home. A car accident, somewhere up near Bredbo. She picked up the keys from the dirt. No one else was injured. "Thirty-one-year-old, Gabriella D'Larghi, wife of Sal." Poor Sal, that little boy, Michael. He was the same age as Fred. She couldn't bear it. Just couldn't bear it.

It couldn't have had anything to do with them.

It was over months ago, after the picnic races. She'd told Sal, no more. But no one was ever to find out, that was her only salvation, the only thing that would make it work.

"It's over, Sal." She'd come to her senses with a bang. Not being able to fall pregnant was messing with her head. She'd just felt so inadequate, as though she was letting Lex down, letting herself down. But it wasn't his fault and it wasn't her fault either. No one's fault. He'd told her one child was as

250

perfect as you could get. They both adored Fred. They were so lucky.

Eventually she'd stopped crossing off the twenty-eight days on the calendar. Four months now, and the tense lovemaking was gone; they were laughing again. And her mother-in-law—at long last, she'd learned to stand up for herself. It had taken her so long. She'd been so weak.

Lex must never find out.

Then Sal had changed. There was a look she hadn't seen before, a look she couldn't quite put her finger on: want, ownership? A vulnerability she couldn't cope with.

Love. You can't choose who you love. Her eyes were wide open now and she knew she loved Lex. And he loved her. And the thought of losing him frightened her to death. She'd come very close.

Oh, Gabriella.

It couldn't have had anything to do with them. Please, she just couldn't bear it.

Chapter 37

There were so many people crammed into the little Presbyterian church, the overflow was spilling out into the grounds. A few chairs had been set up outside, but most were standing, everyone rugged up with coats and hats, windcheaters and scarves. Jessie didn't look around. Sympathetic faces, she was so sick of that expression. "Oh I'm so sorry." Couldn't they think of anything else to say? Did her mother really know all these people?

She stared straight ahead at the stone pillars, worked her way around the leadlight windows. The altar, with its plain white cloth. Her eyes avoided the square screen with all those pictures of her mother, as they faded in and faded out. So happy. No, she wasn't going to cry.

Where was Michael? He'd said he'd come. Today had been so crazy. Last night he'd said he'd come. Fred and Sonya sat next to her, with their father on the end, near the aisle.

Fred was doing a reading. Her dad was doing the eulogy. How could he do that? Not that it was anything to do with her. How many times had he been unfaithful?

Thank God the pictures had stopped, they were making her feel queasy.

They were standing for the first hymn. The organ notes flooded the church. And then the congregation began to sing. It was woeful but the organist struggled on. Jessie raised her voice—this she could do for her mother. The words of "How Great Thou Art" pounded through her.

Music—her mom had given her this love of music, encouraged her, taught her so much. *Thank you for that.*

Michael hadn't come. She didn't turn around, didn't have to. She would know if he was there. Surreptitiously she checked her phone in her bag—nothing. She turned it off.

*

She'd made it through the wake. Jessie stood outside on the patio at Five Oaks, welcoming the biting breeze. It was a windy, gray afternoon. Iron-fisted clouds gathering over the black mountain range, promising rain again today. She needed the fresh, cold air. Everyone else was inside near the roaring fire. A lot had left already. She could see cars trickling down the driveway. If she heard anyone else say, "I'm so sorry," she might puke. If she saw her father bow his shoulders again, struggling so bravely with the weight of all that sympathy, she might scream.

"Hold on, hon, you're in the home stretch now. You can do it." Belinda had come up behind her, holding three steaming mugs of coffee.

"Thank you." The wind was so cold it was making her eyes water. Patti was there too, and they huddled together, warming their hands around the mugs.

"How've you got on this week?" Jessie asked Belinda. "I'll be back at work, not tomorrow, but the next day. What day is it? Everything's a bit hazy."

"That's what I wanted to tell you," said Belinda. "We've had a bit of a breakthrough. You know the report you were working on? I put it to the service clubs in town, Lions and Rotary, and they've agreed to support us, *really* support it. They are taking it to their state bodies, whatever they're called, and we're going to get some substantial backing. One thing they know is how to lobby. They know all the politics backward. We could be going to get somewhere. And today is Friday, so I don't want to see you till Monday."

Jessie gave a little laugh. "Right. That's good. That's very good."

Fred and Sonya had joined them. "I'm taking Son home to relieve the sitter, then I'll be back." Fred leaned over and kissed Jessie on the cheek. "Now, don't you do any clearing up till I return, understand?"

Jessie put her arms round Sonya and hugged her tightly. "I don't know how to thank you, Sonya, for all you've done over the last few days. You've been amazing, more than wonderful, but don't come back, Fred, we'll be right, no one's staying over."

"I loved your mom, too, she was very good to me." Sonya reached out to Jessie and wrapped her arms round her. "Brr, you're freezing. Go inside." They left by the path through the garden that took them round to the back, where the cars were parked.

Belinda, Patti and Jessie stood there silently for a moment. Jessie noticed a car making its way in, travelling against the stream of cars that were leaving. It was black, a big four-wheel drive SUV. Michael's car? Maybe. No-show Michael.

"I think I might just go inside and see if I can find the dishwasher," said Patti. "It must be in there somewhere under all those cups and saucers. Come on, Belinda." Patti dragged her away—they must have noticed the car, too, but they didn't say anything. Jessie couldn't have been the only one to have noticed his absence.

So she was mad with him, upset he hadn't come when he'd said he would. What did it matter? Her feet started walking toward the paddock where he would park. She needed to see him now. There weren't many cars still here, maybe twenty dotted around. She was there waiting when he pulled up. Michael got out and she fell into his arms.

"What are you doing out here?" he said. "It's freezing."

"I saw you coming. Where have you been?"

"I'm sorry."

Jessie hit him on the arm. "Don't say that. I'm so sick of 'I'm sorry.' If anyone else says it tonight, I will punch them. Hard. Now, where were you?"

Michael reached inside the car for his coat, wrapped it around Jessie's shoulders, then bent and kissed her.

She was surrounded with his warmth and his smell and his strength. She sensed his hunger and matched it with her own. The world disappeared. That they were standing in an almost empty paddock as the day turned from gray to black was irrelevant. There was no sun to be seen. No warm colors in the sky. Just rainbows in her head. Michael's lips and his taste and his tongue and his strong arms round her.

He slowly released her.

"I nearly didn't come. But in the end I had to."

"I'm so glad." Jessie buried her head into his chest.

It was such a shock. How did you go from being one person, a whole and independent, living person—to this body, this mind, that had to have another person to survive? To function properly. Breathe, eat, talk, move; exist.

Today would have been totally different if he'd been there. She could appreciate it now. Before, she hadn't known what was missing. She'd been on automatic—nodding, smiling, hugging perfect strangers. Bending under this intense loss—a grief that both hurt and numbed her, but didn't break her. But with Michael there, it was surmountable, with him she'd be safe.

Facing it together, she was stronger. And that revelation was a bit hard to absorb. How could you say that to someone?

"Come in." Arm in arm, they started to walk slowly toward the house.

"How's it been? You okay?" Michael asked, leaning over to kiss the top of her head.

"Terrible, horrible, no good. Did you ever read that kid's book? Never mind. All Mom's pals from the theater came. So many people; her yoga mates and the quilters. What I can't understand is that everything seems so much better now you're here." She squeezed his arm and smiled up at him.

They walked out of the dusk and went straight to the kitchen. Jessie took two beers out of the fridge. It would be a miracle if she ever drank tea or coffee again. Patti and Belinda were in the kitchen, stacking the dishwasher.

"You guys want a wine or a beer?" Jessie offered.

"No thanks, I'm driving home." Belinda had started filling the sink. She was wearing the fancy rubber gloves Clare always wore, the purple ones with fur. Jessie tore her eyes away.

"Well, I'm not," Patti piped up from the bowels of the dishwasher. "I'm basically next door, I'll have a wine, thanks."

"The food was great." Belinda handed her plates. "They're good caterers, aren't they? Those quiches were delicious. Who made the cakes?"

"That was Sonya. Sponges are her specialty, apparently."

"Here you are, Michael, make yourself useful." Patti passed him a tea towel. "And as a reward, I'll get you a piece of Sonya's sponge cake."

"That sounds good," Michael said with a grin and shook out the towel confidently.

"Well, Jessie, I'd say you've been lucky. It looks like you've landed one who knows how to dry up."

Jessie went pink and choked on her beer. It was all very well to admit to herself how much she and Michael were a couple, but she hadn't got used to saying it out loud, as yet. Even to her best friends. "Landed" was so gross. She hoped they weren't going to say anything more embarrassing. Fat chance. She looked for an open bottle of wine.

"You know, Jessie doesn't believe in sex before marriage." Belinda eyed Michael seriously.

Jessie closed her eyes.

"Neither do I," said Michael gravely as he took another plate from Belinda. "Luckily, we think alike on most things, don't we, Jessie?"

"Mm hm. So we do." She picked up a clean glass from a tray and poured Patti her wine. Then she carried the tray of glasses into the dining room. When she got back, they were all laughing uproariously.

"What are you laughing at now?" she asked suspiciously.

Her father walked in behind her. The laughter fell away.

"Hello, Michael. Couldn't keep away?"

Belinda and Patti looked at each other and walked out of the room, closing the door behind them.

"Dad, I asked him," Jessie cut in. "Don't be unpleasant. He's here for me."

"Hello, Mr Cranfield." Michael's hand was ignored.

Jessie couldn't stop herself. "How dare you be so rude to him? Is it too difficult for you, Dad? Does he remind you too much of the woman you had an affair with all those years ago? What's your problem? Is the guilt too much? How you've lived with it all these years is beyond me. Did Mom know? Tell me. I know you swore Olly to secrecy. "

The room turned icy.

"You couldn't leave it alone, could you, Jessie? You just couldn't leave it alone." Her father spoke in a husky voice. "Yes, I'm worried. I'm worried that he's going to be too much like his *father*, not his mother. His *father* was the one who slept with *my wife*. They were the ones who had the affair, if that's how you want to put it. He seduced my wife. Now, do you want a man like that, Jessie? Do you? Or should I say, the *son* of a man like that."

"That's a lie. He's lying, Michael, like he's lied all these years."

"No, Jessie, he's not."

"What?" Jessie turned huge eyes on Michael. "What did you say?"

"Dad told me this morning. That's why I couldn't—I couldn't come."

"So why did you come now?" She was so angry.

"I couldn't stay away."

"I think Dad's right, you'd better go."

"I really think we should talk about it."

"Not until I've got my head 'round it. Please go."

Michael walked out the door. Really there was nothing anyone could say.

Chapter 38

The morning after the funeral the house was silent and empty. There was no sign of her father. Jessie felt she'd been enclosed in a washing machine, a front loader with a glass door. Or as though she'd been dumped in a huge wave at the beach. Nothing made any sense. What was up was down and it didn't stay that way for longer than five seconds. There was no way out. And just when she thought she was out, she got sucked back in again.

She had to apologize to her father. How?

They'd simply ignored each other during the cleanup and getting everything back to order. She'd vacuumed the floors and he'd filled up the ute with rubbish and taken it out to the dump. They'd put away the cups and saucers and the good plates, and washed the tablecloths. Jessie had frozen some of the cakes and quiches, but most of the other leftovers had to be thrown out.

She'd got it so wrong. Had she known her parents at all? Either of them? She thought she had. Her mom was exuberant, charming and, yes, she loved to milk the drama out of any situation. Her dad went along with it, he was the quiet one except when he lost his temper and they all ducked for cover. But they understood that her dad was the decision-maker, even though Mom made more noise. What she couldn't understand was that the two of them had been living on top of this festering carbuncle for thirty years, pushing it under the carpet. Pretending it had never happened.

You don't know your parents and you never have.

Why had she been so eager to believe the worst of her father? That was the bit that was so hard to apologize for.

Jessie walked out of the house, down through the garden, past the shed, where she gathered up a biscuit of hay, and continued on to the horse paddock. There they were again—right in the furthest corner. She whistled and Savior looked up and saw the hay in her arms and cantered over, Dolly following behind.

"Well, hello to you too." She laughed as Savior pulled at the hay and she dropped it to the ground. "What secrets do you two have? I know for a fact that you simply aren't able to have a love affair with anyone. Sex is the root of all evil, wouldn't you say? Wouldn't it be simpler if we were all neutered? Just friends, girls and boys. This lust makes everything so complicated." She kicked the ground with the toe of her boot. "And real and defined."

And that started her thinking about Michael, but she sheared away from that one. Too difficult altogether. Theorizing about love and lust was okay—you didn't need to put a face to it, particularly Michael's face.

Slowly she walked back to the house. The sun had finally appeared, the sky had that freshly washed look and the ground was soft and moist. No growth yet. Not in the middle of winter. There'd been a little frost this morning, she'd seen it out the window but it had gone by the time she'd got dressed. The sooner she moved out again the better. At least she had Olly's house to move in to. You could call it running away, maybe. Or you could call it moving on.

Nearly back, she could hear the phone ringing. It was so archaic being out of mobile range out at the farm. She felt so cut off from her life. She ran in.

"Hello? Hi Sonya ... No, I'm not sure ... You've spoken to him? Okay. See you in an hour. What can I bring? I've got a sponge cake or two in the freezer ..."

Sonya wanted to have everyone to lunch. She'd already spoken to Lex. Where was he? She had to talk to her father. What was she going to say?

*

Jessie heard the ute at five to twelve, which meant there was no time for deep and meaningful conversation before they left.

"Hi Dad."

"Jessie, you're up." He was washing his hands at the sink. "I'll be quick, Sonya wants us over there at twelve, doesn't she?"

"Yes."

"I'm just going to change my shirt."

Jessie watched him go. Who would guess it had been less than twenty-four hours ago that she accused him of all those terrible things? Wasn't that how he'd dealt with all crises? With politeness and basically pretending it hadn't happened? *Well, think again, Dad.* She wasn't going do things his way this time.

She knocked on her parents' bedroom door. "Dad?"

She heard something, it could have been a yes, and she walked in. Her father was standing in front of the wardrobe with a clean shirt in each hand and fat tears silently running down his face.

"Oh Dad, don't." Jessie went up to him and put her arms round him. He patted her awkwardly on the back.

"Jessie, if I could take it back, I would. I should never have told you. Yesterday was the worst day of my life, I wanted to hit out at someone and Michael D'Larghi seemed a good target at the time. It was unforgivable. I didn't mean to hurt you, you're the last person I wanted to hurt." He kept patting her with the shirts.

"I can't believe I leaped to all those stupid conclusions either. Forgive me, Dad, please." She was crying now, too. She sniffed.

"Oh Jessie, there's nothing to forgive. I don't know whether I should have told you straight off or just told you to forget it. But I couldn't let it go. It's not your problem, it was mine. I thought it was all in the past. Forgotten. Then you brought Michael into our lives and it all came back. I got hurt all over again, but you must understand that I loved your mother so much. I just can't bear the thought she's no longer here with me. Oh Jessie."

They stood for a minute before Jessie said, "Come on, decide which shirt, for heaven's sake. Mom loved that blue one."

"She did, didn't she? Blue it is."

Chapter 39

Go, she'd told him. You'd better leave. Well, he didn't need telling twice and if she changed her mind she'd have to be the one to get him to walk back in. And that may not be so easy.

All right. She'd just been hit over the head with an awful fact. And she'd turned to him for help that he couldn't give her.

The truck rolled on toward Sydney in its cruise control mode. He was making good time. It was only eleven and there were a fair few trucks on the road tonight. A lot of chat on the CB about an accident ahead, somewhere near Lake George, but it should be sorted by the time he got there.

What an impossible situation. If he could get her sorted in his own head, it would be a start. He was unable to leave it alone but he had to, at the moment, because he didn't think anything with a D'larghi name attached would be welcome at Five Oaks. But it didn't stop him thinking constantly about her, worrying. She could be a bit impulsive, she needed to look before she leaped sometimes. He wanted to know when she was moving back into town, how she and her father were getting on.

It had been bitter the other night and Jessie had been very angry and he couldn't blame her. The funny thing was, he understood his own father so much better now, as a few of the questions that had been bugging him had fallen into place. That didn't mean he could forgive him.

If she would just talk to him.

No, he should leave it a while longer. Didn't have much of a choice, did he?

The talk on the CB was saying now that the accident was a fatal. Apparently a motorcycle had run off the road. The place was crawling with police and RMS officers. Not good news. He ran through his log book in his head; it couldn't be too bad, he only did one run a week but get those hours wrong and he was in trouble. What with the cameras, the on-the-spot checks by the RMS and the highway patrol, they had you pretty stitched up.

Everything had lost its gloss a bit lately. The project was demanding more and more of his time. Nonna—or Renee, more like it—had gathered that something had gone awry at the wake. Someone must have picked up on the confronta-tion—you couldn't stop a story like that one. They'd been at him to tell them what had happened. They weren't going to hear it from him. Nor his father apparently. How Sal had lived with that secret all these years was beyond him. He supposed if you made a mistake like that, you do live with the consequences. Hell, they were all living with the consequences, thirty years on.

Now the traffic had stopped. He turned up the CB, listening for more information. It looked like it was going to be a long night. He reached for the bottle of water in the cooler. Ringing Jessie wasn't an option as she was still out at the farm. He wasn't going to chance getting Lex Cranfield by mistake. But he had to talk to her. Monday she'd be at work. He'd see her then. If only this mess would sort itself out.

At least it was all out in the open now. The question remained, though: what were they all going to do about it?

Was it something Jessie could put aside, with her mother so recently laid to rest?

Trucks and cars lined up the highway, as far ahead as he could see. The traffic had completely stopped. Drivers were clambering down from their cabs to have a smoke and a chat. A police car cruised slowly past, on the dirt, with blue lights flashing.

Chapter 40

Jessie sat with Belinda going over the last-minute presentation planned for later that morning. She couldn't help looking across the road for a glimpse of a tall figure walking in the door. Michael hadn't appeared yet. Of course, he might have got there early. Earlier than seven, when she'd got there. Not that he'd be interested in seeing her, anyway.

She'd be sitting here watching from afar forever.

Ho, ho, who's feeling sorry for herself?

"Will you stop looking out the window and concentrate?" Belinda remonstrated. "What do you think about these personal stories from the kids in Mittagong?"

"I like the one from Tim, and Anna, maybe one more, but not all of them. Keep it short and sweet. Just say they are three of many."

The dribble of office workers into the café across the road had pretty well finished. It really was the favorite place for Cooma-ites to gather. Jessie sat and wondered again where Michael was this morning. He was running late. She began to worry. He'd never been this late before. Perhaps he'd traded the truck off to Ron in Fyshwyck. Or if he hadn't—where was he?

266

"Hey Jessie! Earth to Jessie, come in, Jessie." Belinda was looking at her curiously.

"Sorry, damn. Now I'm using it."

What?

"That terrible word. Sorry. I hate it. I hate hearing it and I will never use it again. Belinda, I've got to go. I won't be long. Five minutes, okay?"

She grabbed her coat and phone and went out of the office and along the road to D'Larghi Motors. She began to walk through the cars to the back where they parked the truck. And there it was—the truck. She let out the breath she didn't know she was holding. That's all she needed to know. She turned away and ran smack into Michael.

"Jessie, hi." He was holding a takeaway coffee.

She eyed the cup. "How did you get that? I've been watching for you to come back and I—" She closed her mouth. That was enough explanation. She wasn't going to give anything more away. How to leave with her remaining dignity intact was the problem.

"I'm a bit late, there was an accident on Lake George. It put me behind." He grinned suddenly. "Were you worried?"

Yes, of course she was worried. "Not really."

She couldn't help herself. She drank in Michael, his blue singlet and checked flannelette shirt, jeans and dusty boots; the dark stubble. He didn't look tired, not like he should, having driven all night. He looked wonderful.

"How are you, is everything okay after the other night? There was no way I could tell you. We've got to talk, Jessie." He leaned forward and took her hand and rubbed his thumb softly over her knuckles.

"I know. Yes, I talked to Dad, and yep, everything's getting better. Kind of—" Suddenly she became aware they were attracting attention. She pulled away. "Oh, help. We've got a meeting in ten minutes. I've got to go."

"Jessie!" Michael called after her. "Wait!" But she'd disappeared.

*

A little after five that evening Jessie and Belinda walked out of the office and locked the door. They were both jubilant.

"See you tomorrow, and that was one good day's work." Belinda dropped the key into her handbag.

"I know. I think we're finally getting somewhere." A dark figure on a sleek BMW bike pulled up beside them and let the engine idle as it kicked out the support leg.

Lifting his visor, Michael said, "Good evening, Belinda, Jessie. Jessie, I want to kidnap you for an hour. And I want it witnessed that you agreed to the kidnap." He looked totally serious and reached behind him to extricate a helmet and a leather jacket from the bucket at the back of his bike.

"Should I?" Jessie asked Belinda.

"Yes, you idiot. And I'll meet you in Leo's in an hour."

"Okay." Jessie took the helmet and put it on. Her fingers were trembling but she snapped the buckle shut and put on Michael's jacket. It was so satiny and warm and smelled so good. She tucked her pants into her boots and straightened. Michael's visor was back down and she couldn't see his face, so she slid one leg over and clutched him from behind. It reminded her vividly of the trip down the mountain on the back of his skis. He took her hands and arranged them more firmly around his middle, and may have said something but she couldn't hear as he put the bike in gear and gunned the engine.

Lord, the sudden acceleration nearly took her breath away. They braked once for the set of traffic lights and then they were free—the 65 mph speed limit flashed past and she leaned into Michael's back and tightened her hold on him. It was sensational.

The bike wound its way up the mountain, down into valleys, screamed round corners with their knees nearly touching the tar. She had no idea where they were going, just enjoyed the sensation of speed, balance and controlled power taking her breath away, literally.

They were slowing, but she didn't want to let go. When they stopped, she lifted her head cautiously. The rusty old farm gate looked familiar. They'd come here before to look at the nissen huts. Her arms were still tight around Michael's middle and he gently disengaged them and got off to open the gate. They proceeded through the scrub of snow gums and past the huts. Michael stopped and waited for her to get off the bike first. Her legs were trembling.

"Wow. That was," she took a breath, "amazing."

Michael took off his helmet and then hers and kissed her.

Now that was some kiss. He was hungry and in control and the word "surrender" looped around before it scattered to God knows where. She was incapable of thought or any movement. Reality was Michael, his body up against hers, his arms, his lips, his tongue, nothing else mattered.

She pulled away. "No. Don't. Stop."

Michael laughed a little breathlessly, "Don't stop? Or don't. Stop."

"I'm serious, stop now. Don't you see it can never be the same again? You'll be thinking I'm just like my mother. I'll be thinking I'm just like my mother. Why did she do it? It's driving me crazy. Why did she have to do it?"

"Don't blame your mother entirely. It takes two. My father was there, too, you know."

Jessie turned impatiently and walked away. How could he ever look at her and not remember that her mother and his father had had an affair? That they had hurt the people who loved them the most? That they lived in the moment—with total disregard for their families and their children? How had her father ever forgiven her mother?

Michael came up behind her and put his arms around her. "We can get through this. It may take time. Look, this is what I wanted to show you."

Jessie lifted her head. The view stretched out forever to the craggy zig-zag of the Snowy Mountains and the high plains of the Monaro. No trees, just the silvery grass waving in the wind. A few knobs of granite boulders that some giant in some far-off time had scattered on the ground.

"That is incredible," she whispered.

"Great site for a house, don't you think? Our house, no one else's. Our history, no one else's. Our future—just us."

"How can that be, Michael? We are both of us what we came from. We are what we learned along the way. You can't throw it all away and pretend we're other people."

"I'm not asking you to. But we are strong enough to build something new, put the past behind us. I believe that."

"I'm not sure I can."

"I know this has been a rough time for you. I can't tell you how worried I've been for you."

"And our families. Oh, Michael, how do we cope with that?"

"We are together—united—and they come to us on our terms. They will not dictate to us anymore. Just think we can do it, Jessie—thought is a powerful thing. Just think positively and give it some time. I love you."

There it was, in his eyes. She'd seen it before but it was too much and she turned away again.

They walked back to the bike in silence.

*

Michael put the bike back into the shed. He was shaken. He felt like he'd put himself out on the line to dry. What had Jessie thought of it all? He'd delivered her back to Belinda as promised. She'd smiled and said goodbye but she hadn't said "Ring me," or "I'll be in touch." Had he been too strong, too dictatorial, what had she been wanting? Someone who talked things through with her more? He just wasn't sure if he'd done it right.

Renee was digging in her vegetable patch. He walked over and took the shovel from her and started digging. "You shouldn't be doing this."

"Well, thank you, kind, sir." Renee twinkled at him gratefully and went over to pull out the tomato stakes. "It's nearly time to plant some carrots and parsnips, I was thinking. Snow peas do well now, too."

"I'll get you some fertilizer from the yard. And some mulch."

"Have you seen Jessie?"

"Yep." Renee was looking at him, he knew, but he kept digging. "I'm not sure if I did the right thing. I basically put it all out there. Told her we could have a future together."

"Told her ..."

"I know. Maybe I did it all wrong."

"Of course not, she needs time and she needs to know you are there for her. What did she say?"

"Nothing."

"Well that's better than get lost. Let her come to you, Michael. If you've done all you can, let her digest it and make up her own mind. You can't decide for her."

"You're right. Patience. God help me."

"Well, thank you for your hard work but I think you've finished. If you dig any deeper we'll be discovering China." Renee smiled gently at him. "Come on, let's go."

Chapter 41

Jessie grabbed a bridle and went down to the paddock. There they were at the furthest end, as usual. She whistled, glad she'd remembered the biscuit of hay to entice them. As usual, Dolly played her pretend game of don't care. "It's all right, you're not invited. Anyway, you'd only come halfway and refuse to go any further. You stay, my friend. Savior and I are going for a ride."

Once out of the yards and into the pale winter sunshine, she felt better. She wriggled down into the saddle and let Savior have his head. He was keen to get where they were going. He knew. It was their favorite secret place. They used to go there a lot. Savior must have liked the grass or something—maybe the peace. It was a very restful place, and often she'd taken a book along with her and just lain in the grass with Savior munching close to her ear. Looked up at the clouds and read.

They worked their way up and over the plains to the strange gobble of granite boulders, thrusting up out of the ground. Inside was a little lake—well, sometimes it had water in it. Not much bigger than a fifty-meter swimming pool and totally hidden behind the rocks. The grass was always green there. Savior loved it.

It had been a great place to practice her roles. She could shout and cavort as much as she liked. Savior would stop eating and turn his head and look at her as if she were mad. Once she'd taken off all her clothes and sunbaked. That had been a disaster—she'd got quite sunburnt and hadn't been game to tell her mother where she was sore and so had to do without the cream because she couldn't reach the worst places by herself.

Jessie pulled Savior up and slid out of the saddle with an oomph. "Yowie, I haven't done that much riding for a while."

She walked through the rocks to where she could sit down. She'd come to try to work things out.

She'd hated walking away from Michael. Think positively, he'd said.

Ha. Cranfields thought in negatives. No, that wasn't fair. Cranfields weighed everything up and made wise, steady decisions based on hard facts. Or so she'd been led to believe.

She got up and began to walk the length of the lake.

"Fact—my mother slept with Sal D'Larghi. Fact—my father knew. Fact—I know. Fact—Michael knows. So, how are we ever going to forget it?" She leaned against one of the rocks, rubbing the roughness with the palm of her hand.

At least she could throw away all those "I don't like the D'Larghis" ploys. Her parents hadn't not liked Michael or distrusted her judgment, like she'd thought. They were dealing with their own lies and distortions of the truth.

Fact—they'd been living with it all for thirty years.

They'd lived in the same town, together, her parents had lived in the same marriage together, for the last thirty years knowing—how do you do that?

An engine noise broke the silence; it was a long way away but it whined closer and closer. Curious, Jessie took Savior's bridle and walked out to see who it was.

Her father. He got out, the slamming door ricocheting around the rocks.

"Hi Dad. Fancy seeing you here. How did you know where I was?"

"Jessie, this is where you come. We knew you came here, often. Didn't take me long to work out where you'd gone." Her father laughed and shook his head. "Honestly, Jessie, of course we knew where you came to. After you'd gone missing once for a couple of hours, your mother made me follow you and find out where you'd got to. It didn't take long. This is a beautiful spot, isn't it?"

He chuckled and walked into the secluded area. "I used to come here when I was young. It's a bit like a church. You can't get much closer to God up here, anyway." He sat on the grass with his elbows on his knees, picked a stalk of long grass and started chewing. "Sit down, there a few things I need to say."

"I'm not sure I need to hear any more, I think I've heard enough."

Her father ignored her. "After Fred, we desperately wanted another child, or at least, your mother did. My parents were still alive and they were making life very hard for your mother. I didn't realize it then, only later. Making her feel as though she wasn't good enough for the Cranfields. It was a different time." He sighed. "She wasn't getting pregnant. Every six weeks or so, off she'd go to the doctor with her little jar of urine. That's how we found out, in those days. No over-the-counter tests then. And then she'd come home.

"It was my fault—I didn't know how to handle it. My parents demanded respect, which I had been brought up to give them. I didn't realize they were driving a wedge between us, making your mother feel so inadequate." He shook his head in disbelief. "It's all very well to be blaming them, but I have to take a lot of the blame myself. I was unforgiving, impatient, hard to live with. The farm was in drought. Wool and sheep prices were crashing, I sold all the sheep for a pittance and bought into cattle at a premium price; we were in a lot of debt.

"So one day your mother met Sal D'Larghi, who stopped to help her out and change a flat tire." He shrugged. "A bloody flat tire."

"How did you find out?"

"Your mother told me. After Gabriella died. She was distraught, thinking maybe she and Sal had been the reason for her death. I never knew what happened there. But by then it was over, she said. I believed her."

"And Olly, how did she get involved?"

"I'm not sure, but she did, and I asked her not to say anything to anyone. Marriage is a strange, convoluted state, Jessie. I loved your mother passionately. Thank God I realized it wasn't all her fault, and the bottom line was I knew I never wanted her to leave me, ever. You must believe that. It would have killed me.

"Your mother loved me too, you know. Marriage is a bumpy ride sometimes, and you need to hold on to each other tightly through the bad times. But it's different for everyone, and that's a fact. Marriage is not just a once-only choice, you make the choice to stay married again and again.

"One thing I did know—I never wanted our marriage to end." He looked up and searched her face. "What you feel for Michael is yours to sort out. Don't let us spoil it. If it's the kind of love your mother and I had, it is very precious. Basically, there's not a lot you can do. You'll find it hard to deny it and fight against it, believe me. But it is your choice."

*

Riding home a little later, all Jessie could think was that she'd thought her parents had had the perfect marriage. Sure, they argued, but they were comfortable with each other and you couldn't deny there was a spark there. Yet her mother had betrayed her dad's trust. Lex might have forgiven Clare, but Jessie couldn't.

*

Jessie moved back into town but spent the next two weekends out at the farm. She wasn't sure where Michael spent his—he hadn't rung. Neither had she rung him. What were the words of that song she and Michael had sung on that fateful night? Was it only three months ago? About love lasting and hurting? She wished him all the best, really she did. With whoever. Sienna—no, Sienna was not the right person for him. It would have to be someone else.

It had shaken her to the core, what her father had told her. He had loved her mother. He'd told Jessie that the day Clare died had been the worst day of his life because, no matter what she'd done before, and even in the state the stroke had left her, she'd still been there, alive. With him.

Put herself in Gabriella's shoes. What would she do if Michael had an affair? Scratch his eyes out. Or kill the girl. *Both*, she thought despondently. No one knew what Michael's mother had done but it looked like she was leaving, not staying to fight.

I would have stayed to fight, Gabriella.

But she wasn't, was she? She was seriously thinking of leaving, getting her old job back in Sydney. Getting out of town was the only option. Searching endlessly for tall male figures going into Leo's café was slowly driving her crazy. Gazing at her phone for hours on end wasn't doing her any good at all. The only peaceful time was out at Five Oaks, but she was getting restless and it was time to get on with her life.

She still couldn't believe how everything changed after their talk. Her father was a different person in her eyes. You couldn't deny he was missing her mom. They both were.

*

It was nine thirty on Monday morning when she saw her father and Sal D'Larghi walk to the café, pull up chairs at an outside table and sit down. Not believing what she'd seen, she got up and went to the window to make sure. Yes, it was definitely her father and Sal.

"Shit, Belinda, holy shit."

"What's the matter?"

"Oh, Belinda, I've got to go." She grabbed her phone and dialed Michael's number.

"Michael, where are you? Nearly back? That's good. I just thought you should know your father and my father are sitting together at Leo's. They look as if they're having coffee together … I know, it's bizarre. I don't know whether to go over or not … No, I can't see a gun. That's not funny. What on earth are they doing?"

Jessie stood near the window, peering out, and Belinda joined her. "Your dad and Sal D'Larghi. I don't think I've ever seen them together before."

"That's right," Jessie said faintly, "neither have I. Michael said he'd be here in about half an hour and I should wait for him, keep him informed if there's any trouble."

"Why would there be trouble?" Belinda asked her. "They look happy."

Sure enough, they looked, well, like two old friends catching up for a coffee. In a very public place. People stopped and chatted. Jessie watched with her heart in her mouth until finally she saw the familiar, tall figure make its way up from the car yard. She timed her trip across the road to arrive at the same moment.

"Hello, Dad, Mr D'Larghi."

"Jessie." They both rose.

"You must call me Sal. Ah, and here's Michael. Won't you join us? Pull up some chairs, Michael. Leo, more coffee." Sal waved to Leo who was watching with interest from inside.

"Did the trip go well, Michael?" Lex asked.

"Yes, great." Michael sounded bemused, much the same as Jessie felt.

"You're running a bit late, we thought you'd be here before now." Sal smiled.

"Yes, I'm later than usual."

They stayed another ten minutes. It was relaxed and casual.

Then Lex stood up. "Good to see you both." He nodded. "Are you ready, Sal?"

Sal got up too and they walked away together, leaving Michael and Jessie looking at each other.

"I'm not exactly sure—did you hear what your father said to my father just then?" said Jessie.

"No."

"He said something about his grandchildren, has he got any grandchildren?"

Michael raised an eyebrow. "Not that I'm aware of."

"Well, what was that all about?"

"No idea. It's very out of character for my father."

"And mine."

"At least we didn't have to pick them up off the floor. I was worried when I got your phone call we might have to tear them apart." Michael grinned at her and it did such strange things to her stomach.

"So was I."

"My father told me the day of the funeral that he loved your mother. That he hadn't meant to, it just happened."

"And that's supposed to make me feel better or worse?"

Michael shrugged. "It might help you to understand. Basically it was their lives, Jessie, they paid for their mistakes. *We* don't have to."

"I'm thinking of going back to Sydney."

"That's a pity. We'll just have to go back to meeting after midnight for our coffees at the café."

Jessie opened her mouth and closed it. Did she have to get up and shout, for him to understand? Did he not get the message?

"Challenges, Jessie, I told you they turn me on. Whatever fences you put up, I'll find a way to tear them down. Watch me."

She had to laugh. He was impossible.

Chapter 42

Leo's was crowded. Belinda had organized a huge dinner to celebrate getting the go-ahead for their project. The community had really got behind them and at last, after all these years, it was happening. The restaurant was looking pretty festive. Jessie had done the flowers on the tables, and the balloons.

Looking around, she saw Fred and Sonya with the twins in their stroller. Sonya shrugged apologetically; she mustn't have been able to get a sitter after all. Michael was sitting with his family, his nonna and Renee and Ron Fraser. Renee was getting involved with Growcare as a volunteer and helping with the seedlings. Her father was next to Sal again—now that was a very strange union, it was as if they had this weird connection. If she believed in a mystical after-life, she could almost believe her mother had something to do with it.

She was sitting with Belinda when Michael got up, went to the small dance floor and took the microphone that Leo held out to him. Leo slapped him on the back and grinned. Surprised, Jessie looked at Belinda—did she know what was happening? Belinda shrugged but her eyes were dancing and Jessie didn't trust the innocent expression on her face.

"This is a wonderful night, Growcare is opening in six months from now, after a remarkable effort from Belinda Allen and Jessie Cranfield. I have checked with a few people—Belinda and Lex Cranfield, to mention two—and I would like to sing a song for someone very special."

Jessie was startled to hear her dad mentioned and looked over at him to find he was grinning from ear to ear.

Michael smiled right at her and Jessie went pink and felt like she might sink through the floorboards. Leo had his accordion in his arms and the music started. A lively Italian song—"Funiculì, funiculà" was it called?.

Michael started singing with gusto.

> *Mamma Mia, what am I to do?*
> *The girl I love is thinkin' of shootin'*
> *through*
> *I told her No*
> *I told her stay*
> *I said I love you in every way*
> *And I told her it's important—I would*
> *marry you today.*

Everyone started to laugh and clap in time. She looked over at her father, who was sitting with a particularly satisfied expression on his face. He lifted his glass in salute. She shook her head slowly.

> *Mama Mia, what am I to do?*
> *I won't make it—I haven't got a clue*
> *If she says no*
> *My heart will break*
> *Funiculì*
> *Funiculà*
> *And I know that it's important that she*
> *marries me post haste.*

Jessie started laughing. Michael was looking at her with that expression that promised her the world, but this time she met it head on. This time she gave it right back and then some.

"Oh Michael," she breathed. "Who knew?"

Michael grinned at her. "Everyone. I had to ask your father and Belinda and then Leo, and then I had to tell Nonna. Of course then I had to run it by Patti."

"Oh no, stop—I don't need to know." She collapsed, laughing, against him.

People were whistling and stamping to the music. He kissed her and the crowd went mad.

"Funiculì, funiculà, funiculì, funiculà."

They were joined at the hip, so to speak. He had his arm round her and she had her arm round his waist. She knew she would never let him go. She didn't know the words, but it didn't matter. As long as they were doing it together. That was what was important.

Acknowledgments

A huge thank you to Joel and Tara at Momentum for their professionalism and enthusiasm. Nothing really prepares you for that wonderful email—that vote of confidence—that feeling that you've done it. And to Kylie, who did an awesome edit.

I really want to thank two people at "Growing Abilities" in Goulburn, Anne Oliver and Fran Beck from whom I stole the idea for Belinda's "GrowCare" project. I am delighted to announce that the real "Growing Abilities" opened its doors in Goulburn last October. It's a wonderful project with a strong Goulburn community behind it—so many tradies and businesses have donated their time, energy, and experience to get it up and running. Thank you.

And to Skye, my beautiful agent, who kept me grounded and attempted to present me as a professional. And finally to my inspirational husband, the person without whom this book would not have happened. The biggest thank you of all.

www.ingramcontent.com/pod-product-compliance
Lightning Source LLC
Chambersburg PA
CBHW031603240626
47153CB00002B/617